THE RELUCTANT COWGIRL

AUTHOR'S NOTE:

Even though I suppose there are little towns named Shady Grove
in every state, including Arkansas, the particular Shady Grove
in *The Reluctant Cowgirl* is a purely fictional place with purely
fictional people, plunked down in the middle of northeast Arkansas,
somewhere around Sharp County.

A McCORD SISTER ROMANCE

THE RELUCTANT COWGIRL

CHRISTINE LYNXWILER

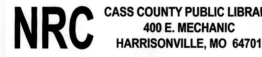

BARBOUR
PUBLISHING

DEDICATION AND ACKNOWLEDGEMENTS:

To Tracy Bateman,
I couldn't have done it without your continuous support
and encouragement—and most of all, your friendship.
You inspire me.

Special thanks to all my critique partners and supportive family.
And to Elizabeth Borngeret for the wonderful
Broadway insight. Any errors are mine and not hers.

© 2009 by Christine Lynxwiler

ISBN 978-1-60260-150-5

Scripture taken from the New King James Version®. Copyright © 1982 by
Thomas Nelson, Inc. Used by permission. All rights reserved.

This book is a work of fiction. Names, characters, places, and incidents are
either products of the author's imagination or used fictitiously. Any similarity
to actual people, organizations, and/or events is purely coincidental.

Published by Barbour Publishing, Inc., P.O. Box 719, Uhrichsville, OH 44683,
www.barbourbooks.com

*Our mission is to publish and distribute inspirational products offering
exceptional value and biblical encouragement to the masses.*

Member of the
Evangelical Christian
Publishers Association

Printed in the United States of America.

CHAPTER 1

"Mark my words. Someday Julia Roberts will be bragging that Broadway star Crystal McCord used to serve her sandwiches."

"Right, Mia," Crystal drawled into the phone as she looked out the dingy cab window at the small theater. Distance-wise, the green awning was a stone's throw from Broadway. But on days like this, that stone seemed to weigh a ton. "Julia Roberts came into the diner *one* time, and I was so nervous I messed up her order. I can't really see her bragging about knowing me. Besides, you're my agent. You have to say that."

The cabbie made a left and swung around to the back of the building. Crystal balanced the cell phone against her cheek and fished his fare from her purse.

"You're too modest. Why do you think I took you on?" Part of Mia's magic as an agent was her supreme confidence in her clients. She counted on it being contagious. And usually it was. "Look. You're a fantastic actress. If this play hadn't closed so quickly—"

"My daddy always said *if* is the biggest little word in the English language." Crystal put her hand to her mouth. Where had that come from? Apparently her brother's e-mail had made her more homesick than she'd realized. And that's why she had to put it out of her mind for now.

"Yes, well," Mia replied, without missing a beat or questioning the quote, "your daddy isn't in show biz. Here we deal in ifs on a daily basis. And like I was saying, *if* this play hadn't closed so quickly, it would have been your fast track to Broadway."

A weary smile lifted Crystal's lips. "*Fast* track?"

At least Mia had the grace to laugh. "You and I both know you've put in a hard six years here. But the media loves an overnight success. So when you *do* hit Broadway with a bullet, we'll spin it that way."

"Almost seven years actually. And I wish I had your confidence."

The cab driver eased his car up to the back door of the theater and stopped.

"Closing nights are always tough." Sympathy laced Mia's voice. "Just get through tonight. I've got leads on several auditions. You'll have a new play by next—" Mia gasped. "Crys, listen to this late review I just found."

Crystal shifted her hand, preparing to flip the phone shut. "I'll have to read it after the performance. I'm here. Besides, good or bad, I'd rather not hear it right now."

Mia sighed loudly. "Fine, spoilsport. Call me later. Oh, and Crystal?"

"Yeah?"

"Break a leg." Mia snickered at her own tired joke.

"Ha-ha." Crystal closed the phone and shook her head. Why had she ever told Mia how sick she got of hearing that?

The cabbie cleared his throat.

Her gaze jerked to meet his impatient eyes in the mirror. "Sorry." She dropped her phone back into her bag, fumbled his fare into his hand, and jumped out. "Thanks."

Crystal waited for an oncoming cab to pass then crossed the street. She jumped as the cab honked at the car in front of it. An answering honk came quickly. She wove her way around a parked moving van.

She was always amazed by how easily plays came and went. Two weeks ago, *Making a Splash* had opened to great expectations. Then the bad reviews had started. As a supporting actress, she'd been lucky enough to escape mention by name, but guilt by association was bad enough.

The aroma of fresh-cooked hotdogs drifted to her from the small vendor by the door, and her stomach growled. She nodded to the white-capped man.

He gave her a toothless grin. "Half price for you," he called.

She laughed. "You only say that because you know I don't eat before the show."

He sent her a broad wink. "When the curtains close, the cost doubles."

"I'll have to take my chances." Today she bantered almost on automatic pilot. She just felt so tired inside. With two fingers she caressed the tiny daisy pendant that hung around her neck. Brad had picked a fine time to be a no-show. Some wannabe fiancé he was.

As if on cue, her purse vibrated. She stepped over to the edge of the sidewalk and retrieved her phone from the big red bag. She pressed a button to read the text message. TEXT ME LATER IF YOU WANT ME TO MEET YOU FOR THE CAST PARTY.

She started to hit REPLY but accidentally landed on the message that had irritated her an hour ago. HELPING DENNIS MOVE TONIGHT. DON'T FREAK OUT. AFTER ALL, I SAW OPENING NIGHT AND YOU WERE GREAT. BREAK A LEG.

Her lips tightened and she shoved her phone back into her purse. She could text him at intermission, and he'd have plenty of time to make it for the cast get-together. Right now, she needed to concentrate on the show.

"It's been nine months." Jeremy Buchanan slammed his fist on the old oak table and pushed to his feet. "Why can't we find her?"

Sam gave him an uneasy look and stood. "Being patient is never easy. This time it was a dead-end lead. But next time. . ."

Jeremy stared at the private investigator, whose Adam's apple bobbed as he swallowed.

Shame coursed through him. The situation he was in was no one's fault but his own. Yet here was a grown man half afraid of him. He nodded and slapped Sam. . .gently. . .on the shoulder. "I'm sure next time *will* be different. I appreciate your not giving up."

Sam nodded, but Jeremy was pretty sure he didn't imagine a bit of hurry in the man's step as he let the screen door slam behind him.

Jeremy crossed the kitchen and stood by the cordless phone, waiting for the call he knew was coming. *Five, four, three, two, one,* he counted down. The phone chimed loudly and he lifted it off the cradle and hit the TALK button. "Hi, Mom."

"Actually, it's me," a deep voice said, embarrassment evident.

Jeremy couldn't resist a sad grin. That had been the way for forty years. His mom had always suckered his dad into doing her dirty work. "Oh. Hi, Dad. Sorry."

"That's okay. Your mom—"

Jeremy heard a murmur in the background.

"We. . ." His dad cleared his throat. "We wanted to know what you found out."

"Nothing. Dead end."

The silence on the phone line hurt almost as bad as the news from the PI had.

"I figured it was."

"Yeah, me, too."

"Hang on, your mom wants to talk to you."

Jeremy tightened his fingers on the phone.

"Jeremy?"

"Hi, Mom. Sorry the news isn't better."

"Don't give up hope, son. God hears our prayers."

Jeremy nodded, even though she couldn't see him. "I know."

"Your dad wants to know if you want to come over for supper."

"Nah, I've got soup in the refrigerator. I think I'll read awhile and turn in early tonight. I promised Jonathan I'd check the hay crop in his bottom field and see if the cold snap the other night got it. But you better have coffee ready when I get done with that," he teased halfheartedly.

"Yeah, we know how cranky you are without your caffeine in the morning." Her teasing was as forced as his, but at least she tried. "See you, then. Love you."

"Y'all, too."

Crystal slipped inside the backstage area. She closed her eyes and let the familiar smell of turpentine and the noise of sound checks calm her like a cup of chamomile tea. She might be tired, but there was no denying her love for the theater.

"Crystal?"

She jerked her eyes open.

Zee, the stage director, frowned at her, his gold eyebrow hoop lifting. "You okay?"

She smiled. "I am. It's just been a long day, and you know closing nights are always rough."

"Hmph," he grunted. "Especially when they're forced on you. But you'll be great. Just like always." She was surprised he didn't ruffle her hair. He wasn't much older than she was, but in spite of the fact that she was twenty-five, most of the show people still treated her like she was a teenager. The joys of being short.

"Thanks, Zee. You're sweet."

"Tell that to Tink. I need all the help I can get with her." A grin flitted across his tan face, the long scar from his ear to his chin puckering slightly.

"I'll put in a good word for you." Crystal laughed and hurried into the crowded dressing room.

Her friend and castmate, Tina, or "Tink," as Zee called her, waved from an empty station. She ran both hands through her dark spiky hair and finished with her arms straight up in the air in a ta-da motion. "There you are."

Crystal motioned toward Tina's hair. "Turquoise, huh? Cool."

Tina fluffed her multi-colored spikes. "Yeah, thanks."

Every few weeks, Tina's highlights changed color. Tonight, they matched her blouse and her eye shadow.

"I'm all done with my hair and makeup. Want me to do yours?"

"Thanks. I'd love that." Crystal sank onto the chair and closed her eyes.

Tina briefly massaged her shoulders. "Girl, you're tighter than a fiddle string tonight," she said, in her thick Texas drawl.

"I know." Crystal sighed and tried to relax.

Tina's hands flew as she brushed through Crystal's shoulder-length hair. "Why do I think that sigh isn't all because the play's closing?"

Crystal jerked her head up to meet the woman's gaze in the mirror.

The heavy black eyeliner around Tina's eyes didn't hide the compassion there. "What's wrong?"

Crystal shrugged. "Nothing really."

Tina snorted. "Nothing, my foot."

Those blue eyes never missed a trick. Crystal sighed again. "Isn't it enough that the play *is* closing? And that you, Zee, and I will have to try to find another job Monday? What if we don't get one together?"

Tina grabbed a folded-up newspaper and stuffed it into Crystal's bag. "I know you don't want to see it now, but read it after the show."

Crystal laughed. "Must be some review. First Mia, now you." She held up her hand. "But you're right. I don't want to know."

Tina snatched a pick off the counter and attacked Crystal's hair, artfully styling it into the homeless look necessary for the first scene. "Don't worry. We'll get a gig together. You audition where you want to, and we'll tag along. We've done it before. What else?"

"Brad texted to tell me he couldn't make it tonight. Something came up."

Tina shrugged. "Wedding-Proposal Ken can't make it tonight, huh? That's a little irritating, and you know the right answer to his question anyway, you just don't want to admit it. I'm pretty sure there's something bigger wrong, unless I'm way off base."

A smile tugged at the corners of Crystal's mouth, but she was careful not to show it. Tina got a kick out of calling Brad "Ken" as in "Ken and Barbie," but other than that, she had good instincts. In every way.

Tina paused with the teasing comb above Crystal's head. "Might as well tell me. You know you want to."

"Maybe you need to go to work for one of those psychic hot-lines," Crystal drawled.

"Very funny. You know I don't believe in that mumbo jumbo. I just know you. Nice try changing the subject though. And if you really don't want to talk about it, far be it from me to be pushy."

Crystal grinned. "Pushy? You?" She considered taking the out. But Tina was her safety valve, and right now she really needed that. "I got an e-mail from Aaron."

Tina tapped her lip with the comb and stared at the ceiling for a second. Then her gaze met Crystal's in the mirror again. "Aaron. Got married a couple months ago. Right?"

"You amaze me."

She shrugged. "I don't have any family but my grandpa to keep up with. So keeping your six brothers and sisters straight is a challenge. Besides, it was an event worthy of your going home for a visit. That in itself is rare enough to make me remember it."

"I visit." Crystal heard the defensiveness in her voice, but she couldn't seem to help it. "Holidays are a bad time to get away in this business. You know that."

Tina opened her mouth then shut it again. She took a deep breath and smiled. "So what did Aaron have to say?"

Crystal closed her eyes for a second as she remembered the e-mail. "He and Bree have gotten a chance to move to inner-city Chicago for a year and do some mission work with at-risk boys."

"Ah, that's sweet." Tina slapped Crystal's arm. "Too bad they don't want to move to the Big Apple. We could use a little more gospel around here, don't ya think?"

Crystal nodded absently. "I guess." Tina and Zee were always trying to get her to go to church with them. In a way, that was probably what had drawn her to them in the beginning. Even though she'd quit going to church when she moved to the city, she still believed in God. She just wasn't sure He cared about people who had turned their backs on Him. "This is a special houseparent program that Aaron and Bree have a chance to participate in."

"Good for them."

Crystal looked in the mirror at the dark smudges under her eyes. "Aaron was twelve and just about to initiate into a Chicago gang when his grandmother died and we got him. So he feels a strong need to do this. Stop boys from getting into gangs. Provide a place where people care about them and give them boundaries."

Tina smiled. "And introduce them to Jesus."

Crystal ignored her comment. "Anyway, Aaron called a family meeting for tomorrow."

"You going?"

Crystal snorted. "To Arkansas? I'll be auditioning and you know it."

"On Saturday?"

"All next week. It would be a waste to just fly there and fly back. Not to mention annihilating my tiny savings."

"So everyone but you is going to be there."

She shrugged. "Probably. But they know I can't make it."

"Can't or won't?" Tina muttered. Before Crystal could respond, she spoke in a normal voice. "So what's the problem with Aaron leaving?"

"He's Dad's right-hand man."

"Don't some of your other sisters and brothers live nearby?"

"Yeah, but they're busy with their own lives. Aaron's been the main one who takes care of the cattle. And Mama and Daddy are going on an overseas trip in a week. I think he's afraid they'll cancel."

"Mission trip?" Tina asked, her voice dry, as she deftly started on makeup.

Crystal nodded. "With a second honeymoon tacked on for good measure."

"Honeymoon or no honeymoon, your family's so holy, 'The Hallelujah Chorus' must burst out spontaneously every time they're together. I bet they bug you worse than we do about going to church."

Crystal frowned. "Not really so much."

"It's not because they've given up on you, honey," Tina drawled as she smoothed in the foundation on Crystal's face.

Heat spread from Crystal's neck to her face. Tina had an uncanny way of taking the words right out of Crystal's mind and speaking them aloud. She glanced in the mirror and cringed inwardly. Not much chance her embarrassment would escape unnoticed, since the pale makeup clashed violently with her red face.

Tina made no comment about the color change. "Your biggest sin is you're too hard on yourself."

"I'm not hard on myself."

"Yeah, and I'm not from Texas," Tina drawled as she unfastened the Velcro at Crystal's neck and whipped the white cape off her with a flourish. "Ta-da. The most beautiful homeless woman I've ever seen."

CHAPTER 2

Director's meeting in two minutes," a deep voice yelled from the hall.

The room erupted into pandemonium.

Cries of, "Throw me my shoes," and "Does my hair look right?" whizzed across the room like arrows. Tina linked her arm in Crystal's, and they hurried out the door ahead of the mass exodus.

Five minutes later, Crystal pulled her knees up to her chest as she nestled in the theater seat and listened to Ray reminding them about blocking and cues. Out of habit, she again put her hand to the diamond daisy on a silver chain around her neck. Three months and three bouquets of roses after her agent introduced them and they started dating, she'd finally told Brad she preferred everyday daisies to hothouse roses. When they'd gone to Arkansas for Bree and Aaron's Valentine's Day wedding, he'd presented her with the diamond necklace.

She'd laughingly accused him of missing the point. But there was some truth to her accusation. She glanced behind her at the empty theater. The seats just waiting to be filled. Why was it so hard to explain that something as simple as filling a seat and being supportive meant more than expensive gifts?

Ray's tone shifted, and Crystal's attention jerked back to the present. "I may be flipping burgers tomorrow, but tonight I'm proud to be your director." He smiled, but tears glittered in his bloodshot eyes.

Crystal felt her own eyes watering. Starting over was never easy. She thought that was one reason she felt so tired and depressed. Each cast became a family, and closings were almost like divorces.

"Let's make them sorry they forced us to close."

Everyone nodded.

"Because if I really do end up being your manager at the little burger joint down at Forty-third and Seventh, we're both gonna regret it."

Crystal laughed along with the rest of the cast as they filed out and hugged the director. But by the time the curtain rose a few minutes later, she was back to an emotional train wreck. Hard to believe what high hopes she'd had opening night. Fickle didn't begin to describe this business. And tired didn't begin to describe how she felt when the second curtain call was over.

"You are *not* going to miss the farewell party," Tina insisted as they wiped off their makeup.

"Yes I am," Crystal assured her, tears too close to the surface to trust a longer explanation. "I've already told everyone good-bye."

Tina stared at her.

Apparently she'd have to risk tears, or Tina wasn't going to let the subject drop. "I have a splitting headache. And I just need to go home."

Tina nodded. "Okay. Let me call you a cab."

Crystal forced a smile. "No cabs for me. I need to save money now. Tomorrow, I'll be back to waitress pay full-time, if they'll have me." In between plays and on her off days, she worked as a waitress at the deli near her apartment. Even though the job brought more blisters and exhaustion than it did tips, for now it was all she had.

"Or you could go home for a couple of weeks. . .see what the family meeting brings. Zee and I wouldn't mind taking a short vacation until you get back."

Crystal laughed. "Or I could fly to the moon. One's about as likely as the other."

Tina grabbed her cell phone out of her pocket. "Fine. Give me a sec to tell Zee I'll meet him at the party, and I'll run you home."

Crystal reached out and touched Tina's phone. "Thanks, but no thanks. It would take more than the threat of a short walk to the subway to get me on that Hawg." Tina's bright red Harley Davidson was three times as big as she was, but she controlled it like it was a bicycle. That still didn't mean Crystal wanted to get on it.

"Walking in the city's more dangerous than riding with me. I guarantee you that."

"I know. But it's not far. I'll be fine."

Tina shrugged. "Girlfriend, when you open the dictionary to the word *stubborn*, if your picture's not there, it should be."

"Thanks." As Crystal walked out the door, she shot her friend an impish grin. "Stubborn is what gets us where we're going. Especially in this business."

Jeremy flipped the switch that plunged the downstairs into darkness and carried the phone upstairs with him. A beam of silver light shone through the window at the top of the stairs. He started to his room and stopped, unable to keep himself from going to the room next door instead.

He turned the knob and stepped inside. And waited for the familiar scent. His heart squeezed in his chest. All that was left was the smell of a closed-up room.

He touched the light switch then dropped his hand, allowing the moonlight to soften reality. The twin bed creaked under his weight as he sat and picked up a small gray elephant. With his face pressed against the soft toy, he prayed, words he'd prayed hundreds of times before.

"Amen," he whispered. He felt a split second of peace before doubt and anger flooded in. He shoved to his feet, frustrated with his inability to control his thoughts. All day long, he worked hard and concentrated on keeping things going on his small cattle farm. But when darkness came, anger—raw fury at Lindsey for turning his life upside down—came with it. Especially on nights like this when bad news was his only companion.

He peered out of the window. In the distance, his mom and dad's guard light emitted an eerie orange glow. They were good neighbors and normally they minded their own business. His friendship with them was one of the bright spots in his life. But their pain magnified his own. Next time, he'd have Sam meet him somewhere else or just tell him the news—or lack of—over the phone. No use in getting their hopes up over and over.

He glanced upward at the blanket of glistening stars. Was she looking at the same stars? Was she scared? Had she forgotten him?

Outside the theater after saying good-bye to everyone, Crystal automatically looked to the sky. Her daddy always told them that no matter where they were in the world, if they were lost at night, all they had to do was follow the stars. But after sundown in the Big Apple, the bright lights made it seem like day everywhere but in the darkest alleys. And there, the buildings were so tall that even the sky was obliterated by brick and mortar.

She wrapped her jacket tighter around herself and walked faster. Almost as much as she missed her family, she missed the stars. Especially on nights like this. The strong March wind blew a stray flyer across her feet, and she instinctively recoiled then shook her head. Just thinking about home made her jumpy. Maybe that was why she knew her future was in New York City, not on a ranch in Arkansas.

As she reached in her bag to grab her subway pass, her hand closed on the folded newspaper Tina had shoved in there. Once she was on the train, she slid into a seat and unfolded the paper. "*Making a Splash* isn't making much of a splash with audiences," she read. "Herman Lowder's play lacks—"

Crystal frowned and skipped down to where her name was circled in red.

"Despite the fact that *Making a Splash* flops like a fish on dry land most of the time, Lowder's play has its moments. For instance, any moment where Crystal McCord has face time on the stage. Her performance seems so effortless that one has to wonder if she might really know what it's like to be homeless and alone."

She stuffed the paper back into her bag. The last sentence was too close to true for comfort, but at least when her name had finally made it into the review, it wasn't negative. She felt a strong desire to call someone. But as she went through her list—her agent, her roommate, her mother—she knew the one person she wanted to call wasn't reachable by phone anymore. What was wrong with her tonight? Maybe the unexpected closing of the play had reminded her too much of other abrupt endings.

She shifted in her seat and pressed in Brad's number but hit END before it started ringing. Since she hadn't planned on going to the after-party, she hadn't texted him at intermission. And he hadn't contacted her, either. It would do them good to just take the night off. She didn't have an answer for him yet anyway, and if they got together tonight, he'd probably expect one.

The subway jerked to a halt and she thrust the phone in her bag. Outside, she instinctively glanced at the sky again. To her amazement, two tiny lights flickered, higher than the city spires. Were they stars? "You feel small, don't you, little guys?" she whispered. "This place is great, but sometimes it does that to you."

Ten minutes later, she slid her key in the lock and stepped into the two-bedroom apartment she shared with Sabra. A good night's sleep would help her to make sense of everything.

A giggle followed by a masculine chuckle drifted from Sabra's closed door.

"Great," Crystal murmured and walked softly into her own tiny room. Once inside, she shut the door and collapsed onto her bed.

Why had she jumped so quickly into this unofficial rental agreement with her fellow waitress? She stretched out on the soft mattress and knew the answer immediately. The first few years she'd been in the city, she'd lived with four other girls in a boardinghouse room. As the newest paying tenant, her "bed" had been a sleeping bag in the corner. Somehow loneliness in a crowded room is magnified. And she thought she'd smother with it if she didn't get some privacy. But she'd put one foot in front of the other. And learned to be a better actress.

Eventually, as her roommates had moved on, she'd worked her way up to a real bed, but when Sabra offered to share this rent-control apartment with her, even though Crystal didn't know her very well, the lure of having her own room had been too much to resist.

In spite of their differences, they got along most of the time, and in fairness to Sabra, the redhead did make a point not to have men in the apartment while Crystal was there. But tonight, thanks to the play going kaput and her skipping the cast party, she was home three hours earlier than expected.

"You pay rent," she muttered to herself. "You don't have to hide." She pulled on an old Razorbacks sweatshirt and a matching pair of maroon sweatpants. When she opened her door, she could hear Sabra talking in her bedroom, so she tiptoed over to the bathroom. Just as she reached it, the door creaked open.

Her breath caught in her throat. Sabra must be on the phone in her room. Unless she had two visitors.

Either way, Crystal stared at the floor. In her peripheral vision, she could see feet and ankles. And thankfully, the tattered hem of a pair of jeans.

She blew out her breath. Not as bad as it could be.

Her gaze traveled up to where the man had frozen in the act of patting his wet hair with a white towel that draped across his tanned chest. She stared at his brown eyes huge in a pale face. Those oh-so-familiar eyes.

Her heart skipped several beats before the metal walls came down around it and the door clanged shut. She was wrong. This was ten thousand times worse than she'd imagined it could be.

"Brad," she whispered.

CHAPTER 3

Crystal's hand flew to her daisy necklace and she tried to find the right words to say. She stared at the man who had proposed to her a week ago. . .the man who was supposedly still waiting for her answer. . .and drew a blank.

She'd shared her heart with this man. Told him things no one else in New York knew. He'd held her while she cried, and for a little while she'd had a semblance of peace.

"Helping Dennis move?" Her heart sat like a heavy block of ice in her chest.

He shook his head. "Crys, this isn't what it looks like."

"So you're not sleeping with Sabra?" Her teeth ground together as she said the name.

He pursed his lips as if considering the question. "Well. . ."

Even though she'd known the truth the second she saw him with wet hair and just his jeans on, she'd still hoped. Hoped there was some crazy reason for him being here like this. Disgusted with herself for being so naive, she blinked hard against the tears.

He held out his hand. "This was all a mistake. Let me make it up to you. Please." He widened those brown puppy dog eyes in a way she could never resist.

"Only guess what?" she blurted out. "I'm resisting."

"What?" he said, his brows drawing together as he reached for her arm.

"Never mind." She took a quick step back. "Get out."

He shook his head. "You don't mean that. You're just mad. And I don't blame you."

"You don't blame me? Well, that's mighty big of you." How could she have thought even for a second that this was the man she was going to marry? She'd wasted a year of her life learning to ignore his little habits that annoyed her. "Some things can't be ignored."

Brad looked puzzled again, but then he sighed. "Of course not," he said soothingly. "I wouldn't expect you to ignore this. But we can work through it."

"I hate tennis."

"What?"

"And brunch." She knew she was on the verge of hysteria, but that was the thing about hysteria, there was no rhyme or reason. She could feel the hot tears splash onto her cheeks.

His eyes widened. "Brunch?"

"What's wrong with breakfast? Bacon and eggs, sausage even, with homemade biscuits and gravy?"

He frowned. "Crystal. Are you okay?"

"Am I okay?" She motioned toward his bare chest. "You're standing here half dressed, and you're asking me if I'm okay?"

"I'm sorry, honey. I didn't intend for this to happen. I love you. It's just that. . ."

Betrayal replaced the hysteria with fury. "Just that what?" she snapped. "That Sabra threw herself at you and you couldn't resist?"

She heard a door behind her open and spun around as Sabra, wrapped in a tiny pink robe, red hair tousled, stepped into the hallway.

"Brad, what's going on?" Sabra stopped as she saw Crystal.

"Apparently what's going on is you decided that what's mine is yours," Crystal said flatly. "I think a better question might be, 'How long has this been going on?' "

"Crystal—" Sabra started to say, but shrank back as Crystal stepped toward her.

"How could you?" Crystal didn't even try to stop the tears now. "When you had the flu, who brought you 7UP? Who sat beside you and held a cold rag on your head? Who cleaned it up when you couldn't make it to the trash can?" She clutched her stomach, the queasiness easy to remember. "I should have known what kind of friend you were when I got it the next day and you had 'plans.' "

Sabra's face paled. "I didn't mean for this to happen."

"You didn't mean for me to get the flu either," Crystal said quietly, "but it still made me sick."

Brad sighed loudly. "We didn't do this to you on purpose."

Crystal turned back around toward him. "No? I thought you loved me. You asked me to marry you!"

He looked from Crystal to Sabra then back again. "Crys. . ." He shifted from bare foot to bare foot. "I do love you." His face reddened.

Crystal stared at him, her blood pounding in her ears. *Now* he was embarrassed? Unbelievable.

"You're the one I want to marry. This. . ." He gestured toward Sabra without really looking at her. "This means nothing to me."

Sabra gasped. "Dude. You're calling me nothing?" she screeched. "I'll show—"

Crystal spun around and cut her off. "Don't bail on him now." She reached up and wrapped her hand around the diamond daisy on her necklace. The feel of it around her neck was like an iron manacle. Gritting her teeth, she pulled, ignoring the pain of the delicate silver chain cutting into the back of her neck. One more yank and she tossed the charm, chain and all, at Sabra's feet. "Here's a sign of his deep commitment. It's all yours."

Brad started forward. "No! That's yours."

Crystal shoved him back then jerked her hand away as she touched his bare shoulder. "Let her have it. She's earned it. Since I don't have thirty pieces of silver lying around, this is the best I can do."

Sabra slouched a little and jutted out her chin. "Crys, he's right. It didn't mean anything." She shot daggers at Brad with her eyes. "To either of us, obviously. It was a mistake—"

How do you sleep with your friend's boyfriend by mistake? Crystal thought cynically. Suddenly, her anger waned. She felt too tired to say another word.

Brad took a step toward her. "You know what, honey? I really should go and let you cool down."

As soon as he said the words "cool down," white-hot anger flared inside Crystal like a fanned flame. "Yes, *honey*. You should go. Let me get your clothes for you."

She spun around and marched into Sabra's room. Her stomach churned as she saw Brad's folded Hollister T-shirt on the dresser beside his Birkenstock shoes and leather wallet. The neatness screamed of planning and forethought. Pre-meditated betrayal.

Fury pushed her forward. She scooped it all up into her arms. Her gaze fell immediately on the open window. Still holding Brad's belongings, she stumbled over to look out. Two stories below where people were hurrying by. Going on with their lives. Unaware that hers had taken a major detour.

"Hey!" she yelled. "Look out below." A couple of people glanced up, but most just kept going.

Brad and Sabra skidded to a stop in the doorway of the bedroom. Crystal plunked his shoes out of the window one by one and glanced back to see her ex-boyfriend watching her with shock. Sabra looked almost bemused, like she wasn't sure who Crystal was anymore.

"You can't do that," Brad said.

"Watch me." She turned back to glance down at one shoe wedged in a shrub. If she remembered correctly, a prickly holly. She tossed his T-shirt out. The yellow shirt with the white bird on it fluttered to the ground in front of the bushes.

"Not the wallet, not the wallet." Brad rushed toward her.

"Glad to see *something* is important to you." She let the shiny black leather billfold slip from her hand and watched with satisfaction as it fell with a *plunk* behind the shrubbery. She was 90 percent sure that was a "sticky bush," as she and her brothers and sisters always called hollies with sharp leaves.

"You crazy—" he yelled then turned and sprinted shirtless and barefoot down the hall. Within seconds, she heard the front door slam.

She brushed past a speechless Sabra and darted down the hall to her own room. Her breath came in short spurts as she locked the door and leaned against it.

Eyes closed, she imagined the starry night sky, the sound of horses neighing softly in the corral. She pictured the familiar surroundings, focusing on the smell of fresh hay and dirt. For a split second, a memory of Brad there with her for Aaron and Bree's wedding sliced through her distracting technique, but she pushed it away.

"Crystal," Sabra whined from outside the door, "you and I have to talk."

Crystal ignored her and stepped to the closet. She stood on tiptoes and slid her big black overnight bag off the top shelf. She took her three favorite outfits from the closet, rolled them up, and stuffed them in the bag. Three pairs of shoes went in on top of them. She dumped her top drawer in next then jumped back as her gaze fell on a tiny stuffed black-and-white dog.

A sob started, and she wrapped one arm across her stomach. With two fingers, she lifted the toy and tossed it into the trash can. He'd taken her to the carnival only because she insisted that it reminded her of home. Another sob hit and she couldn't stop it. Finally she just let them wash over her. She worked as she sobbed, tossing in designer jeans, polo shirts, and tees indiscriminately. When the bag was overflowing, she leaned hard against it, slid the zipper shut, and sat on the bed next to it.

The crying stopped as quickly as it started, and she stared at herself in the mirror. It was over. And she had no desire for it to be otherwise. It still hurt, but letting herself feel pain opened up a Pandora's box she wasn't ready to face. So for now, she picked up her cell phone and called a cab. Now to face Sabra again.

Clutching her bag and purse, she opened the door. Sabra, looking pretty relaxed on the couch, fumbled for the remote and muted the TV. She jumped to her feet. "Hey."

"I'll be back in about a week to get what I can't carry tonight." Crystal stopped and looked back. The thought of leaving anything in Sabra's apartment made her physically ill. "On second thought, I'll have someone come by tomorrow and get the rest of it." Tina and Zee would do it. For once, she was glad that she'd accumulated little since she'd left home.

"Seriously?" Sabra said the word like "searslee."

Crystal grunted under her breath. To think, until she'd bumped into Brad in the bathroom doorway tonight, the most irritating thing about her roommate had been Sabra's high-pitched slang. Sometimes perspective was a painful concept to grasp.

Sabra blew out a loud breath as if irritated by the whole situation. "Listen. You don't have to go. Good roommates are hard to find."

Crystal stared at her. "Tell me about it."

She hurried out the door without looking back.

Out on the street, a yellow cab was just pulling away. The one she'd called? The thought that someone would steal her cab hit her like the last straw. "Hey!" She whistled and waved.

The yellow car slowed. Crystal yanked the back door open and skidded to a stop. Brad stared up at her. Fully clothed. "Crystal. I'm glad you changed your mind. I love—"

He started to climb out, but Crystal reared back and slammed the door with all her might.

Another cab eased up to the curb and she jumped into it. "Lock the doors, please, and be sure they don't follow us." She motioned toward the car in front of them.

The driver's dark eyes looked puzzled, but he nodded. "Where to?"

"Arkansas."

He tapped the brakes and met her gaze in the mirror this time. "Ma'am?"

She sighed and collapsed against the worn seat. "The airport."

He accelerated and she closed her eyes.

She knew she really had no right to ask for help. But right now she didn't know where else to turn.

Lord, help me, please.

I'm going home.

Jeremy opened his truck door and froze, his hand cupped over the metal frame. Instead of sliding in, he grabbed his hat off the seat and headed for the barn. Maybe being out in the cool morning air would blow away the cobwebs of another restless night.

In his stall, Nacho gazed up at his master and whinnied softly.

"Hey, brother." Jeremy hooked an easy arm around the paint's neck. "How 'bout a ride this mornin'?"

He worked quickly in the stillness of the barn, keeping his mind on the familiar task before him, as he saddled the horse. Before Lindsey had taken Beka, he'd often wondered how people go on when they lose someone they love. Now he realized they had two choices. Go on or give up. Quitting was out of the question as long as there was hope. And the only way to keep going, for him anyway, was to consider each new day as another day closer to finding them.

He put his foot in the stirrup and slung himself up onto Nacho's back. Just like they always did, his anger and worries faded to the background as he and the horse worked together as one.

Tiny splotches of green along the branches of the trees and the short sprigs of grass popping up in old Mr. Marshall's yard caught his eye as he galloped by. They reminded him of the last picture Beka had colored for him. Almost a year later, the faded paper still hung on his refrigerator, its corners slightly curled.

As he neared the bridge, spring seemed to kick into hyperdrive. More and more green flashed by him. He slowed Nacho to a walk.

Honeysuckle mixed with the scent of the river as they clip-clopped across the wooden bridge. Jeremy took a deep breath. His life was in Sam's hands, and disappointments like last night made it hard to keep on believing. Over coffee, his mom had accused him of taking on too many jobs in order to keep his mind occupied. He snorted aloud at the memory. Nacho shifted slightly under him, responding to his master's unease.

As if work could keep his mind off of Beka for more than a second. He helped Jonathan when he could because the McCords were good neighbors, and when it was time to do things on his own ranch or his father's, Jonathan and the boys were the first ones there.

He laid the reins gently against Nacho's neck and guided him into the narrow dirt path that led to the McCords' bottom field. As he neared the moorings of the bridge, a tiny black compact car caught his attention. Who would drive a car like that down a field road? The tags identified the vehicle as a rental. Hair stood up on the back of his neck. This was private property. And none of the McCords would be driving that car.

He shifted his hat back on his head and examined the riverbank. Nobody. "Whoa," he said softly. Nacho stopped immediately. He patted the horse's neck as he slid off and let the reins fall to the ground. Some things in life were more certain than others. He knew he could count on the fact that Nacho would be standing right here when he returned.

He'd almost reached the car when he saw her.

Beside a brushy tree on the bank with her back to him, the woman stood as still as a tree herself. Blond hair barely touched her shoulders. Her clothes went with the car, black and way too dressy for this particular locale.

Either she hadn't heard him or she hoped that if she didn't acknowledge him he'd go away. And for a second he wanted to. The oddity of the whole picture screamed complications, and Jeremy needed to simplify his life. Not complicate it.

"Excuse me, ma'am."

He thought he saw her flinch, but she still didn't turn, nor did she answer.

He took a couple more steps toward her to make sure she heard him above the rushing water. "Ma'am? Are you okay?"

"I'm fine," she said, still not turning around.

Walk away. She said she was fine. But her tear-clogged voice and slumped shoulders said otherwise.

He took another step toward her. "Are you from around here?" He and his parents had just moved here two years ago after they'd sold the gas rights to their property in south Arkansas. Maybe she was a native he just hadn't met yet.

"I used to be." She still didn't face him, her blond hair shifting around her shoulders with the breeze. "Whatever happened to cowboys being the strong silent type?"

So she *had* seen him ride up.

"I'm sorry, ma'am. But this is private property."

She turned around to face him, her blue eyes glistening. "I think the owner will let it slide this time."

CHAPTER 4

He took a step back as he recognized her. "Crystal." Jonathan McCord's oldest daughter's appearances in this part of the country were as rare as a March snow. Jeremy had only finally met her at her brother's wedding a couple of months ago. "I didn't know you were home."

She sighed. "Neither does anyone else. Yet."

He shifted from foot to foot. Why hadn't he trusted his instincts to avoid complication earlier and walked away? "You okay?"

A smile tilted her lips slightly. "I'm not sure yet. I'll let you know."

He looked past her at the water, an old rope swing swayed gently in the wind. "Do you always stop by here when you come home?"

She turned to face the river. "No. Only when I need somewhere *private*"—even though she stressed the word, she glanced over her shoulder with a sheepish grin—"to gather my thoughts."

"I'm sorry."

She looked back at him again. "I was teasing."

"I know. But I'm still sorry for suggesting you were trespassing. And for interrupting your peace and quiet." He doffed his hat to her even though she wasn't looking at him. "Have a nice visit." He turned to walk away.

"Jeremy. Wait."

He stopped and faced her. "Yes?"

"I actually owe *you* an apology." She sank onto the bank, pulling her knees up to her chest.

"Me?" He stared at her, a study in contrast sitting on the ground in her dressy clothes.

She nodded and patted the grass beside her.

Feeling a little like he was obeying a royal summons, he walked over and lowered his lanky frame to the ground next to her.

"At Aaron's wedding. . .Brad. . .my—the guy I was with. . .was not really nice to you." Her face reddened.

"And it's your place to apologize for him?" Even though he didn't hold a grudge, he hadn't forgotten the man who'd made a federal case out of Jeremy getting a cell phone call from Sam during the reception.

She kind of laughed. "Well, I guess not anymore."

As her words sank in, he nodded. She'd been way too classy for that poser. Anyone could see that. "Good for you."

She made a face. "It wasn't exactly my doing."

Okay, anyone *else* could see that. He, of all people, knew that love really was blind sometimes.

"Although he did want me to take him back, even after I caught him with my roommate. . ."

"Ouch."

"At least I had sense enough not to consider it." She plucked a piece of grass up and examined it, then tossed it five feet short of the water.

"That's smarter than I've been at times."

"Oh, hey"—her eyes softened and she touched his arm—"has there been any word about your daughter?"

He flinched. "No."

"I'm sorry." She fiddled with the grass blades as if searching for exactly the right one.

He cleared his throat. "Thanks for thinking about her."

"I bet you get tired of people asking."

"Not really." He shrugged. "Sure it hurts, but that way I know I'm not the only one who remembers she's missing."

"You're definitely not."

"So does your family know? About Brad?" Jeremy asked, as much to change the subject as anything.

"Huh-uh." She jerked her head from side to side quickly. "I hate the idea of them thinking I got my heart broken and ran home." She cut her gaze toward him. "Because that's not true."

"What would you like for them to think?"

She seemed to consider his words. "That I came for a surprise visit."

"So not only do they not know you're here, they don't know you're coming?" he asked.

"Right."

"Then I'd say this counts as a surprise visit, wouldn't you?"

"And you really think I could pull that off?"

He grinned. "You are an actress, aren't you?"

Actress or not, her smile was one of the most genuine he'd ever seen.

"Thanks."

He pushed to his feet and offered her a hand. "Anytime."

"Anytime? You may regret saying that when I call you at three in the morning to dump my problems on you." She slid her tiny hand into his, and he lifted her effortlessly to her feet.

He raised an eyebrow. "Three in the morning, huh? I'm usually awake around then anyway."

Sympathy flitted across her face again, and he regretted his words.

He pushed his hat down tighter on his head. "I'd better get

going. I hope you have a good visit with your family."

She glanced back at the river as if drawing strength from the steady stream. "Thanks. Me, too."

He stood still for a few seconds, waiting for her to move or speak, but she'd apparently forgotten him. Or dismissed him.

"Bye."

She jerked her attention back to him. "See you."

He walked out into the field, squatted down, and brushed back a little dirt. A tiny blade of grass poked up right below the surface. As he looked closer, he could see several green sprigs already breaking the surface around him. His shoulder muscles relaxed. He hadn't planted too early. Future weather cooperating, Jonathan would have a good stand of hay in this field.

As he started back to Nacho, he saw Crystal getting in her car. Even though Jeremy had only met her once, he was surprised he hadn't recognized her immediately, even from the back. Her breathtaking beauty and poignant grace made it hard to mistake her for anyone else.

He climbed astride the horse and settled into the saddle. As he watched the cloud of dust Crystal's car stirred up, he considered their conversation. He, of all people, knew how deceptive beauty and even sweetness could be. He'd do well to remember that this was just another girl who went her own way without regard to others' feelings but came running back to safety when her heart was broken.

"As long as I don't forget that, we'll be fine," he whispered to Nacho. "Let's go."

The horse broke into a gallop and, for the next few minutes, Jeremy cast his cares to the wind.

Crystal guided the tiny rental car into the first driveway, parked out by the barn, and killed the motor. Her eyes closed and she fell back against the headrest as she mentally chided herself.

Why had she even stopped at the river? If one place summed up everything she'd lost, everything she'd run away from, if all her happy childhood memories could be rolled into one location, that swimming hole would be it. When she stood on the bank, she hadn't seen placid water and an old rope. She'd seen tan legs and arms and white grins, heard loud yells and laughter, and felt overwhelmed by a mixture of nostalgia and grief. So why hadn't she driven on by?

At least then she wouldn't have spilled her guts to a cowboy. Jeremy Buchanan seemed genuinely nice and, what with his ex-wife stealing their daughter, he'd obviously seen his share of pain. But that was no excuse for telling him all about Brad. She couldn't remember the last time she'd done something so out of character. Unless it was throwing Brad's stuff out the window. She smiled. That was pretty different for her.

Her cell phone rang. She glanced at the caller ID and tensed. It was Brad. Without waiting for it to stop ringing, she hit IGNORE. She had nothing to say to him. Amazingly, she didn't even feel red-hot anger when she thought about him. She just felt. . .nothing. And right now she had bigger fish to fry, as her granny used to say. She had to face the family.

Jeremy had at least given her a good idea. She flipped down her visor mirror and scrutinized the tense face staring back at her. Could she convince her family that this was just a happy surprise and not have to bare her fresh wounds for everyone to sympathize with? The idea had merit.

She took her compact out and touched the sponge to the puffy circles under her eyes. A dab of color on her lips and, ta-da, she was ready to see the family. Her legs wobbled as she climbed out of the car and started down the pea gravel path to the house.

Who was she kidding? There were hundreds of highways she could have taken after she rented the car at the Memphis airport.

And right now, she was having to force herself to keep from running back to the car as fast as her high heels would allow and peeling rubber to the nearest road out of Shady Grove.

When she stepped up on the back porch, the laughter and loud conversation drifted out, pulling her forward. She'd missed them so much. For a few seconds, she stood at the door and listened, not for distinct words but just to the timbre of the familiar voices. Her daddy's deep rumble. Her mama's softer alto. And unless she missed her guess, the teasing tones belonged to the twins, Kaleigh and Chance. Even though they were in their early twenties, the two redheads never missed an opportunity to give each other a hard time.

She started to knock, but then she twisted the old metal door-knob instead and pushed the door open.

Everyone stopped talking, and she knew instantly what they were thinking. Since they were all there, who could be coming into the house unannounced? A pang sliced through her heart that she'd let herself become so distanced that a stranger would be more expected than she. She stepped inside and smiled at her family gathered around the long kitchen table.

Nine pairs of eyes were fixed on her. Beside the stove, her mama gasped, and still holding a spatula, ran across the room to pull Crystal into her arms. "So good to see you," she whispered against her hair.

Crystal nodded, blinking hard against the tears she'd thought she'd banished. "You, too."

Over her mama's shoulder, she could see Matthew waving.

"Hey." Luke saluted her with a forkful of gravy and biscuit. "Good to see you, kid."

Luke never missed a chance to rub in the fact that he was a few months older than she. He'd been twelve to her and Cami's eleven when their parents had adopted him. For some reason he'd been a little in awe of Cami, but he'd loved to tease Crystal and had claimed a whole year on her and called her "kid" ever since.

"My turn." A smile teased the corners of her daddy's mouth. His blue eyes sparkled. Her mother reluctantly released Crystal, and her daddy folded her into his big embrace. She breathed in Old Spice and Coast soap and smiled.

"Hey, Crys," Aaron called from the end and gave her a thumbs-up. "Glad you made it."

Beside him, his wife, Bree, waggled her fingers and grinned.

Lynda McCord spun around to face her oldest son. "You knew about this?" She waved her spatula at him. "You rascal."

Everyone, including her daddy, turned to stare at Aaron. Just as he'd known they would. Crystal gratefully took the opportunity to breathe.

Aaron shrugged and put his arm around Bree. "Would I spoil a surprise?"

A smile split Crystal's face. He'd make a great houseparent. Honest but diplomatic.

Kaleigh's fiery red ponytail bounced as she pushed her chair back and stood to hug Crystal. "Glad you're here," she said. "PM in the pole barn after breakfast," she whispered.

Crystal nodded. *PM* had always been their signal for a "private meeting," usually in the largely unused pole barn farthest from the house. "Private" as in no parents allowed. Thanks to Aaron's e-mail, Crystal knew that this particular meeting was about the newlyweds' immediate opportunity to move to Chicago and how that would affect their parents' planned Peru mission trip and the subsequent second honeymoon in Rio de Janeiro that the kids had given them last Christmas.

Crystal released Kaleigh and reached down to tap knuckles with Chance.

"What's up, sis?" he said softly, part greeting and part true question. Concern clouded his green eyes.

She forced a grin and shrugged. Chance had been the one she

was most worried about fooling. There was no chance that Aaron wouldn't know something was wrong, since they e-mailed almost daily. The others she could keep the truth from for a while. But at twenty-three, even though he was a joker, Chance was intuitive and sensitive to his brothers' and sisters' feelings. Crystal knew from experience that being tuned in to a twin's emotions made it easier to pick up random signals from the rest of the family, too.

Before Chance could question her further, Elyse rose gracefully from the chair on the other side of him, her cream-colored broomstick skirt swirling above her ankles. Crystal studied her sister with pride. Officially a dog trainer, unofficially, according to local legend, a "dog whisperer," the tall brunet had no idea how beautiful she was. Painfully shy when the McCords had first adopted her fourteen years ago, Elyse was finally almost as at ease with her own family as she was her four-legged friends. But she'd still predictably waited to be the last one to greet Crystal. "You staying with me?"

"Where else?" Crystal said it as a quip, but everyone in the room, with the possible exception of Bree, surely realized that since Luke was living in the small barn loft apartment, Elyse's place was her only choice. Unless she wanted to try a bed-and-breakfast in town. And she thought that would surely force her mama into pushing the issue of her not staying in the house.

She smiled at Elyse. "If you think the newest member of your family won't mind company. I can't wait to meet her. Aaron says you have her eating out of the palm of your hand. Literally." She refrained from saying that Aaron had called the recently rescued bichon frise "that vicious little ankle biter."

Elyse's brown eyes widened, but a soft grin played across her sculptured lips. "He's exaggerating, believe me. I've almost gained Nikki's trust, but I'm still not quite there. If you come over to the cottage in a little bit, I'll introduce you and you can unload your stuff."

Crystal nodded. Of course, her one satchel might give away the fact that this was an unplanned trip.

"So how long are you staying, kid?" Luke drawled from across the table, a smile splitting his unshaven face.

"Just a few—"

Mama neatly scooted his elbows off the table as she walked by and handed Crystal a full plate. "Right now, we're just glad she's here for breakfast, Lucas."

Crystal stared at the plate. Her stomach growled a noisy greeting, and her mouth watered. She hadn't eaten a bite since she'd thrown Brad out of the apartment last night. Actually since a couple of hours before the play. The smell of homemade biscuits and gravy mixed with bacon and eggs drove every other thought from her mind.

"Thanks, Mama." She took the plate and sank into the empty seat next to Elyse. "I've been dreaming about your breakfast." She smiled at the others. "I'll do the dishes, since I didn't help cook."

"You heard her," Kaleigh said with a sassy grin. "I'm off the hook."

"You're off, I'll give you that," Chance teased.

Everyone laughed, and Crystal relaxed her shoulders. The hardest part about coming home was always the awkward first few conversations. Usually she barely stayed longer than that.

For the next half hour, she ate and drank quietly and listened to her family, so different yet so close. When she and Cami were eight and her parents had decided to first foster then adopt Aaron, the idea of getting a big brother had been exciting. The reality had been a little different, especially when five more kids had been added to the family over the next few years.

But her love for them had grown every day they were together, and in these past few years they were apart, it hadn't faded any. If anything, she felt more attached to them because she didn't take their existence for granted.

41

CHAPTER 5

Crystal clutched the large, rough, wooden, rectangular "button" on the barn door and took a deep breath. How many times had she made the trek through the field from the house to this old barn? She looked down. Never in high heels. But she'd been here more times than she could count. For her and Cami's ninth birthday, Daddy had built them a stage in this unused barn. A simple wooden platform running the length of the far wall, with steps going up on each side, the "stage" was humble. But the twins had soon filled it with players, some willing, some not so much. She smiled at the memory.

She dropped her hand, suddenly unsure she could go in, even though she knew she was late for the meeting. She'd accepted the fact that she couldn't bear to go into their old bedroom, but would this be what her visits to the ranch would always be like? Standing outside familiar doors, afraid to go in?

Sudden anger flared up inside her and she yanked on the unlatched wooden door and it swung open. Inside, she squinted. Sunlight filtered in through the eaves and dirt-covered windows, but it took a few seconds for her vision to adjust.

"What took you so long?" Kaleigh asked from her perch on the bare stage. "The dishes were almost done when I left."

Crystal glanced around at her other brothers and sisters already settled in on the mishmash of old chairs and sofas arranged in front of the platform stage. She plopped down beside Matthew on the nearest couch and waved away the dust that rose in the air. "I'm guessing y'all haven't had very many meetings here since I've been gone," she coughed out. She didn't wait for an answer because a part of her didn't want to know if they'd gone ahead with the family tradition without her. "Mama changed her mind about going into town with Daddy."

A collective groan murmured through the room. Their parents had gone into town every Saturday after breakfast for as long as anyone could remember. It was a tradition rarely broken.

"I insisted she go with him, but I finally had to go settle in for a nap on the couch before Mama would believe it was okay for her to leave."

Matthew shook his head. "After all those Saturday morning meetings we had when we were kids, wouldn't it be funny to get busted for them now?"

"We'd have had to convince them we're getting the Pole Barn Players together for a reunion performance." Kaleigh pushed herself off the stage, landing on her feet on the concrete floor. Dust whooshed out around her. She swept into a silly bow.

Crystal grinned. Some things hadn't changed.

Aaron coughed. "Sure, like lying wouldn't make me feel even more guilty." He took Bree's hand. "I feel bad enough even thinking about leaving right now. Maybe we should just let this chance go by. There'll be others."

Crystal shook her head. "This position is tailor-made for the two of you, and we all know it. You have to be in Chicago a week from Tuesday. That part is already decided."

The others nodded.

Aaron gave them a doubtful look. "In that case, we have to tell

CHRISTINE LYNXWILER

Mama and Daddy today that we're leaving. And to keep them from canceling their trip, before we do that, we have to figure out who's going to take care of the ranch while they're gone."

Silence reigned in the room for about thirty seconds. Plenty long enough for Crystal to brace herself not to volunteer. She had to get back to New York and start auditioning. If you weren't on stage, you were being forgotten.

As if to prove the point, Kaleigh climbed back up on the stage and waved her hand in the air. "Chance and I can take turns helping out on weekends."

"Then who would show all the city slickers how to catch a fish?" Luke asked with a grin.

Crystal cringed. He was right. Kaleigh and Chance had put their river-rat childhood to good use when they started K&C Guided Fishing Tours back in high school. Now it was paying their way through college. They couldn't afford to jeopardize that.

Even she was a better choice than they were.

Luke shook his head. "Besides, you need to be concentrating on your schoolwork. The last thing you need to do is run home every weekend. I can handle things."

Kaleigh plopped back down on the edge of the stage, a dejected look on her face.

Crystal turned to Luke. "Aaron said you were working pretty long hours these days on that all-natural health center." Actually what he'd said was that Luke was almost killing himself to make up for several rainy weeks in the early spring. And that he'd already gotten a big chunk of his fee upfront and spent it on materials for the house he was going to build for himself.

"Maybe I can cut back."

"And still be ready for the grand opening in July?" Crystal shook her head. There had to be a better solution. One that didn't involve Crystal being forced home. *Please.*

Matthew cleared his throat. "I can come every other weekend."

"From Tennessee?" Elyse said softly. "Matthew, that's not logical. Vet school is too hard for you to be running back and forth." She stood and looked out the window. "I can handle the ranch."

"Hon. . ." Bree pushed to her feet and put an arm around Elyse's waist. They stared together out of the grimy window. Crystal glanced at their view. Cows grazed on the early spring grass. "You're busy, too."

Elyse shrugged gently away from Bree and turned back to the group. She raised an elegantly arched eyebrow. "I know what you are all thinking. But there's more to this ranch than"—she waved a hand over her shoulder as if she hated to say the word then laughed—"than cows." She smiled at the group. "Go ahead and laugh."

"We're not laughing," Crystal protested. Although they were all smiling. "And even though your schedule is packed, since you live and work right here, you're the most logical one to help out. But there are almost a thousand cows here. What if one of them got into trouble on the back forty?"

"That's why we hire people. I'd call one of the guys. They have cell phones, all except for Slim." Determination outlined her face, and it was impossible not to admire her courage in the face of her absolute terror of cows.

Crystal slumped. She knew they were all waiting for her to offer. Apparently they didn't know she was more afraid of coming home than Elyse was of cows. She bit her tongue.

"Sure you could do that," Aaron allowed. "But honestly, Elyse, with calving season coming up, you wouldn't have time to put in the hours needed, even if you weren't afraid of cows."

He scanned the group, but it seemed to Crystal like his gaze rested on her the longest. "Any more ideas?"

"I can't do it." She bit out the words.

"Oh no. Of course you can't," Elyse exclaimed softly. "You've got the play."

Aaron raised a brow as if wondering when she was going to tell everyone what he already knew.

Crystal squirmed. "*Making a Splash* actually closed last night." She shot Aaron a glare. "But I *am* about to start auditions."

"Oh, Crys. I'm sorry about the play." Compassion flooded Kaleigh's green eyes. "Are you okay?"

"I'm fine. There'll be another one soon. Who knows? Maybe Broadway this time."

"Well, you definitely can't come home to stay then, even for a while," Elyse said firmly. "We'll figure something else out."

Crystal waited for relief to untie the knot in her stomach. But it just seemed to get tighter.

A knock on the barn door made her jump.

"Come in," Aaron called, seemingly unsurprised.

This morning's handsome cowboy sauntered in like he owned the place.

Crystal stared at Jeremy Buchanan, suddenly flustered. Was that an almost imperceptible shake of his head?

He nodded to everyone. "Did I just wander onto the set of *The Waltons* reunion movie?"

"Just don't be calling me Jim Bob," Luke joked.

"You prefer Mary Ellen?" the cowboy quipped back as he closed the door behind him.

"Crystal, you remember Jeremy from the wedding, don't you?" Aaron said.

Could she just say yes or should she 'fess up to stopping by the river for a good cry before she arrived? "Actually. . ."

"It's great to see you again," Jeremy said with a big grin. "Home for a surprise visit?"

Oh boy. He'd encouraged her to bill her homecoming as a happy surprise instead of a heartbroken sister act, and now he was going to tease her about it?

"Yes, as a matter of fact I am." She returned his grin.

Aaron cleared his throat, his brows drawn together. Probably wondering what all the grinning was about. "I asked Jeremy to come by. He volunteered to handle things around here for the next few weeks." Aaron shot his friend an exasperated look. "But he refuses to take any pay."

Matthew shook his head. "Man, you can't do that. You've got your own things to manage."

Jeremy shrugged. "Since I don't have any livestock yet, except for a couple of horses, my ranch almost takes care of itself. Y'all help me whenever I need it. I'd like to repay the favor."

Crystal hadn't thought she could feel any smaller. How would their parents react when they found out she'd allowed a neighbor to step in when she was currently unemployed and homeless? Without allowing herself time to think, she shot to her feet. "Jeremy, thank you for offering, but it won't be necessary."

Everyone turned to look at her. "I'll do it," she said firmly.

"You?" Jeremy said, his dark eyebrows rising. "You're going to run the ranch?" His mouth twitched, and she had the uncomfortable feeling he was trying not to make a smart comment.

She saw her brothers exchange similar looks.

"Uh-oh," Luke muttered, but his dimples flashed.

Hands on her hips, she raised an eyebrow at Jeremy. "You don't think I can?"

He shrugged but she saw his glance go down to her stilettos. "I wouldn't imagine you get a lot of ranch experience in New York City."

Okay, now he was getting personal. The way he said "New York City" reminded her of that old *picante* sauce commercial. She lifted her chin and gave him her most confident smile. "Well, whatever you think," she said. "But I'll handle things here until Mama and Daddy get back."

"What about old what's-his-name?" Luke teased. "Think he'll mind commuting back and forth to Arkansas to see you?"

She met Jeremy's gaze. "That won't be a problem." Let the family draw whatever conclusions they wanted to from that answer.

Jeremy ducked his head. "I'll help you take care of things if that's okay."

Aaron shot her a silent plea. She knew him well enough to know he was reminding her of everything the man had been through.

She gritted her teeth. "Thanks, Jeremy. That'll be fine."

She sank back onto the couch as conversation continued around her. How had her whole life turned upside down in less than twenty-four hours?

"An undercover cop thought he saw Lindsey in a little blues joint down on Beale Street in Memphis last night."

Jeremy's heart thudded against his ribcage. "Did he take her in for questioning?"

"He's undercover," Sam's gravelly voice reminded him through the cell phone line. "And he's not sure it was her."

"Did he see a little girl?"

"No. But that's not surprising. It's hardly the kind of place for kids."

The thought of Beka being in a place like that, or worse, left at home in who knew what kind of rat hole to fend for herself, made his gut clench with anger and fear. "Give me the address."

"I can leave in a couple of hours to drive over and check it out."

Jeremy did some quick calculating. In Little Rock, Sam was about the same distance from Memphis as he was. "I'd like to go myself this time."

Silence. "You tried that before. Remember?"

Jeremy ran his hand across his eyes. How could he ever forget those first few months? He'd jetted from possible sighting to possible sighting until he'd finally collapsed from exhaustion and despair. "I'm stronger now. And I need to do something."

"I understand." Sympathy laced the deep voice. "Do you want me to meet you there?"

"Thanks anyway, Sam. Just give me the address."

Sam rattled off the address and Jeremy wrote it down.

The PI cleared his throat. "Listen, man, I know how upset you are with your ex-wife, but don't do anything stupid if you find her. She's the only one who knows where your little girl is."

Jeremy stared down at the paper clenched in his tight fist. He had enough restraint not to hurt Lindsey. But he felt pretty sure that when the police locked her up and threw away the key, she'd tell them where to find Beka. And then, as far as he was concerned, she could rot in jail for the rest of her miserable life.

Inside the smoky room, Jeremy stopped to get his bearings. "Blues joint" was an overstatement. Up on the tiny stage, a woman sang, or tried to between coughing fits, to an almost empty house. He scanned the few occupied tables. Lindsey definitely wasn't here tonight. He walked up to the bar and slid a twenty and Lindsey's picture across the scarred surface. "Have you seen her?" he said quietly.

The bartender, who barely looked old enough to get in the door, much less be working here, picked up the picture and ran his hand across his Mohawk haircut. "No." He tucked the twenty into the front pocket of his baggy jeans.

Jeremy scooted another twenty along with his card toward him. "Will you call me if you do?"

The young man's eyes lit up. "More where that came from if I do?"

Jeremy nodded.

"Fo' shizzle."

"Does that mean yes?"

The boy rolled his eyes and nodded.

Jeremy turned to walk over to the nearest table.

"If you're not lookin' for trouble, ya need to get on."

He glanced back at the boy. "Why?"

"People don't come here to be interrupted by strangers."

He cut his gaze toward the table again. The boy was right. "Fine. Call me if you see her."

"You keep payin' and I'd turn in my own mother."

Now why didn't that instill great confidence in him?

When Jeremy was halfway across the dim room, the singer finished up her song and stepped down off the stage.

"Hey, handsome," she called.

He almost kept walking, but the opportunity was too appealing.

"Hi," he said softly, stepping over toward the light.

She followed him. "You a cop?"

He shook his head. Up close he could see that, like the bartender, she seemed to be in her early twenties. But her eyes looked much older.

"In that case, you wanna have some fun later?" She coughed then tossed him what was, no doubt, meant to be an alluring smile.

He shuddered. At one point, she'd been an innocent little girl like Beka. What had her life been like to lead her to this point? "Actually I'm looking for information." He held up the picture of Lindsey. "Have you seen her?"

"I thought you said you wadn't a cop." She pursed her lips in a pout and ran her hands down her faded, wrinkled purple dress. The plunging neckline showed her bony sternum and nothing else.

"I'm not." He offered her a twenty and his card. "Would you call me if you see her?"

She snatched the money from his hand and he shoved her the card. She took it more slowly. "Sure. Why not?"

Back in the car, he turned the air on high and stared at the graffiti-covered building. Had Lindsey really been here last night? Had she had Beka with her?

After only ten minutes inside, the hopelessness of the club had permeated his clothes and his skin. And the memory of the singer made him sick. Was his little girl going to end up like that? Not knowing that her daddy was looking for her, longing to bring her home?

CHAPTER 6

Crystal lay in bed waiting for the tap on the door she knew was coming.

Tap. Tap. Tap. A dog barked. "Shh. . ." She heard Elyse say softly. Then, "Crys? You getting up for church?"

Crystal put her hand over her eyes. "I don't think so. I think the jet lag has gotten to me." It was true. Even though she'd slept at a hotel near the airport last night, there'd been very little actual sleep.

"You sure? I can wait if you want to go."

The longing in Elyse's voice made Crystal's stomach churn, but she pulled the covers up tighter. "You go on. I'll get up and take a shower in a little bit and meet you at the house for lunch."

She sensed rather than heard her sister linger outside the guest bedroom door for a few seconds. "Okay. See you then." Disappointment was obvious in her voice.

When Elyse was gone, Crystal tried to relax. In New York, she'd gotten to where she barely even noticed Sundays, other than as a well-deserved day off. But here it was like someone had turned her conscience up to hyperdrive. She'd been lying awake for an hour, racked with guilt as she heard her sister getting ready for church.

She was going to have to get a handle on that if she was going to stay here.

"Or you could start going to church again," she could almost hear her friend Tina saying. She turned over and pulled the edge of her pillow over her ears. Not that it helped, since the voice was coming from inside her head. But she knew it would take more than putting in an appearance at church to make things right between her and God. So that was that.

She punched the pillow and closed her eyes. Now if she could just go back to sleep.

"I can't believe we're leaving tomorrow." Her mother turned toward the suitcase on her bed as she said the words, taking great pains with arranging the pair of jeans Crystal had just folded.

Crystal glanced over at her tense profile. "You nervous?"

Her mother bit her lower lip. "Don't tell your daddy, but I am a little." Concern filled her eyes. "You do know you'll need to stay in the house, right?"

Crystal closed her eyes and took a deep breath. She'd known this was coming. Had actually thought of it a split second after she volunteered to take care of things while her parents were gone.

And when she'd flown back to New York this past weekend to tell Mia and pick up her things from Tina, it had been this thought above all others that had most tempted her to call Aaron yesterday and chicken out of coming back. But she hadn't. So here she was.

She opened her eyes. "I was hoping maybe I could just stay out at Elyse's and walk over here every day to check on things. I'm already settled in there."

Her mama didn't say anything. She just reached over and added a pair of casual black pants to the suitcase.

"I know you'd feel more comfortable if someone stayed in the house," Crystal said. How did Mama still do that? Make them toe the line without saying a word? "I'm just not sure I can do it." Her voice cracked and she put her fingertips to her throat, as if to add strength.

When her mother finally turned to face her, tears sparkled in her eyes, but she was smiling. "Oh, honey, you're so much stronger than you think you are." She motioned toward the queen-sized bed. "You can sleep in here if you'd rather."

Crystal nodded. She'd probably end up on the couch downstairs, but there was no point in worrying her mother. "I'll be fine." She folded the last of her dad's casual shirts. "I guess I'd better go out to the barn. Aaron's going to remind me what it takes to run this place. I promised I'd take notes." She dropped a kiss on her mama's smooth cheek and started toward the door.

"Crys. . ."

She spun around.

"I'm glad you're home. I know it will be a lot of work, but I wish you'd relax and enjoy it."

Crystal smiled. "I will, Mama. I'm looking forward to a little break from the city." And she was. As long as that's all it was. "I love the ranch." Again, true. The house may suffocate her, the river might sadden her, but the ranch, with its honest labor and never-ending circle of life, made her feel rejuvenated in a way The City That Never Sleeps couldn't seem to do.

As if reading her mind, her mother frowned. "We're proud of your success on the stage, honey. You know that. But you have other talents besides acting."

Crystal frowned. "I made a choice to follow a bigger dream."

"Are you still writing?"

Crystal shook her head.

"Do you ever think about working with children?"

Crystal forced a chuckle. "I was a kid myself when I thought I wanted to do those things." Why couldn't her mom just be happy that she was achieving some measure of success in New York? She might eventually make it to Broadway. What mother wouldn't be thrilled about that?

"Honey, you and I both know you loved working at that childrens' theater when you first went to New York." Compassion filled her mother's eyes. "Cami wouldn't want you to keep on living your life for her. In spite of what she might have said to you that last day, she was always a believer in y'all each doing your own thing."

Crystal winced and wrapped her arms around her waist. She'd quit the children's theater and started waitressing because she was getting too comfortable there. She could see she'd never push herself hard enough to make it on Broadway if she stayed there. And she really didn't want to talk about what Cami and she had disagreed about "that last day."

"Uh-hum." She started to dart for the door, but her mother took two quick steps and cut her off as if she were a confused calf that needed to be herded into the trailer.

Her mama touched Crystal's shoulder. "Talking about her helps."

Crystal twisted her mouth. "Not for me so much."

Her mama sat on the bed and patted the spot beside her.

Crystal sank onto the hand-pieced quilt with a sigh.

Her mother reached over and pushed Crystal's hair back behind her ear. "When's the last time you said Cami's name?"

A few months ago, actually, when she'd told Brad right before their trip to Arkansas for the wedding. Of course that was the only time she'd spoken of her sister since the move to New York. But it wasn't like she was around family.

Crystal frowned. "I'm not still grieving, if that's what you mean. How could I be? It's been seven years."

"Seven years you've spent in a time warp."

"I didn't run away to New York. You know we planned to go right after graduation."

Mama stared into her eyes, and Crystal squirmed under "that" look. Her face grew hot. "I just did what we planned. I'm living our dream." Of all people, her mother knew how long they'd counted on making it big on Broadway.

"You did what Cami planned for the two of you. You're living *her* dream."

Crystal flinched. It was partly because of a conversation just like this with her mama seven years ago that had made her mention to Cami that maybe they shouldn't be so quick to go to New York. That maybe it wasn't the best thing. And because of that conversation, she hadn't been with Cami when she died.

"Living her dream, without her." Her mother never took her gaze away from Crystal's face.

Crystal picked at the tiny stitches around the big star in the middle of the quilt.

"I remember when your granny was making that quilt," her mother said. "Years later, it almost killed me when she called me into her room and insisted I take it for mine and Jonathan's bed when she was gone."

Crystal traced the star with her finger.

Her mom chuckled. "Not long after she passed, I found you and Cami in here, lying on your stomachs on the quilt, telling your favorite 'Granny' memories. I let the chores wait while I plopped down between you and joined in."

A smile lifted Crystal's lips as it always did when she thought about her granny. The woman had been strong and courageous, working beside her husband on the ranch and thanking God for every minute of it. "I remember that day. We laughed so hard. You know, we always felt sorry for the others because they never knew Granny."

"That was a loss, all right. But you two kept her memory alive with your stories. I guarantee you, if you ask Aaron or Luke or even the younger ones, they'll say they felt like they knew her."

Crystal's smile faded. "That's not the same thing, Mama." She lifted her chin and met her mother's gaze. She was a grown professional woman, a breath away from Broadway, not a troubled teenager who needed to be tricked into healing. "I really need to go see if Aaron's ready."

Her mother nodded. "You're right." She pushed to her feet and turned back to the suitcase. "We can talk more when I get back from our trip."

Crystal nodded, grateful for the reprieve. When her parents got home, she'd be gone back to New York before there was time for more talk.

Jeremy stepped out onto the porch, pulling the door shut behind him. And almost collided with his dad. "Hey. I didn't know you were here."

"Got a minute to talk?" Worry lined his dad's face.

Jeremy glanced at his dad's truck, parked squarely behind his in the driveway. Why did he feel like that was no accident? He jangled his truck keys a little but nodded. "What's going on?"

"You know we're going to Florida next week."

Jeremy nodded.

"You sure you won't reconsider and come with us? We'll only be gone a couple weeks."

"I appreciate it, Dad. But I'd better stay around here. Keep an eye on our land."

"Speaking of our land, I thought you and I might go out to the sale barn at Ash Flat and check out a special Black Angus consignment sale they're having."

Jeremy took a deep breath. "I'll go with you if you're looking to increase your herd, but I'm going to wait a while." He resisted the urge to say, "Like I told you before." He knew his parents had his best interests at heart with their offers of vacation and their urgings to buy cattle. But they didn't understand.

"You know, son, when they discovered natural gas on our place down south, I thought we were the luckiest people in the world. You and I agreed that we could finally live our dream of moving up here and having adjoining cattle ranches."

Jeremy had heard it all before and knew exactly where his dad was going with this, but he just stared out at the rolling hills of his land. The new green grass was undisturbed for as far as he could see.

"In order to be a cattle ranch, it has to have cows." His dad's chuckle was forced. "A year ago, you were ready to fill this land with livestock. It's time to make that dream a reality."

"Ten months ago, everything changed. I told you and Mom then that I didn't want to be tied to a working ranch, that I was going to wait until I found Beka before I went ahead with my business plan. You know that financially I can afford to do that."

His dad looked down at the ground and scuffed at a rock with his boot. "We're not talking about finances, son. We're talking about you having a life."

"I have a life." Finding Beka. And putting one foot in front of the other until that day came.

"We just thought you might. . ."

"Give up?" Jeremy could hear the anger in his voice and he tried hard to rein it in. "Is that what you want me to do?"

His dad's tan face paled to a sickly gray. "Everything changed for us, too, when Lindsey took Beka," he said. "And we would never give up on bringing that sweet baby home. You know that."

"I know. We will find her," Jeremy whispered, the lump in his throat not permitting anything louder.

His dad put his hand on Jeremy's shoulder and squeezed. "I believe that. I just hate to see you in limbo until that day."

"No more than I hate to be here. But in the meantime, I'll help you. And I'll help the McCords. And I'll keep looking for Beka every chance I get."

His dad nodded. "I'll let you get back to what you were doing, then." He turned to walk to his truck, suddenly looking older than Jeremy had ever seen him.

Jeremy squeezed the keys in his hand. "Holler if you want me to go with you to the sale barn."

"We'll save that for another time." His dad climbed in his truck and left as quickly as he'd come.

Jeremy stood for a minute and watched him drive away. In spite of his attacks of doubt, he did believe what he'd told his dad. They would find Beka. And when they did, he'd fill this ranch with cattle. But until that day, he would avoid complications and stay focused.

Crystal McCord's face immediately popped into his brain and he chuckled, the tightness in his chest loosening a little. How would she feel to know that the word *complications* brought her to mind?

"You've got to be kidding me." Crystal barely stopped short of stomping her pointy-toe high-heel boots on the wooden floor of the barn office. "Hello? I was raised on this ranch. Do you really think I need a babysitter?"

Aaron smiled and shook his head. "C'mon, sis. You know better than that. But Jeremy needs to stay busy right now. And helping you get your ranch legs is the best way I could figure out to make that happen. I told him to stick close to you for a week and then he'll let you manage things on your own, if you want."

She frowned. "You're not trying to play matchmaker, are you? I know how newlyweds are, but Aaron, I assure you, I couldn't be less interested in a relationship right now."

He raised an eyebrow and fiddled with a notebook on his desk.

"So you and Brad are over? I figured, but you never really said."

She gave him a terse nod. Considering that Brad still called at least once a day, in spite of the fact that she ignored every call, he might not have gotten the message yet. But they were definitely over. "That doesn't mean I'm looking for a cowboy to fill the gap. I'm going back to New—"

"Whoa, whoa." He put his hand out as if soothing a skittish colt. "I'm not matchmaking. If you're not interested in a relationship, how do you think Jeremy feels? His ex-wife prances back into town and steals the daughter she left without a thought three years before. It's been a long time with no word. Other than anger, that man's heart has to be numb with grief."

She blushed. "I'm sorry. Of course it is. And I'm with you on his needing to stay busy. But a week?"

He picked up the notebook and stood. "It's for a good cause, I promise. Besides, who knows? You might actually need his help at some point. So don't burn any bridges."

She sighed. "Give me some credit. I know I don't know everything. It's just that. . ." She studied his face and opted for total honesty. "Getting used to the ranch again will be hard enough without a constant companion."

"Got it," he said and made an imaginary mark on his notebook. "Cancel the golden retriever I hired for you."

She laughed. "Very funny."

"It's good to hear you laugh."

She sobered. "I laugh."

"Not often enough."

"I wish you and Bree didn't have to leave tomorrow. It would be so nice to spend more time with you."

"Chicago's not nearly as far away as New York is. We'll come home often."

She cringed inside at his implied excuse for her long absences.

They both knew distance had nothing to do with it. "But I may be gone by the time you get back."

He shook his head. "We'll have a welcome home party for Mama and Daddy. And you'll still be here then."

"Am I late?"

Crystal spun around just as Jeremy stepped into the tiny office.

Aaron grinned broadly. "No, not at all."

The two men shook hands.

Jeremy tipped his hat to Crystal. "You getting settled in?"

She nodded absently.

Aaron handed Crystal a notebook. "I thought I'd show you both the routine at once. If that's okay. . ."

What was she supposed to say? Jeremy was staring at her as if expecting her to protest. But Aaron had gone to all the trouble of setting it up. And she had no real reason to resist. Probably her own insecurities made her more prickly about accepting help than she normally would be. She took a deep breath and nodded. "That sounds great."

Jeremy's eyebrows shot up beneath the brim of his hat.

She smiled. So the cowboy had been sure she was going to throw a prima donna fit. She could already tell he was going to have to work on not stereotyping her.

Two hours later, bouncing along a dirt path between Jeremy and Aaron in the old farm truck, she stared at the pages of scrawled notes. "There's more to this than I remembered."

Aaron clutched the steering wheel as the truck hit old ruts and tried to swerve to the side. "You can do it."

On the other side of her, Jeremy frowned. "If you don't think you can handle it. . ."

For a second, the temptation to give up before she started was overwhelming. He was obviously offering to let her off the hook and take the job himself. How easy it would be just to say, "You know what? I don't think I can." She could be on her way back to New York by this afternoon.

No more worries about staying in the big house with only memories for companionship after her parents and Aaron and Bree left tomorrow. No more concern that she might not be able to make herself go back to the city when this was over. No more trying to convince a cowboy that she could run a ranch.

"I can handle it," she said softly then tossed him a saucy grin for good measure. "After all, I've got you for the first week at least to keep me in line."

CHAPTER 7

Aaron slowed at a red metal gate, and Jeremy jumped out before they came to a stop.

Crystal watched the cowboy effortlessly yank the big gate open then felt Aaron's gaze on her.

"No fair flirting just to annoy him, Crys."

She laughed. "That wasn't flirting, big brother. That was teasing."

"Just remember, he's not your brother. And in spite of what I told you in the barn, he might think more of it than you mean."

How ironic that she was receiving this lecture. She'd heard Cami get it so many times but never dreamed it would ever be directed toward her. "I'm just trying to be a good sport."

Aaron nodded. "Fine. But be careful. Jeremy's been through enough. And for that matter, so have you. I don't want either of you to get hurt."

She watched the cowboy walking back to the truck. "I'd say it's too late for that."

"Let me rephrase then. I don't want either of you to hurt the other."

Jeremy climbed into the truck, effectively ending their private conversation.

Crystal quietly took notes the rest of the time.

When they parked in front of the barn and climbed out of the truck, Jeremy turned to face her. "Since you'll be pulling airport shuttle duty, want me to meet the hands in the morning and give them their schedule?"

She nodded. "If you can take care of tomorrow, I'll be ready to work bright and early on Wednesday."

"You can count on it." He flipped his phone open. "Do you mind giving me your phone number and taking mine? Just in case you need me, or vice versa?"

As she retrieved her phone from her back pocket and they exchanged numbers, she was struck by how quickly she'd accepted the thought that she might need to call him. He had a way of fostering confidence. Sort of like Brad had. Only she had a feeling that if Tina could meet the cowboy, she'd find there was nothing Ken-like, nothing plastic, about Jeremy Buchanan.

"Now that we've exhausted all the boring details of my life and we're almost back home, let's move on to something more interesting." Elyse kept a tight grip on the steering wheel, but she glanced over at Crystal. "What's been happening with you?"

Crystal sighed. "Well, I told you the play closed. And my agent had a meltdown when I told her I was taking some time off."

"Aw, Crys. I'm sorry."

"That's life. I'm actually looking forward to a little break from the city." She stared out the window at the budding trees, growing thicker by the mile, as they left the Memphis airport far behind and got closer to home. "As long as I'm sure I'm going back."

Elyse glanced at her. "Daddy and Mama didn't look like they were harboring any secret plans to run away forever when we left them at the airport, did they?"

Crystal grinned. "Not that I could tell."

"So you'll be going back in six weeks."

"Right." Why wasn't Crystal that sure? She couldn't wait to get back to the theater life, but she felt tired every time she thought of facing the auditions and callbacks.

"Am I right in assuming you and Brad are history?"

"Definitely history," Crystal said, almost feeling bad by the lack of any residual feeling for Brad. Even when she'd gone back to New York last week to get her stuff, she'd had no desire to see him, but at the same time no flutter of anxiety that she might run into him when she'd gone to their old haunts.

She turned to stare out the window again. Was her heart defective? Maybe she would never love a man enough to really care that he was gone.

Elyse put her turn signal on and leaned forward to check for oncoming traffic. "Wanna talk about it?"

Crystal shook her head. "Not really. He wasn't what I thought he was. The end."

"Good riddance to bad rubbish," Elyse said. "Isn't that what we always said when some guy in junior high or high school turned out to be a jerk?"

"Yep. And that about sums it up still. Some things never change." She sighed. "And some things change too much."

Elyse glanced across at her. "Worried about spending nights at the house?"

"Who, me? Worry?" Crystal couldn't believe the quaver in her voice.

As they turned off the highway onto the gravel road, Elyse cleared her throat. "You know you're welcome to keep staying with me."

Crystal nodded. "I know. But Mama really wants someone in the house while they're gone."

"Do you want me to stay there and you bunk at my place? Who would know?"

A smile tilted Crystal's lips. "That's incredibly nice. But I'd know. And Luke would know. And your newest family member would definitely know. She tolerates me, but if you weren't there, she'd go berserk."

"Can you do it?"

Crystal considered her sister's question carefully. She hadn't spent a night in the house since Cami died. At first, she'd escaped to the barn loft apartment. Then despite what she'd claimed to her mom about just following through with plans, for all intents and purposes, she'd run away to New York. "I can sleep on the couch. As long as I don't have to go in our room."

"I don't see why you should have to."

"Is it still the same?"

Elyse glanced over at her. "What?"

"The room. Did anyone clean it out?"

Elyse shook her head. "Mama said you'd do it when you were ready."

"Hmph. I'm never going to be ready."

"Never is a long time," Elyse said.

The cow bawled again pitifully and thrashed around on the grass.

Jeremy groaned, too. When he'd happened upon the cow in the process of giving birth, he hadn't been worried. There'd be hundreds of calves born this spring on the ranch. But there'd be one less if things didn't turn around soon for this one.

He knelt down beside the laboring cow. "Hang in there, little mama. We'll get some help." He snagged the phone from his back pocket.

Nacho whinnied.

"If this were the Old West, I'd send you back to the ranch for help," Jeremy muttered to the horse. He skimmed through his address book. How had he ended up not getting any of the McCord employees' numbers? In the last ten months, he'd gotten so distracted, it was a wonder he could run his own cattle-less ranch, much less help anyone else. At least he had thought to exchange numbers with Crystal. He scrolled down to her name and hit SEND.

"Hello?"

"Crystal, it's Jeremy. Are you home from the airport yet?"

"We just drove in. What's up?"

"We've got a cow birthing about half a mile from the house right next to the old caverns. She's having a hard time. Do you have Slim's number?"

Silence. "Slim doesn't have a phone, actually. I have Joe's and Mike's, but they're all working out by the Dewey place. What do you need?"

"Someone to call the vet." He glanced back at the cow, thrashing around and trying to get to her feet. "And in the meantime, another pair of hands. She's already delivered the water bag, but I'm afraid the calf's stuck."

"I'll call Doc Johnson, throw on some jeans, and be right there." She hung up before he could say anything.

Ten minutes later, a huge cloud of dust on the horizon caught his attention. Within seconds, the old farm truck emerged from the grayness, careening wildly across the pasture. He pushed to his feet and took Nacho's reins in his hand. The horse was trained not to bolt, but at the speed that truck was coming, all bets were off. "Whoa, brother," he whispered softly. "She's in a hurry."

He had to give her credit for slowing down before she got close to the cow, coasting to a stop fifty feet away.

She dragged an old brown leather bag out of the truck and took off toward him at a run. "How is she?"

"Hanging in there. But no real progress. Is the vet on the way?"

Her delicate shoulders lifted as she led the way toward the cow.

"He was out of the office. I left the information with his emergency service."

He frowned at her jeans, designer unless he missed his guess, and her stylish white button-down shirt. Had he sounded that panicked on the phone? "I could have waited for you to change clothes."

She grimaced. "I did. My wardrobe is a little limited these days." She squatted down and touched the cow's swollen belly.

"You look great. I just hate to see expensive clothes get ruined."

"I gave twenty dollars for the pants, but you're right, they were two hundred originally. Don't worry, I shop in thrift stores." She winked. "I'm an expert at good deals." She rubbed her hand gently across the cow's abdomen.

He grinned. "Smart woman. Does your expertise extend to birthing calves?"

Before she could answer, the cow bellowed loudly. They both jumped back as she struggled to her feet.

"Good for you," Crystal murmured, patting her flank. "You're a fighter, aren't you, gal?"

He nodded toward the brown duffel bag sitting on the ground. "What's in there?"

"You're looking at the official McCord calf-birthing kit. Handed down through the generations." Her blue eyes danced.

"You're kidding."

"Yeah, I am. I just stuck some stuff in here when you called." She opened the satchel, took out a bottle of rubbing alcohol, and poured it on her hands, working it up to her elbows. "But the lighter we can keep things, the more relaxed we'll be. And the more relaxed we are, the more relaxed she'll be." She handed him the bottle.

He glanced over at her as he washed his own hands. "You learn that from your sister? Assuming cows and dogs have the same rules?"

For a moment, he was struck again by the absurdity of this pint-sized beautiful blond taking the whole situation in stride. Her hair looked like she'd just stepped out of an upscale salon. Her face was flawless, but there was a determined set to her chin he'd never noticed before.

"No, I learned that from Daddy. And Elyse would tell you, cows and dogs definitely don't have the same rules." She retrieved a package from the bag, ripped it open, and handed him a pair of rubber gloves.

His eyebrows shot up, but he took them. "I'm guessing you were a girl scout?"

"Nope." She slid her own gloves on with a snap. "Farm girl."

He nodded slowly. He was right. There was definitely more to Crystal McCord than met the eye.

"Which end do you want?" she asked.

"You're doing a good job of keeping her calm. If you'll keep doing that, I'll see what I can do to help her."

She nodded.

"C'mon, Bess," he whispered to the cow. "You can do it."

"Bess? Seriously?"

He glanced around the cow toward Crystal. "What's wrong with that?"

She had her back to him, but her shoulders lifted. "My granny's name was Bess. She always said it showed lack of imagination that every man in the country had to call a cow by her name."

"Excuse me." He patted the cow again. "C'mon, Anastasia. Let's get this baby out."

Crystal had her back to him, but he was pretty sure the muffled sound he heard was a snicker.

Twenty minutes later, with hardly any progress, all mirth was gone.

"What do you think?" Crystal murmured.

"I think you're as good with cows as your sister is with dogs. At least she's staying calm. Just keep doing what you're doing." Jeremy tensed his shoulder muscles and released them then flexed his neck. Sweat trickled down between his shoulder blades. "The calf seems to be caught. I'm doing what I can, but if it doesn't come soon, we're going to have to try pulling it. So pray."

"Let me know if I need to get the ropes from the truck." He couldn't see her face, but her voice sounded strained.

Since he'd started ranching, he'd seen his share of death, but this little life they were fighting to save had become intensely important to him in the last hour. Maybe after the heartache of the past several months, he just needed to see faith and hope rewarded.

"Please," he whispered. A minute later, he felt movement beneath his hands. "It's coming," he said and suddenly Crystal was beside him guiding the slippery calf to the ground.

The cow turned her wild-eyed glance toward the bundle on the ground. Jeremy and Crystal stripped their gloves off and watched in silence as Anastasia took care of her tan and white baby.

"How can anyone see this and claim there is no God?" he asked quietly, swallowing against the lump of emotion in his throat.

She shook her head, and he thought he saw a hint of moisture in her eyes. "I don't know."

"You okay?"

She nodded. "I'm just so glad it all worked out. I was pretty nervous."

No wonder she'd gone into acting. "You deserve an Academy Award then, because you sure didn't seem like it." He smiled at her. "And you handled Anastasia like a pro."

"Nice name, by the way. Granny would have been proud of you." She pushed a stray strand of hair out of her eyes. "I was always the tomboy who followed Daddy around like a shadow. I've helped on more births than I can count. But it's been awhile." She sank down on the grassy hillside.

"Guess it's like riding a bicycle." Jeremy could feel the grin stretching his lips. Funny. He'd grinned more since Crystal McCord had breezed into town than he had since Lindsey took Beka. For some reason, the thought wiped the smile from his face. He couldn't afford to lose his focus. "Anyway, I'm glad you were around."

"Me, too." She pointed and he followed her gaze.

The calf, front legs still bent, extended his wobbly back legs and pushed himself up. Just before he stood upright, he trembled and fell back to the ground. But in less than a second, he tried again. On the third try, he stood, shaky but standing.

Jeremy smiled. "It looks like our job here is done."

She nodded but kept her gaze on the calf, getting a good start on his first meal.

He adjusted his hat. "So I guess I'm going to call it a day and go get cleaned up."

She waved absently. "Good deal."

"See you in the morning." He climbed up on Nacho's back and shifted the reins. When he was almost to the main road, he glanced back at the tiny white dot that was Crystal still sitting on the hill watching the cow and calf.

One advantage of farm life—usually things were exactly what they seemed to be. Especially for the last several months, that fact had allowed him to operate on automatic pilot. But with Crystal McCord around, he had a feeling those days were long gone.

CHAPTER 8

Crystal lifted the oblong casserole dish out of the hot soapy water and handed it to Elyse.

Her sister ran it under the faucet. "So you helped Jeremy deliver a calf today?" Elyse's voice shook a little.

Crystal smiled. "You make it sound so scary. The cow was glad to have our help. And we didn't have to do much. It could have been a lot worse."

"Yeah. You could have gone back to New York, and I could have had to help him." Elyse shivered.

Crystal decided a change of subject was in order, for both their sakes. She didn't want to think about how badly she needed to be back in New York. And she knew Elyse would rather not think about cows.

She passed Elyse a plate. "As crazy as it may sound, it feels good to be doing dishes with you again. Don't tell the others, but I always kind of liked kitchen duty, especially before Mama got a dishwasher."

Elyse arranged the glass pan in the draining rack and swiped her hair away from her face with the back of her hand. "I'm glad my lack of a dishwasher is good for something. Even if it's just a shot of nostalgia for you."

"Aw c'mon, admit it." Crystal slid the last plate beneath the bubbles and attacked it vigorously. "There's something cathartic about washing dishes by hand. Life seems so simple when you're up to your elbows in suds."

Elyse shook her head. "Give me a tub full of soapy bubbles over a sink full of soapy bubbles any day."

Crystal laughed. "Remember how Mama used to say, 'Calgon, take me away'?"

Elyse nodded. "We had no idea what she meant. But now that's exactly how I feel sometimes."

The phone rang.

"That's what usually happens when I try for a bubble bath, actually. The phone rings." Elyse wiped her hands on a dish towel. "Can you handle the rest while I get this?"

"You betcha. It's good for my psyche, remember?"

Elyse chuckled as she picked up the phone.

She hung up just as Crystal draped the dishcloth over the back of the sink and gave a contented sigh that always accompanied a job well done.

Elyse grinned. "Nice and shiny."

Crystal took the good-natured teasing for what it was. It was good to be home. "Thanks."

"That was Rachel Westwood on the phone."

"The chiropractor Luke is building an office for?" Luke had declined their supper invitation because he was working late.

Elyse nodded.

Crystal's stomach lurched. "Is Luke okay?"

"I'm sure he is. She was calling about her chocolate lab."

"What's wrong with it?"

Elyse slipped on her shoes. "He's cowering in the bedroom. She was telling me about it at church the other day. She and her husband can't figure out why he's suddenly started doing that sometimes.

73

I made her promise next time he took refuge in the bedroom she'd call me."

Crystal looked at the time on her phone. "It's a little late for a house call, isn't it?"

Elyse glanced up at the kitchen clock and shrugged. "It's only eight. If I don't see him during an actual episode, I won't know why he does it."

"Then I guess you'd better go." Which meant she'd better go, too. Back over to the house to face the long night.

Elyse grabbed her car keys. "Come with me. We can stop on the way home and get ice cream."

"Really? Are you sure that would be okay?"

"I know it would. Rachel has some friends over, and they'll be happy to meet you."

"Meet me?"

"My sister, the New York actress."

Crystal laughed. "I'm sure you're just being nice, but I'll ride along with you if you're sure you don't mind."

Twenty minutes later, they stood on the porch of the big ranch house. Elyse rang the doorbell.

The door swung open and a thirty-something redheaded woman with beautiful green eyes smiled at them. "Come in." Inside the house, she shook Crystal's hand. "I'm Rachel Westwood. You must be Crystal."

Crystal nodded.

Rachel motioned toward the handsome cowboy who'd walked into the foyer to stand beside her. "This is my husband, Jack." She turned to him. "Honey, introduce Crystal to Allie and Daniel while I take Elyse to the bedroom to see Cocoa. Maybe she can coax her out."

"We've tried everything. . .even doggy treats," Crystal heard her say as she and Elyse headed down the hallway.

Crystal followed Jack into the living room, where a couple looked up from a basketball game on TV. A black labrador lying on the rug gave a cursory bark but didn't get up.

"That's Shadow," Jack explained. "Whatever is upsetting Cocoa apparently doesn't bother her."

The man on the couch picked up the remote control and hit the MUTE button. He and the woman stood as Jack introduced them to Crystal.

"These are our friends, Daniel and Allie Montgomery. We've all discovered a common love of Razorback basketball. Or at least Daniel and I have. Rachel and Allie tolerate it, I think."

"Don't let me keep you from your game." Crystal motioned toward the remote. "You can turn the sound back on."

Allie chuckled, her blue eyes twinkling. "Don't be silly. It's halftime or Daniel wouldn't have turned it down."

Crystal smiled. "I totally understand. We McCords are Razorback fans, too, even though football is more our game."

"It's so nice to meet you, Crystal," Allie said. "We've heard so much about you."

"I hope it wasn't all bad."

"Bad? Are you kidding me?" Allie shook her head. "We're all hoping you'll decide to put on a workshop while you're here."

Crystal tilted her head. "A workshop?"

"A woman used to come down from Chicago and do a drama day camp for the local kids when I was growing up. Before your time." Allie laughed. "We loved it."

"I didn't know that. We—" Crystal cleared her throat. "I took classes at the Imperial Studio of the Arts in Pocahontas when I was young. I don't think we ever had anything like that here in Shady Grove then."

Allie shook her head. "No, she quit after us. Hmm. . .maybe we drove her out of town."

"The truth comes out," Daniel said dryly.

She slapped at him. "Not me, of course, but maybe Lark or Victoria." She glanced back at Crystal. "Two more of my and Rachel's friends. You'll love them. Although, Daniel's right. Together, we could usually find some kind of trouble to get into."

"Some things never change, do they, man?" Jack said teasingly.

Daniel laughed, but he put his arm around Allie's waist.

"Are you guys ganging up on Allie?" Rachel asked as she and Elyse came back in the room, followed by a friendly-looking chocolate lab.

Jack snorted. "Who? Us?" He held out his hand to the dog. "Hey, buddy. You feeling better?"

Cocoa cast a nervous glance around the room but trotted over to his master. Shadow stood and padded across the room to Elyse.

Rachel beamed. "Elyse figured out what was wrong."

Jack glanced up from where he was rubbing the dog behind the ears. "What?"

"March Madness—it's our basketball kick, combined with the new surround sound system."

"Huh?"

"The whistles. He hates the refs' whistles." She turned to Elyse. "So if we turn off surround sound while we watch the ball games, do you think it'll be okay?"

Elyse nodded, her own attention focused on Shadow. Crystal noticed her olive skin took on a hint of red with all eyes on her. "That should be fine," she said softly. "If not, you can just get Cocoa settled in the bedroom with some toys and food and water before you start the game."

"Not that we'll have to worry about that anymore until next season unless the Hogs do better this second half," Daniel said.

Jack winced. "Ouch. True. But it's a big relief to know what was causing her to bolt for the bedroom."

Allie nodded. "She was giving us a complex. Every time we come over lately, she starts acting funny."

Daniel scooted his wife over against him. "Good to know he's just allergic to basketball and not us."

"We'd better go," Elyse said softly.

As if she understood Elyse's words, Cocoa trotted over to her. She bent down and told both dogs good-bye then straightened.

Admiration flitted across Rachel's face. "Thank you again, Elyse."

"It was my pleasure."

"Nice meeting you," Crystal said.

Everyone echoed her words.

"Let me know if you decide to put on a workshop, Crystal," Allie called.

"What kind of workshop?" Elyse asked as they pulled out onto the road.

Crystal told her about their conversation.

"That sounds like something you'd love," Elyse said.

"It would be fun, I think. But I can't do it while I'm supposed to be watching the ranch."

"No, but you could do it when Mama and Daddy get home."

"Bite your tongue. I have to go back to New York the second they get back. I'm really close to the possibility of a Broadway role, Elyse."

Elyse nodded. "You can't take a chance on missing that opportunity. Not after you've worked this long for it."

After a quick pass through Dairy Queen to get ice cream, they headed home. As they pulled into the driveway in front of the McCord house, Elyse looked over at Crystal. "Want me to come in with you?"

"I don't know," Crystal joked. "Are you going to tell me a bedtime story?"

Elyse chuckled. "I could throw the chew toy for you until you get tired."

"Hmm. . .I think I'll be okay." She reached over and gave her sister a sideways hug. "You were great tonight."

"Thanks. 'Night."

When Crystal's foot touched the third step of the front porch stairs, she stopped and shifted her weight on it again then smiled. That board still squeaked. After all these years. Some things never changed. She scanned the huge wraparound porch. Like the way the moonlight made the oak-plank floor look silver.

She slid her key in the front door lock and pushed the door open. She stepped into the dark house, flipping the light switch on the wall as she went. Elyse's taillights reflected in the glass door as she closed it.

Without allowing the quietness to seep into her mind, she took the stairs two at a time and grabbed a blanket, a quilt, and a pillow from the hall closet. She cast a glance at the surrounding doors, some open, some closed. One door in particular drew her attention. It was closed. Which was just how she intended to leave it.

She balanced her burden going down the stairs. "Look out, couch. Here I come."

She made her bed on the sofa in the living room then settled in for a good night's sleep.

An hour later, she was still lying there, fighting demons and arguing with naysayers in her mind. Finally, she sat up and curled her legs up under her. She glanced over at her daddy's ratty recliner. She'd sat in here a lot with him, both of them reading Zane Grey or C. S. Lewis.

A scene flashed through her head. Graduation night after the ceremony. She'd come home instead of going out with friends.

And she'd been right here on this sofa when the call had come.

Her daddy had been reading the newspaper before he answered the phone. She could still see the sports page flutter to the floor as his face turned the oddest shade of gray she'd ever seen. He'd hung up the phone and given her a look so terrifying that she'd burst into tears before he said a word.

She pushed the memories from her mind and jumped up, snatching her blankets and pillow off the couch. For a second, she stood in the living room, clutching her bedclothes. Such a big house. But nowhere she wanted to sleep.

She tiptoed to the front door and opened it. The quiet yard loomed big, swathed in shadows and moonlight. She dragged her blankets with her over to a double rocker with a padded seat.

She sat quietly for a while, wondering what God would think if she asked Him to give her peace. He'd probably think she was a little late in the asking. And He'd be right.

Finally, she put her pillow down at the end of the rocker, stretched out on her side to look out at the night sky, and tugged the blankets snug around her. She lay quietly in the dark and watched the twinkling stars waltz to the crickets' symphony. She'd followed those stars home.

Now what?

CHAPTER 9

I ain't wakin' her up." Slim shifted his chew of tobacco and spat on the ground.

"Wakin' who up?" Jeremy said as he came around the barn to where the cowhands were huddled.

Slim jabbed a thumb over his shoulder toward the house. "Sleepin' Beauty."

The other guys laughed.

Slim scowled. "Laugh if you wanna. But I don't see any volunteers."

Jeremy glanced toward the house. "How do you know she's still in bed? Maybe she's on the phone or something."

"Ain't in bed. She's zonked out right on the front porch."

Alarm shot through Jeremy. What if Crystal was sick? Passed out cold while these bozos stood around and laughed? He ignored the other men and ran toward the porch.

When he turned the corner, he skidded to a stop. She was lying in the big wooden rocker, a down-filled blanket wrapped around her like a cocoon. Definitely asleep. He tiptoed toward her. Her blond hair framed her face; long, sweeping eyelashes touched her cheeks.

On the third step, the wood squeaked loudly. He froze.

Her bright blue eyes popped open and focused on him immediately.

"Good morning," he said softly.

She frowned and looked past him at the yard. "Morning?"

He watched her face as reality dawned. She almost fell as she scrambled to sit upright, still swathed in the blanket.

He rushed toward her. "Hey. . .it's okay."

She leaned forward and peered out at the barn where the guys were still huddled. "Hmph," she offered, a half laugh, half grunt. "I feel like an idiot."

"You shouldn't. Sometimes when sleep finally comes, it hits like a hammer."

She nodded, her smile embarrassed. "Thanks. If you'll excuse me, I'll be ready to work in about ten minutes."

"Want me to go ahead and get the assignments off of Aaron's desk in the barn and hand them out?"

She clutched the blanket around her neck and rested her chin on her fists. "Would you? That would be so great."

"Sure. Aaron said it's been a while since the north-side fences have been checked. Okay if we do that today?"

"Sounds perfect. I'll be down there in a few minutes."

On his way back to the barn, Jeremy chuckled to himself.

Sleeping Beauty.

Slim had pegged that right.

Crystal ran through the living room, grabbed some clean clothes, and ran up the stairs. "Haven't you ever heard of an alarm clock?" she grumbled to herself.

Why had she assumed that as soon as the sun rose over the horizon, she'd wake up? Actually, she'd felt certain she wouldn't sleep at all. But one thing she'd never imagined was being found on the porch swing like a bum on a park bench. Her face reddened at the memory as she tore off her Razorback sweat suit. After a quick shower, she wriggled into her jeans and shirt and looked in the mirror. Definitely a ponytail day.

Less than twenty minutes after she woke up on the porch, she walked into the barn office. Not bad for a girl who used to take major grief in the mornings for hogging the bathroom.

Jeremy looked up from the desk. "You just missed Slim and the guys."

She grimaced. "Probably just as well. I guess they saw me snoring on the porch?"

" 'Fraid so." He winked. "Slim was trying to bribe one of them to wake you when I got here." He shoved the chair back and stood.

"Oh no. I'll never live this down."

"Well, I just wouldn't break into song with birds flying around or go near any spinning wheels," he called over his shoulder as he walked out the door into the main tool storage area.

She groaned again and followed him. "Sleeping Beauty?"

"The one and only."

He tossed her a pair of heavy leather gloves, which she stuck in her back jeans pocket.

While Jeremy heaved a roll of wire into the back of the little four-by-four farm-utility vehicle, she flipped open the toolbox and gave the contents a cursory inspection. Several pairs of fencing pliers and plenty of wire clips. Perfect. She lifted the toolbox in beside the wire and turned to face him. "You're awfully familiar with fairytales."

He glanced up from where he was now checking the gas and oil in the small chainsaw. "I've read that one and watched the movie often enough to recite it by heart."

"Beka's favorite?" As soon as the words left her lips, she realized he might rather not talk about his daughter.

But he smiled. "She loves it."

"She'll be back with you soon to watch it again."

"From your mouth to God's ears."

She blushed. Maybe once upon a time. But no more.

He loaded the chainsaw in the back of the tiny vehicle and motioned to her to get in. He opened the driver's door, slid in under the wheel, and then froze. He glanced at her. "I didn't think to ask. Did you want to drive?"

She shook her head and fastened her lap belt. "You're not typical, you know that?"

"I'm not?" He started the motor and backed out into the main barn area. "Why?"

She shrugged. "Even before New York, the local boys"—she raised her eyebrows—"not counting my brothers of course—treated me like I was a 'little lady.' Aaron spent half his time getting Luke out of fights he'd get into defending my tomboyishness."

He laughed and hit the gas. "I can see Luke doing that." He glanced across at her. "So I don't treat you like you're a 'little lady'?"

She laid her head back against the seat. The breeze felt so crisp on her face. "I thought you were going to. When you made that"—she deepened her voice in an imitation of his—" 'not many ranches in New York City' remark." She cut her gaze toward him, curious to see his reaction.

"Hey, can't a guy be surprised? I make it a habit not to judge a book by its cover. But in your case, it's pretty much impossible not to." He pulled up to the closed gate leading from the barn lot into the pasture.

"Thanks for trying." She jumped out and opened the red metal gate. As soon as he drove through, she pulled it shut and climbed back into the utility vehicle.

He pushed his hat back on his head a little and looked at her. "You up for a detour?"

She motioned toward the wide open spaces around them. "Being here for the next six weeks is a *major* detour, believe me. But what did you have in mind?"

A frown flitted across his face so fast she thought she might have imagined it. "Nothing big. I just thought we might swing by the cavern area and see if we can see Anastasia and baby."

"I'd love to. Do you think we'll be able to find her?"

"We'll give it our best shot."

Twenty minutes and six Anastasia look-alikes later, Crystal was starting to think that the cow had been a figment of their imaginations. Every time they got close enough to a cow to really identify her, the markings were different. Three of the faux Anastasias even had tiny brown and white calves. "You can tell it's calving season around here," she grumbled as they drove over another hill.

The utility vehicle stopped suddenly. "That's her, isn't it?" Jeremy said, pointing to the cow and calf nearest them.

"Yes. Definitely."

"The calf looks great."

"Happy," Crystal agreed.

"Happy?" Jeremy frowned at her. "How can you tell when a calf is happy?"

"Oh, never mind. But the little guy needs a name."

"Naming a calf out here is asking for heartache."

"You're the one who named his mama."

He sighed. "Only because you made fun of me for calling her Bess."

"Prince."

"What?"

She lifted her chin. "We'll call him Prince."

"You're naming a calf Prince? Like the singer?"

"No, silly. Like the happily-ever-after kind."

"Don't look now, but your tomboy image is getting a little frilly around the edges."

She laughed. "I am what I am. I really don't worry about that anymore."

"I'm glad." He sounded really pleased with her answer.

And she was ridiculously pleased that he was pleased.

By quitting time, she was so tired she didn't care who was pleased about what. Amazing what a day of hard physical labor could do to a body. She'd kept in shape in New York. Or so she thought. Until now.

When Jeremy suggested calling it a day, it was all she could do to keep from clapping. "Sounds like a plan," she said, with what she hoped was a jaunty smile but was probably more of a grimace.

"You okay?" he asked as they approached the barn lot.

"Fine. You?"

He nodded, but when they pulled up to the gate, he jumped out and opened it, quickly climbed back in and drove through, then got out again.

"I could—"

He was gone to close it behind them then back in a flash.

"I could have gotten the gate."

"Different activities work different muscles. You're probably going to be pretty sore tomorrow from hauling those limbs off of the fence."

"Tomorrow?"

He chuckled as he maneuvered the little utility vehicle into the barn. "You look like you could fall out any minute. Do you want me to pick you up some supper? I usually run into town and grab a bite."

She shook her head. "I just need to get a shower. Mama left a big pot of stew in the refrigerator. But thanks anyway."

"Okay, then. You go on to the house and I'll put everything away."

Grateful, she started out the door then turned back. "Um, Jeremy. . ."

He looked around at her and cocked his head.

"That is one huge pot of stew. I called a while ago and tried to get Luke and Elyse to eat supper with me, but he's working late and she's got a dog club meeting. So I was wondering. . ." *Do you want to stay for supper and keep me from having to spend the evening in that empty house alone?* "Are you hungry?"

A grin split his tan face. "So I'm a last resort to avoid eating by yourself? I'm flattered."

Heat rushed up her neck, but she forced a smile. "Not really the *last* resort." She nodded outside where they'd driven past Slim and the other guys packing up for the day. "If you're not hungry, I'm sure somebody out there would like to eat supper with Sleeping Beauty."

His grin grew wider.

"They would," she insisted. "Mama makes the best beef stew in the country and everybody knows it."

"I'm sure they would eat with you even if your mother was the worst cook there ever was." Jeremy took off his hat and ran his fingers through his hair. "I'll run home and take a shower and be right back. Truth is my house gets pretty empty at night, too."

She'd known that was the case. Had counted on it, actually— this makeshift supper helping both of them. But in keeping with the light air she was going for, she put her hands to her heart. "Now it's my turn to be flattered. Supper will be ready in about an hour."

"Great. See you then."

After he left, she took a quick shower because her aching muscles made it plain that if she gave into the bubble bath temptation, she'd never get out. After she dried off, she examined her meager wardrobe. What did a country girl turned city girl turned country girl wear to a non-date meal in the kitchen with a good-looking but totally friends only cowboy? The first thing she grabbed. In this case, jeans and a plain blue T-shirt. She pulled her damp hair up into a messy bun and put a little clear gloss on her chapped lips.

In the kitchen, she turned the burner on under the stew and snagged a loaf of wheat bread from the bread keeper. She slathered the slices with garlic butter and sprinkled shredded cheese on top. When the preheat light went off on the oven, she slid the pan of toast inside and set the timer.

She set plates and bowls and silverware on the table as she listened to the *tick-tick-tick* of Mama's old-fashioned egg timer. Just like the timer in her mind counting down the days until her parents came back and she went back to the city.

As she set the table for two, she remembered Aaron's warning her about flirting with Jeremy. Surely even her cautious brother would agree that tonight's invitation hadn't been flirting. And Jeremy obviously understood that, too. She'd seen the compassion in his eyes. He might not understand why she didn't want to be alone, but he could sympathize. And beautiful friendships had started based on less than that.

CHAPTER 10

Jeremy stood on the porch and considered tossing the fragrant blooms into the shrubs next to the house. He'd had the truck windows down on the way over here, and when the scent of newly blossomed honeysuckle had drifted in he'd given in to the impulse to stop and break off a small limb to bring to Crystal. But now that he was on the porch, misgivings outweighed good intentions. Her enthusiasm for the ranch made him forget that she'd spent the last several years, no doubt, accustomed to hothouse bouquets in elegant vases.

Before he could decide, the door abruptly opened. "I thought I heard you lurking out here." Her face lit up when she saw the honeysuckle. "For me?"

He nodded and shoved it into her hands. "Be careful. The stem may be sharp."

She held the blooms to her nose and inhaled. "Thank you. Is there any better smell?"

Jeremy smiled. "My grandma used to say that honeysuckle was what she always imagined heaven would smell like."

She nodded and stepped back. "Come on in while I get something to put it in."

He walked into the living room, but her voice drifted back to

88

him. "I thought we'd eat in the kitchen if that's okay."

He followed her slowly into the big kitchen and smiled at the huge, long wood table in the center. Hard to believe he'd never been in the McCord house before as many times as he'd been at the ranch. It was as warm and inviting as the family itself.

He glanced toward the booth in the corner, a small ceramic-top table set for two. Beside it, Crystal was squatted down with her head in a bottom cabinet.

"Found it," came her muffled but triumphant voice. She emerged with a glass gallon jar, the kind his mom made tea in. "Perfect."

"Nice vase," he said with a wry grin.

"The best." She ran the jar half full of water at the sink, set it on the counter, and plunked the honeysuckle branch into it.

"I'm glad."

"Ready to eat?" She slipped a potholder on her hand and pulled a pan of cheese toast from the oven.

"Now that's what *I* imagine heaven will smell like," he said, breathing in deep.

She laughed. "It does smell good. I've forgotten how hungry working outdoors makes me."

They sat across from each other at the small booth.

He glanced at her. "Is it okay if I ask the blessing?"

An expression he couldn't define flitted across her face, but she nodded. "Sure."

When he finished, they dug into their stew. Halfway through, he laughed. "My dad always says you can tell how hard people have been working by how little conversation there is at the dinner table."

She looked up with a grin. "We worked hard, didn't we?"

When they finished, he pushed his empty bowl away. "I see what you mean about your mama's stew. That was delicious," he said.

"Why did you let me eat so much? I feel like I could sleep for a week."

"Or a hundred years?" he teased.

"No fair bringing up the whole Sleeping Beauty thing again."

"Did you fall asleep out there on purpose?"

She shrugged, absently fingering her napkin.

He peered closer. He hated to be nosy but couldn't help but press a little. "Is there a reason you don't want to sleep in the house?"

"It's just big and empty." She pushed to her feet and threw her napkin on the table. "Want to go sit in the living room? I'll do the dishes later."

"Aw c'mon." He stood. "Why would anyone choose to do dishes alone when there's someone here to help? I'll wash and you dry."

She cocked her head in that way he was becoming accustomed to and studied his face. Apparently deciding he was sincere, she started clearing the table. "We could use the dishwasher, you know."

"I'm used to washing them by hand." He rinsed the sink out with hot water and put the stopper in.

Within ten minutes, everything was washed and dried. He squeezed the dishcloth out and washed the table off while she put the last few things away.

As they walked into the living room, from the corner of his eye he saw her cover a yawn. "I'm going to go and let you get some rest."

Panic flashed in her eyes. "You don't have to leave yet."

He frowned. "Crystal, is everything okay?"

"Of course! I just hate for you to eat and run."

He kept his gaze on her face. "I'm starting to wonder if you think the house is haunted."

Her laugh was strained, at best. "Don't be silly."

Jeremy frowned. "I'm kidding, but. . ."

Her blue eyes were wide and her mouth taut. She obviously wanted him to drop the subject.

"Nothing."

She ran her fingers through her hair. "Are you a Razorbacks fan?"

"Yes, ma'am." Basketball season was over and football season hadn't started, so where was she going with this?

"How do you feel about trivia games?"

"If it's Razorback trivia, I feel like I can beat you. You've been out of state for a long time."

"I had ESPN, a subscription to the *Arkansas Democrat-Gazette*, and a brother who recorded all the games I couldn't get on cable." She grinned. "I'll be right back." She disappeared down the hall.

He studied the comfortable living room. A fireplace mantel full of photos caught his eye, and he stepped over to examine them closer. He picked up one he was certain was Crystal when she was a little older than Beka's age, dressed in a Tinkerbell costume. Right beside it was another one of her, at the same age, in a long blue Wendy-type nightgown. The picture beside it brought his eyebrows together. It looked like Crystal standing beside herself. He glanced behind it and there were several of the same two girls as teenagers.

"Here it is," Crystal called from behind him. "Prepare to lose."

He turned around with the last picture in his hand. "You're a twin?"

She stopped in her tracks and stared at him. "Um. . .I was."

How did a person stop being a twin? Had her sister run away? Been disowned?

"She was killed in an accident when we were eighteen." Crystal still clutched the game in her arms.

He set the picture back on the mantel. Even though the accident happened seven years ago, he could tell her grief was very fresh. "I'm sorry."

"Me, too." She sank onto the couch.

He sat down beside her. "This is why you don't want to stay in the house."

She nodded. "I went to New York right after," she whispered.

"And only came home when you had to," he finished.

She nodded again.

"What was her name?"

"Cami."

He took the game from her, opened the box, and slid out a card. "What football coach led the Razorbacks to the most wins?"

"Frank Broyles," she said quickly.

"That one was too easy. I demand another chance to stump you." Without waiting for her to answer, he pulled another card. "Oh, here's a good one. What former Razorback quarterback went to the pros as a wide receiver?"

"A wide receiver. . ."

"Are you stumped already?" He winked at her.

She rolled her eyes. "You wish. Joe Ferguson was a quarterback who went to the pros, but he went to the Buffalo Bills as a quarterback," she mused aloud. Her face lit up. "I know. Matt Long."

He snapped his fingers in mock disappointment. "I almost had you."

"In your dreams." She laughed and slipped a card out. "Scared yet?"

"Shaking in my boots, but bring it on." It was so good to hear her laugh.

"Three brothers played for the Razorbacks and two of them went on to play for the pros. Who are they?"

"Three brothers. . ."

She looked around. "We need a timer."

He chuckled. "Whoa there, Miss Competitive. I know the answer. The Burnett Brothers."

She raised an eyebrow. "You don't know their first names?"

He laughed. "Picky, picky. Bobby, Bill, and Tommy. And just for the record, Bobby and Billy were the ones who went pro."

"Lucky guess." She quickly pulled another card. "I had to answer two. So do you."

"Like I said, bring it on."

She looked at the card and her eyes widened in disbelief. "This is so not fair."

Her outraged look had him laughing before she even sputtered out the question.

"What Razorback quarterback went on to play as quarterback for the Buffalo Bills?"

"Hmm. . ." He pretended ignorance until he thought she was going to hit him. "A good friend told me the answer to this one. Joe Ferguson."

For the next hour, they pursued trivia and let the more serious matters fall to the side.

When the clock struck nine, he stood. "Want to sit on the porch for a while?"

"I'd love to." She scooped up a pillow and blanket off the end table and carried them out with her.

"You sleeping on the porch again tonight?"

"No. When I get so sleepy I can't stand it, I'm going to move onto the couch."

He walked out and settled on the porch swing.

She put her bedding on the double rocker and came to sit beside him.

They sat in silence, the swing gently swaying, and listened to the tree frogs and crickets.

"Sounds like rain's coming," he said softly.

She motioned toward the sky. "No stars tonight. You're probably right." She covered another yawn and laid her head back against the swing.

For the next ten minutes, he guided the swing gently with one foot on the wooden porch.

"Thank you," she said, her voice slurred. Soon, her head rested against his shoulder.

He waited a few minutes then walked her into the house like he used to with Beka when she'd fall asleep in the living room. Crystal collapsed onto the couch, and he tiptoed back out and got the bedding. She didn't stir even when he put the pillow under her head and covered her with the blanket.

He looked down at her, the second time in one day he'd seen her asleep. Both times he'd been struck by the pure beauty of her face, but tonight he was struck by the vulnerability there as well. Even in sleep, there was sadness and a sense of the burden she was carrying. As he watched her sleep, he knew he recognized these things because he saw them in his own mirror every day.

Crystal woke to the sound of pounding rain. Dusky light cast shadows around the room. Where was she?

She lay still for a minute, taking in her surroundings. Her gaze finally fell on the mantel, and she remembered. Jeremy. She'd fallen asleep on the porch swing. He must have helped her to the couch.

What time was it now? She squinted at the grandfather clock in the corner. Ten. Ten? She glanced toward the window. Sheets of rain were coming down, but the sky wasn't dark. That didn't compute.

She sat up and groaned as her muscles ached in protest. As the cobwebs cleared from her mind, she mouthed, "Ten." Ten in the morning. This time her groan had nothing to do with her muscles. She'd overslept again. Albeit a little more privately.

She jumped up and hobbled over to the door. Apparently Jeremy had locked it behind himself last night because she had to unlock it to open it. A small paper bag fluttered between the screen door and the wooden door.

A note was scrawled on the paper:

Hope this isn't cold by the time you wake up. The guys went home to wait the rain out. They'll be back if it quits and so will I. Call if you need anything.

J.

CHAPTER 11

Crystal peeked inside the bag. A cup of something delicious smelling from Coffee Central and a large muffin. She lifted the muffin out. A sunshine muffin, unless she missed her guess—raisins and walnuts, tiny chunks of apple. Her mouth watered.

After a quick shower, she microwaved the coffee and muffin and headed out to the porch with her late breakfast. She sat in the porch swing and ate while she watched the rain come down. In the distance, she saw Elyse's tiny cottage. She dug her cell phone out of her pocket, scrolled to her sister's name, and pushed the button.

"Hello?"

"Want to go into town for lunch?"

Elyse's soft laugh echoed through the line. "What are you? A duck?"

Crystal smiled and leaned forward to put her hand in the drip. A fine mist sprayed her face. "I love rainy days. They feel so full of possibilities."

"Like the possibility of staying warm and dry?"

"So how soon can you be ready?"

Elyse sighed. "An hour."

"I'm going to call Luke and see if he's around and wants to go, too, okay?"

"That would be great, Crys." She hesitated for a minute. "It's so good to have you home."

"Thanks. It's good to be here."

An hour later, Luke pulled up to the porch and honked. Crystal put the hood up on the bright yellow slicker she'd found in the front closet and ran to get in.

"Hey, kid. What's the big idea, dragging us out in the rain?"

"Nobody made you come."

He grinned, his dimples flashing. "You mentioned food, didn't you? I had no choice."

"Someday, a girl is going to figure out the way to your heart really is through your stomach, and you'll be completely defenseless." Not that they hadn't tried. According to Elyse, half the women in the church singles' group had tried to cook their way into poor bachelor Luke's heart.

"Yeah, well, it's cheaper for me in the long run just to go to a restaurant. Believe me."

He revved the motor and they bounced down the back road to Elyse's house. The windshield wipers screeched but did little to wipe away the deluge of water.

Crystal's seat belt locked in on the last pothole they hit before they pulled up at Elyse's. She unfastened it and scooted over to the middle to rebuckle. She waved to Elyse, who ran toward them holding a huge black umbrella over her head. "Think you could slow down a little once she gets in, bro?"

Luke chuckled. "If I don't, she'll get out and walk. So yeah, I definitely will."

Crystal smiled. Elyse's aversion to any kind of risk was as much a part of her as Luke's aversion to any woman who wanted to settle him down was of him. One of the great things about her family was that they loved each other in spite of individual quirks. Or maybe partly because of them.

Elyse wrestled the huge umbrella into submission, slid it behind the seat, and climbed up into the truck. She carefully fastened her seat belt before she turned to greet Crystal and Luke. "Are you sure we're not crazy for getting out in this weather?"

Crystal shrugged. "Look at it this way—we'll have Coffee Central to ourselves. And the little takeout menu said they have panini. Do you know how much I've been craving panini?"

"I don't even know what a panini is," Luke grumbled.

"Where did you get a takeout menu from Coffee Central?" Elyse asked as Luke pulled carefully onto the gravel road.

"Um. . .I. . ."

"It was probably in the Coffee Central bag Jeremy left on the porch this morning," Luke piped up.

Crystal snapped her head around to look at Luke. "When did you see the bag?"

"When I came up to find out what you were fixing for breakfast," he said, grinning.

"You read the note?" she said.

"What note?" Elyse asked.

"My note," Crystal snapped then regretted it immediately. "A note that Jeremy wrote on the bag. It was no big deal, just work stuff."

"He wrote you a note about work on a Coffee Central bag and left a takeout menu?" Elyse's expression was so puzzled that Crystal almost laughed. Almost.

"There was coffee and a muffin in the bag," Luke volunteered as he flipped on his blinker to signal turning onto the highway leading to town.

"Cappuccino," Crystal corrected.

"I couldn't tell."

She shot her brother a glare. "I guess I should be glad you didn't take a sip to see."

He snorted. "You should be glad there was still a bag there at all, as hungry as I was."

Elyse shook her head. "I'm starting to think I'm sorry for asking where you got the menu."

"It was no big deal."

"You said that, kid," Luke drawled.

"And I meant it."

They rode in silence the rest of the way into town.

Luke pulled up to the door. "How's that for curbside service?"

"Thanks." Elyse retrieved her umbrella and climbed out as she opened it. "Want to share with me?" she asked Crystal.

Crystal shook her head. "Thanks anyway, I have my jacket."

She unbuckled as Elyse hurried in the door. Just before she got out, she felt a hand on her shoulder. She turned around to face Luke.

A sheepish expression flitted across his face. "Sorry I got in your business. I should have left the bag alone."

She smiled. "It's okay. I know you. You had to see what was in it."

"Pretty much."

"At least you didn't eat the muffin." She flicked the brim of his hat. "That's saying a lot."

"Thanks."

"Thanks for the curbside service." She put her hood up, took a deep breath, and jumped out. "We'll get a table," she yelled as she slammed the door. Clutching her jacket tight around her, she ran through the blinding rain into the building.

Once inside, she slipped the dripping jacket off and hung it on a hook next to Elyse's umbrella. Dry never felt so good.

She hurried down the aisle that led to the coffee shop. The little eatery was the hub of a big wheel, with aisles of books shooting out all around it like broad spokes. Crystal sighed. The perfect place to spend a rainy afternoon.

She'd barely settled at Elyse's table when Luke joined them.

"How'd you stay so dry?" Crystal asked, trying to imagine his carrying an umbrella.

"I keep a trench coat behind the seat."

"I'd like to have a picture of that," Elyse joked.

Crystal nodded. "Luke McCord, undercover spy."

"Or hard-boiled detective," Elyse added.

"Speaking of hard-boiled. . ." Luke picked up a menu and flipped through it. "Wonder what they have to eat in this place."

Crystal rattled his menu. "Hey you. We're teasing you. You can't ignore us. Why aren't you making witty comebacks?"

He looked up at her. "Maybe because I'm weak from hunger and rebutting your silly jokes would burn up more calories than I can afford to lose."

Were those worry lines around his eyes?

"I'm glad you're taking a day off," Elyse said softly. Crystal guessed that she could see the strain on their brother's face as well.

"Hmph." He twisted his mouth. "I'm not 'taking' a day off. I have no choice."

Crystal nodded. "I guess you can't do much carpentry work in the rain."

He looked at her like she'd grown an extra head. "There's plenty of inside work to be done. But until they get the driveway poured, there's no way into the site when it's coming down like this."

"Are you very far behind schedule?"

He shrugged. "Define *very*. I'm not ready to ask Rachel to move the grand opening date. But if the weather doesn't cooperate between now and then. . ."

"It will." Elyse touched her brother's sleeve. "Don't worry."

"I'm not worried," he growled. "I'm starving." He cut his gaze toward Crystal. "Some of us didn't get muffin and coffee care packages from a secret admirer."

Crystal gasped. "Lucas Michael McCord, you take that back." She stopped and met Elyse's startled brown eyes. Then they both burst out laughing.

"You sound like a ten-year-old," Elyse said.

Luke nodded smugly, but not before she saw his dimples flash. "Why do you think I call her kid?"

"Um, are y'all ready to order drinks?" The waitress smiled at them, keeping her gaze mostly on Luke.

He and Elyse both ordered Dr Pepper.

"Sweet tea," Crystal said quickly. That was one thing she'd missed terribly. Sweet tea in the North just wasn't the same.

"After we eat, I have to run down to the building supply and pick up a few things," Luke said when the waitress was gone. "Hope that's okay."

Crystal looked around at the books in every direction. "I think I'll stay and read while you're gone."

Elyse followed her glance. "Me, too. I never have enough time in here. And I don't have any sessions scheduled today."

"Dogs just woke up this morning and decided to behave?" Luke teased.

Elyse put her hand to her mouth in mock surprise. "Why didn't I think of that? National Good Behavior Day for dogs. And here I thought everyone rescheduled because of the rain."

Crystal sat back and sighed.

Luke whipped his head around to look at her. "What?"

She smiled. "It's just good to be home. I've missed being with y'all so much."

He hmphed. "Couldn't prove—Ow." He glared at Elyse. "Missed you, too," he said gruffly.

"I'm sorry I stayed away so long," Crystal said. "And I'm sorry Elyse kicked your shin."

"Ankle," he muttered.

Crystal laughed. "Either way, I'm sorry. I'll be home more often from now on." One thing had become apparent over the last few days. She hadn't avoided the pain and grief when she left. She'd just carried it with her.

When they'd finished the last bite of their panini and paid the waitress, Luke pushed back his chair. "I'll be back in about an hour."

"We'll be here," Elyse said. She looked at Crystal. "If you need me, I'll be in the dog section."

Left to her own devices, Crystal wandered through the aisles. She picked up several books, but none really appealed to her. Then suddenly she saw them. On the clearance rack. Three different books about drama for children.

She thought about what Allie Montgomery had said about a local drama day camp. Working at the kids' theater in New York had been so much fun. And this would be a much more short-term commitment. Crystal might not be able to do it this summer, but some other time, between plays, when she wanted to make an extended visit to the ranch, teaching a camp would be the perfect excuse.

She grabbed all three and made her way to a comfy-looking plush couch she'd passed a few minutes before and sank down on it with her books. Within minutes, she was lost in the world of introducing children to drama through workshops, summer camps, and community performances.

She was skimming the third book when she heard someone say, "Crys?"

She glanced up at a woman with short dark hair and dancing brown eyes. She was average sized, maybe a little bigger, but neat and pretty.

"Crystal McCord?" The woman said, her voice not quite so confident.

Crystal stared at her. Those eyes. . . "Phoebe?"

"Yes. Oh, it's so good to see you."

Crystal stood and numbly allowed the woman to enfold her into a hug. "You, too."

Even as she said the words, she realized they were a lie. It wasn't good. She felt caught off guard, blindsided. Why hadn't she considered the possibility of running into high school friends? Shady Grove was a small town.

"So you're an actress in New York, huh?"

Crystal nodded again, wanting to ask about Phoebe's life, but her tongue was stuck to the roof of her mouth.

"I married Derek Mullins about a year after. . ." Pain flashed across her face, looking out of place on her pleasant features. "Graduation."

Crystal nodded inanely, wondering if she looked like a little bobble-head figure on a car dash. They both knew what Phoebe didn't say. A year after the accident.

"Are you. . . Do you. . . ?" Crystal motioned toward Phoebe's leg.

"I get along fine. You probably heard I had several surgeries on it. Now I set off the metal detectors at the airport. But I can walk. And I'm thankful for that."

And you're alive, Crystal thought.

As if reading her thoughts, Phoebe said, "It took me a long time to get over the fact that I lived." She wrinkled her nose. "My therapist said it was classic survivor's guilt."

Crystal stared down at the brightly colored books splashed across the tan couch.

"Can we sit for a few minutes?" Phoebe motioned toward the sofa.

"I. . . Okay." Crystal sat stiffly, perched on the edge of the couch.

Phoebe settled in as Crystal had done earlier and picked up

one of the books. She started idly bouncing it on her knee. Crystal remembered the habit like it was yesterday. Phoebe may not seem like it, but she was nervous. The thought calmed Crystal a little. Some things weren't easy for anyone to talk about. It wasn't just her.

"Over the last seven years, especially for the first year or two, I couldn't quit wondering why. Why hadn't I argued when Cami called shotgun? Why hadn't I just had a party at my house like Mama wanted me to? Why hadn't I called you when you didn't show up and insist you go? Maybe if we'd gone right back and picked you up, those drunk kids would have been in the next county by the time we got to that spot in the road."

Tears sparkled in Phoebe's brown eyes now. And even though every word felt to Crystal like the stab of a knife, she was just getting started.

"You know, I always envied you and Cami for the closeness you had. Yet every time people would say, 'There go the Three Musketeers,' instead of, 'There go the McCord twins,' I felt incredibly blessed."

Crystal sat, stone still, her eyes dry.

Phoebe bent the book in her hand back and forth and bounced it on her knee again. "Most people don't have one friend like that in a lifetime, but I had two. Then I lost them both the same night." She sighed and held the book still. "I've wanted to call you so many times, Crystal. But when I got out of the hospital, you were gone. I kept thinking that after you got past the worst of the grief, you'd call."

But I never did, Crystal thought, for the first time feeling guilty that she hadn't. "I'm sorry."

Phoebe shook her head impatiently, her dark Dorothy Hamill haircut bouncing. "I don't want you to be sorry. I've just missed you."

Crystal felt like an elephant was sitting on her chest. Being friends with Phoebe again would be worse than going into the room that she and Cami had shared the first eighteen years of their lives. "Maybe we can stay in touch," Crystal said and stood.

"Wait." Phoebe motioned her to sit again, and even though Crystal wanted to bolt she sat. "I need to tell you something." She plucked at the smooth fabric of the couch. "It's about my last conversation with Cami."

CHAPTER 12

No." Crystal could hardly believe she'd said it, but she lifted her chin, tears filling her own eyes for the first time since this awful conversation had begun. "No," she repeated. "That's really not necessary."

Phoebe reached over and touched her arm. "Please."

It wasn't her plea, but Phoebe's ice-cold hand that broke through Crystal's determination not to hear. Cami and Crystal used to tease Phoebe mercilessly about how her hands got cold when she was nervous or scared.

Crystal sighed and sat back. Apparently that was all the encouragement Phoebe needed.

"She told me about the argument you two had—that you wanted to wait a while before going to New York."

Crystal wrapped her arms around her ribs. "That was really just cowardice on my part. She knew that." She instinctively defended her twin.

"I asked her why she'd gotten so upset at you about it. She just twirled her hair around her finger, in that way she had, and said, in her most philosophical voice, 'Phoebs, Crys will live her dream wherever she is, but I'll never make it all the way to Broadway without her there to push me.'"

Hot tears splashed down Crystal's face and a sob caught in her throat. Her dream? No childish dream she'd ever had had compared with Cami's dream—for both of them—of Broadway. Which was what made the whole thing so crazy. Unlike Phoebe, who wondered what would have happened "if" this or that, Crystal knew. If she hadn't tried to back out of going with Cami to New York after graduation, they'd have gone out together graduation night, and the accident would have never happened. And they'd both be almost to Broadway now. Instead of Crystal doing it on her own.

"Not thirty seconds before that car hit us, Cami said she was going to call and see if you'd reconsider going with us." Phoebe rummaged in her big bag and pulled out a small pack of tissues. Her hands shook as she handed Crystal one and took one for herself. "She never got a chance to make that call, but I always thought you should know that she intended to."

"Thank you," Crystal choked out.

Phoebe stood. "I'm going to go. I know I forced myself on you." She fished in the bag again, brought out a receipt, and scrawled a number on the back of it. She dropped it on the couch. "Give me a call if you ever want to talk again."

And with that she was gone, leaving Crystal in the middle of a public place, tears pouring down her face, her mind reeling. She found the bathroom without running into anyone and splashed cold water on her face until the tears stopped. She stared in the mirror. Her eyes, the supposed windows of her soul, looked wild. *And rightly so*, she thought, as her stomach churned. She wanted to be home, maybe on the porch, wrapped in a blanket, so she could sift through the things Phoebe had told her.

She bumped into Elyse right outside the bathroom. Her sister had the three books from the couch in her hand. "Look what I found on the sofa—" She grabbed Crystal's arm. "Are you okay? What's wrong?"

Crystal shook her head. "Nothing." Nothing new. "We'll talk later."

"You saw Phoebe, didn't you?"

Crystal nodded.

"Okay, we'll talk later." Elyse held up the books, plus two of her own. "Luke called, he's waiting outside. Want me to get these three with mine and we'll settle up at home?"

"Please."

"You want to go on out to the truck?"

Crystal shrugged. "I'll just wait for you."

At the truck, she stepped back and let Elyse get in the middle. She recognized the defense mechanism for what it was. This way she'd have a buffer between her and Luke, be dropped off at the house first, and disguise the fact that something was wrong.

She sighed. Sadly, she'd become a master of disguise over the last seven years.

Jeremy looked over at Crystal. Day before yesterday, they'd been fixing fence yet had managed to keep up a continuous conversation. But today, as they'd traveled on horseback taking inventory of the cattle, she'd been so quiet. Had the muffin and cappuccino been over the top? She'd thanked him but said little else all morning.

He reined Nacho in beside a wet-weather creek. "Feel like taking a break?"

"Sure." She brought her mare to a complete stop and slid gracefully to the ground.

He dismounted. "Have I offended you in some way?"

She looked up quickly from where she was tying the horse to a small tree. "No. Why?"

"You're quiet today." He lifted the lid of the small cooler in his own saddlebag, brought out two bottles of water, and handed her one.

"Thanks." She sank onto the gravel bank and opened the lid.

He sat down beside her.

They stared in silence at the water. "This reminds me of the day you came to Shady Grove a couple weeks ago," he said softly.

She nodded. "Me, too."

"Did you find what you were looking for here?"

She opened and closed her mouth as if she wanted to say something but decided against it. "Sometimes I think I found more than I was looking for."

His heart ached at the poignant tone in her voice. Did her enigmatic answer have anything to do with him? Or was he assuming too much? "What do you mean?"

She cocked her head and gave him what he was coming to think of as her "measuring" look. "Yesterday, at Coffee Central, I ran into the girl who was in the car accident that killed my sister."

"I'm sorry." He felt like a heel for pushing her but figured if she hadn't wanted to talk about it she wouldn't have told him. "Was she the driver?"

Crystal shook her head. "No, another friend of ours was driving. He was killed, too. Phoebe was in the backseat."

They stared at the tiny brook rippling madly over the rocks in response to yesterday's big rain.

"I should have been there, too, but Cami and I. . ." She cleared her throat and took a small sip of water. "We had an argument that day."

"Crystal, I'm sorry. If you don't want to talk about it, I understand."

Her lips twisted into a self-deprecating sneer. "Thanks, but I think I've probably 'not talked about it' for long enough."

"Was it a big argument?"

"Nothing we couldn't have worked out. Although I'm not sure my heart really believed that until I talked to Phoebe yesterday."

She motioned toward the bright green trees on the other side of the water. "It's almost like yesterday's rain washed away the last dregs of winter, isn't it? Everything looks so fresh and beautiful."

Jeremy looked over at her. She had that right. "Spring's my favorite time of year."

"Mine, too." She touched his arm. "Thanks."

His brows drew together. "What for?"

After a morning of mopey silence, her brilliant smile was like sunshine after rain. "For graciously letting me talk about it then just as graciously letting me change the subject."

He held his hands out, palms up. "Hey, I'm here to serve," he said jokingly.

But as they stood to go back to their horses, a shiver went up his spine. Why did Crystal McCord's silences and smiles matter so much?

"Chance McCord! If you don't get out of that bathroom, I'm going to start breaking your fishing lures. One at a time."

Crystal heard a muffled protest from the bathroom as she walked by. She glanced at Kaleigh, fist raised to pound on the door again, face almost as red as her hair. "Yes, I will. I know where the key to your tackle box is. I have to get a shower before church, too."

"I'm out of Mama and Daddy's bathroom," Crystal said quietly.

Kaleigh spun around. "Oh, okay. You look great."

Crystal smiled. "Thanks. Are you sure it's okay?" Crystal smoothed the dress down with her hands. It had been so long since she'd gone to church, she felt she'd stick out like a sore thumb, but she'd promised Aaron she'd try. And especially with Kaleigh and Chance here, she didn't want to bring up a lot of questions.

"It's perfect. The little black dress everyone wishes they had. Or looked like that in," Kaleigh said, her hand still raised to bang on the door. "Sorry for yelling. He tricked me by giving me the last piece of cinnamon toast so he could beat me to the shower."

"Possibly getting you back for the time you convinced him you saw a monster bass in the cow pond so you could watch what you wanted to on TV?"

Kaleigh grinned. "He stayed out there all night with his rod and reel." She lowered her fist. "Fine. I'll shower in Mama and Daddy's bathroom."

Crystal nodded and went on downstairs. Since yesterday afternoon, she hadn't had to worry about the house being too quiet. The twins had taken a rare Saturday afternoon and Sunday off to come home for a visit. And Matthew should be here from Tennessee when they got home from church.

The three sisters had gone into town yesterday to get groceries. They'd gotten silly and laughed about everything under the sun. Crystal couldn't remember when she'd laughed so hard. She couldn't believe the years she'd wasted staying away. At times being here was very painful, and she was still making her bed on the couch. But the pain was worth the joy of spending precious time with her sisters and brothers. And at least she wasn't still sleeping on the porch. So that was progress, however small.

In the kitchen, she peeked at the big roast with carrots and potatoes she'd put in the Crock-Pot when she first got up this morning. It already smelled delicious. Elyse was making homemade rolls. Kaleigh was taking care of the other veggies. Luke was bringing a gallon of sweet tea. With any luck, from Coffee Central. Matthew was supposed to pick up a Milky Way cake on his way in. And best of all, as it should be when the women cooked, the men had volunteered to do the dishes. That was always fun to watch.

Crystal sighed as she put the lid back on the Crock-Pot. Mama had sounded so proud when Crystal had talked to her last night and she'd found out they were all preparing Sunday lunch together at the house. And especially when she'd realized Crystal was planning to go to church this morning. But Crystal could hear the homesickness in her voice. She'd reminded her mother that they'd been gone almost a week already and the next few weeks would be over before she knew it.

As Crystal remembered their conversation, she felt again the same jolt she'd felt then. It would be over soon. And when it was over, how would she go back to New York and leave the ranch and family she loved? She'd done it before wearing the protective armor of fresh grief. But after she'd grown used to seeing Elyse and Luke regularly and the others on occasional weekends like this one, how would she do it?

She'd have to remind herself how thrilling it would be to act on Broadway. And remind herself that New York isn't another planet. She could visit more often. That's what understudies and days off were for.

She poured a second cup of coffee and sat down at the kitchen table. What about Jeremy Buchanan? She couldn't imagine going back to not knowing him. In the short time since she'd met him, he'd proven himself a good man and a wonderful friend.

"What are you so lost in thought about?" a deep voice said from the doorway.

She looked up at Chance and tried to figure out what to say. "The future."

"Deep subject." He poured a cup of coffee and came to sit beside her. "Anything in particular?"

She looked into her brother's green eyes. "Just wondering what life will be like when I get back to New York."

"Without Brad the cad, you mean?" He winced. "Sorry. I picked that up from Kaleigh."

Crystal snickered. "Very fitting. My friend, Tina, used to call him Ken."

Chance's eyebrows drew together. "Ken?"

"As in Barbie's Ken. Plastic. Like when he had a big plan to get rich on Wall Street, she started calling him Day-Trader Ken. Or more recently, Wedding-Proposal Ken."

Chance started to grin then frowned. "He proposed to you?"

"Oh yeah, about a week before I caught him with my roommate."

"Did you say yes?"

She shook her head. "I hadn't given him an answer yet. But I was going to say no."

Chance took a gulp of his coffee. "Why didn't you just say no right up front?"

She sipped her own coffee and considered his question. "Because I was trying to be sure that marrying Brad would be worse than being alone."

Pain flashed in his eyes. "You could always come home to stay, Crys."

She glared at him. "You know I can't. I'm going to see this through to Broadway."

"And then can you come home?"

She just stared at him. "Come home? Do you think Cami would have made it to Broadway and then quit?"

He shook his head. "But you're not Cami." He reached over and squeezed her hand. "We love you for you, Crys. It's not up to you to preserve Cami's memory by being a living monument to her."

"I think you've been listening to Mama too much. Broadway is my dream. And that has nothing to do with Cami." Heart pounding in her throat, she glanced at the kitchen clock. "Elyse should be here any second to get us. Do you think Kaleigh's almost done?"

"I'll go see." He bounded out of the room. "Hurry, slowpoke. Time to go," she heard him call up the stairs.

"I'm not a slowpoke," Kaleigh's voice drifted down. "You're just a bathroom hog."

A familiar stab of jealousy took her breath away. The twins gave each other a hard time, but they were best friends as well as siblings.

As she sat in the kitchen and listened to her younger brother and sister's good-humored fussing, she realized she'd lied to her mother. She was still grieving. And since she'd come home, she was realizing more and more that she'd lost more than her sister and best friend when Cami died. She'd lost her way.

CHAPTER 13

Jeremy had always spent Sundays with Beka. Through the week, while he and his dad worked on getting their new land into shape, his mom had kept Beka, sometimes even on Saturday. But Sunday mornings, the two of them would get up and get ready for church—"Does this dress look pretty on me, Daddy?"—and go together to Sunday school. Then after church and a big lunch at his parents' house, father and daughter would do something fun, just the two of them. They'd flown kites, gone fishing, built snowmen, swam in the river, and even gone to the Little Rock Zoo and the Memphis Zoo.

Now since Beka wasn't here anymore, he couldn't face all the sweet little girls in their pretty dresses, holding their daddies' hands and skipping into their Sunday school classes. It was just too hard. So he waited and went to worship.

And usually he slipped in right before the service started. As he pulled into the parking lot, he glanced at the clock. Today was no exception.

In the crowded auditorium, Jeremy glanced around for a place to sit. He spotted a familiar blond head halfway up the aisle with an empty seat beside her. He started forward then stopped. Sitting with her now would just make it harder when she went back to New York. At least as it was now, he could pretend that he saw her for work and that their suppers were just a continuation of that. He slid into the pew next to the back by two women he recognized as friends of his mother.

Willing himself to concentrate on worship was hard this morning, even though he knew it was only right. But he managed to keep his mind on the service, and when the hour was up, he felt refreshed and uplifted. And closer to God than he had in a long time.

When he bumped into Luke in the foyer, the contractor clasped his hand. "Hey, thanks for taking such good care of Crystal this week. Work's been crazy and I haven't been around as much as I wanted to be."

Jeremy returned his handshake, wondering what Luke would say if he knew how much of Jeremy's spare time was spent thinking about his sister. "I enjoy working on the ranch." Not to mention talking to Crystal.

Luke looked around. "I need to talk to your dad about some repairs he wants done at his house. Do you know where he is?"

"You'll have to wait a couple weeks. They flew out yesterday to Florida."

"No problem. I'll catch him when he gets back." Luke looked a little embarrassed. "I was just going to have to ask him to be patient with me anyway. Like I said, things are crazy at work."

"I'm sure he won't mind." Over Luke's shoulder, Jeremy could see Crystal walking slowly toward them. Her black dress was simple, but somehow she made it look elegant and. . .beautiful. Suddenly he became aware that Luke was saying something. "What?"

Luke glanced back to see what had caught Jeremy's attention, and a knowing smile flitted across his face. "I was asking you if you had plans for dinner. Don't you usually eat with your mom and dad on Sundays?"

"Yeah, I usually do." He tried not to notice that Crystal had reached them. "I'm just going to run into town and get a bite to eat."

"We've got enough food to feed one more hungry cowboy, don't we, sis?"

Crystal looked startled but nodded. "Sure."

Jeremy felt his face grow hot. "Oh, thanks. But I don't want to push in on a family gathering."

Luke laughed. "Our motto is 'The more the merrier.' "

Jeremy glanced at Crystal, trying to read her expression.

She put her hand on his arm, her smile genuine. "We really would love for you to come, Jeremy. There's plenty of food."

He knew he probably shouldn't go, for the same reason he hadn't sat with her. He also knew that his weak resolve didn't stand a chance. So at least for now he was going to quit fighting. He'd see her while he could and deal with his heart when she left. "I'll run home and change and see y'all in a few."

"Don't take too long. The food goes fast," Luke teased.

"So Luke invited your cowboy to lunch?" Kaleigh looked up from where she was putting together a broccoli-and-cheese casserole.

Crystal, on tiptoes getting plates out of the cabinet, came down to earth with a thud. "He's not my cowboy." And she didn't know why the thought of his *being* her cowboy made her heart skitter at such an alarming rate. She set the plates on the counter and started gathering silverware from the top drawer.

Kaleigh lifted the glass casserole dish and walked across the kitchen. "Would you open the oven for me?"

Crystal yanked the oven door open. Maybe the heat hitting her face would disguise the redness she could feel in her cheeks.

As she closed the door, Kaleigh slipped the oven mitt off her hand and turned to face her. "Why not?"

Crystal pretended to misunderstand. "Why not what?"

"Don't play dumb." Kaleigh grinned. "Why is he not your cowboy?"

"Because I'm going back to New York in a few weeks." Sometimes the obvious had to be stated.

"He doesn't fly? Or he doesn't know the way to New York?"

Crystal sighed. "Long-distance relationships never work."

"Never is a big word," Kaleigh said.

What was it with her sisters and waxing philosophical about the word *never*? Or was it just that Crystal used the word a lot?

"What have you got to lose by trying?" Kaleigh prodded.

My heart. But Crystal wasn't interested in being quite that honest, so she just shrugged. "I don't see you in a relationship. Why is that?"

She glanced at her sister. It sure wasn't because she didn't have plenty of opportunities. Her flaming red hair and startling green eyes were trumped only by a smile that lit up any room. When she first came to live with them—a freckle-faced river rat straight from her grandfather's houseboat—they'd all thought she and Chance were twin boys, but by the time she hit adolescence, she'd blossomed into a living doll.

Now it was Kaleigh's turn to blush, something she did easily. She retrieved the raw vegetables from the refrigerator. "I'm too much of a rebel and I don't know how to compromise."

Crystal frowned. "Who told you that?"

"The last three guys I dated." She arranged the carrots on the veggie tray.

"They probably just wanted to play video games and watch *Star Wars* over and over."

Crystal's words had the desired effect. Kaleigh giggled as she spread out the broccoli and cauliflower. "Pretty much."

"Some things shouldn't be compromised." The thought of her

sister settling for anything less than her heart's desire in a boyfriend made Crystal furious. But hadn't that been what she'd done herself with Brad?

Kaleigh chopped the tomato with enthusiasm. "Yeah, like work ethic and good taste."

Jeremy has work ethic and good taste, Crystal thought inanely.

Kaleigh gave her a sideways glance. "So do you like Jeremy? If you weren't going back to New York, I mean?"

"You know what daddy always said about *if*."

The woman who had owned Jeremy's house before him had apparently loved flowers. Before she'd moved to Texas to be near her grandkids, she'd planted wildflower seeds by the bucket around the perimeter of the yard. He cut one of each kind of flower. At first he felt embarrassed by the motley crew of blooms in his hand. But when he put them all together in an old glass pitcher, he was happy with the results. Crystal would love this.

Not that it was just for her, of course. He balanced the arrangement beside him on the truck seat and reassured himself that it was a hostess gift and nothing more. It could even be for Luke, since technically that was who had invited him.

It actually was Luke who opened the door when he arrived at the McCords' house. Matthew and Chance glanced up from the couch where they were sitting. When they saw the flowers in his hands, they exchanged looks that said volumes.

Suddenly embarrassed, Jeremy quickly thrust the bouquet into Luke's hands. "Here, this is for y'all."

Luke just as quickly placed it back in Jeremy's hands. "We know who this is for, man. She's in the kitchen." With one hand on Jeremy's back, he propelled him gently toward the kitchen.

Jeremy didn't argue. If he was honest with himself, he knew

who they were for, too.

Just as he walked in, Crystal said, "I *am* going back to New York. That's what matters."

He'd never doubted it, but that didn't stop his stomach from clenching at hearing it said so directly. The youngest sister looked up at him, and her face turned as red as the tomato she was chopping.

Crystal's eyes widened. "Jeremy. . .those daisies are beautiful. Well, they all are." She flashed him a smile that made the whole room seem brighter. "But daisies are my favorite."

"I picked them out of my yard. Well, not out of my yard, of course, but around my yard, in the flower beds." He shoved them toward her.

Unlike Luke, she took them. "Thank you." Crystal caught her sister's eye. "For thinking of us. That was so sweet. Wasn't it, Kaleigh?"

Kaleigh mumbled something Jeremy couldn't quite make out. Then she took a visible breath and laid the knife down. "I'm going to go call Elyse and see if the rolls are almost ready," she said and quickly left the room.

"Can I do anything to help?" Jeremy knew he should probably go back into the living room with the guys, but right now he just wanted to enjoy a minute alone with Crystal.

Crystal raised an eyebrow. "Help at your own risk, because today's agreement is the girls do the cooking and the guys clean up after. I'm not sure helping now will get you out of KP."

"I'll take my chances," he said. "What can I do?"

She tilted her head. "Do you know how to set a table?"

Was this a trick question? "Not if Emily Post is coming to dinner. But if it's just going to be us and your brothers and sisters, I can probably manage."

She laughed and handed him the silverware and napkins. "Perfect. Give it your best shot. Holler if you need anything."

"Plates, maybe?"

"We do a buffet-style line, so the plates stay in here. And honestly, we're not picky. Just make sure we all have something to eat with and something to wipe our mouths with."

He stepped into the dining room and set out seven place settings with silverware and napkins. Was it crazy that he was happy that she trusted him to set the table? That she hadn't just shooed him into the living room to sit with her brothers? Probably. But he couldn't keep a smile from his face as he tried his best to remember a manners class his mom had enrolled him in one summer during junior high.

"Someday you'll be glad you learned these things," the teacher had assured him. He'd never believed it. Until now.

"Wow," Crystal said from behind him as he put down the last setting. "You'd do Emily Post proud. I'm impressed."

He chuckled. "Let's just keep this between us, okay? I don't want to get a rep with the guys. I can hear it now—the Kitchen Cowboy."

"Sleeping Beauty has met her match," she said, laughing.

He turned to follow her back into the kitchen. "Glad you finally admit it."

"In terms of teasing potential, that is," she said over her shoulder.

He groaned. "What happens in the dining room stays in the dining room." Just as the last word left his mouth, he looked into the startled faces of Elyse and Kaleigh.

Crystal burst out laughing and she lowered her voice to a whisper. "Jeremy's afraid word will get around to the guys that he knows how to set the table." She put her finger to her lips. "So shh. . ."

Her sisters nodded. Elyse turned back to putting ice in glasses.

Kaleigh grinned. "Your secret's safe with us." She glanced at Elyse then at Crystal. "Ready for me to ring the bell?"

They both nodded and she ran out the back door.

"A bell?" Jeremy's brows drew together. "For real?"

Before they could answer, a loud ringing filled the air.

"It's a McCord tradition," Crystal explained. "The dinner bell tells you that you've got five minutes to get in and get your hands washed or you're going to lose out."

"Cool." *Like so many things about this family,* Jeremy thought. He knew most of them were adopted, but the bond between them seemed as strong or stronger than any blood tie he'd ever seen. "You have a neat family," he said to Crystal as she came to stand beside him.

She beamed up at him. "Thanks. I think so, too."

Kaleigh slipped in the back door just as the door between the kitchen and living room opened and Luke, Chance, and Matthew walked in.

Crystal scooted closer to Jeremy, and everyone formed a loose circle.

When they were all still, Luke cleared his throat. "Let's pray."

They bowed their heads and he blessed the food. At the end, he said, "And, Lord, please be with little Beka"—Jeremy felt Crystal's hand slip into his and squeeze, and he swallowed against the lump in his throat—"and bring her home to her daddy safe and sound."

When Luke said, "Amen," Jeremy sent him a grateful look and nodded. He glanced down at Crystal's hand still in his. "Thanks," he whispered and gave her hand a squeeze.

"You're welcome," she whispered back, and then she was gone like a whirlwind, giving orders and organizing food lines.

But he could still feel the imprint of her hand in his.

CHAPTER 14

Crystal couldn't believe it. This was Jeremy's last official day as her "shadow." Besides delivering Anastasia's calf together, last week they'd fixed the fence and counted cows and calves. This week, they'd corralled cows that needed shots and now they were helping Dr. Johnson take care of those same cows. Every task for the past week had been something different. After the second day, she realized Aaron had planned it that way on purpose, giving her a good refresher course in all parts of the ranch.

As much as she'd protested about having Jeremy help her, she hated to admit that she was going to miss him. Not just at work, either. They'd eaten supper together several nights. She couldn't see that continuing, since he wasn't going to be working with her anymore.

Jeremy sauntered up and adjusted his cowboy hat. "I think we should leave the cows up tonight just in case any of them have a reaction to the meds."

She nodded. That was the way her daddy always did it.

He pulled a bandanna from his back pocket and wiped his forehead. "We can let them out in the morning."

She glanced at him quickly. Had he said *we*?

"If it's okay with you, I thought I'd go ahead and work the rest

123

of this week." He shifted from foot to foot. "Unless you'd rather I didn't."

"That would be great. I mean, if you want to." Inwardly she groaned. She sounded like a love-struck teenager. Which she definitely wasn't. She just dreaded facing the house alone again. And Elyse and Luke were both gone so much.

"Elyse has a meeting tonight, doesn't she?" Jeremy asked, again seeming to read her mind.

"Yes."

"So you want to run into town and get a bite to eat at Pizza Den? It's not fair for you to have to cook every night."

He'd been baching way too long if he thought the simple meals she'd been fixing for them after work were cooking. "Pizza sounds great."

"I'll pick you up about seven."

"It's a date." As soon as the words came out, she felt her face flush. She could have talked all day and not said that. "I mean, not really, of course. That's just an expression. . ." she finished lamely.

He chuckled. "I know. See you at seven."

Mortified, she watched him leave then went in to try to figure out what to wear to a meal that was definitely not a date.

In the end, she settled for a plain white T-shirt, a long, flared turquoise skirt, and her turquoise sandals. When she heard Jeremy pull up in the driveway, she threw on the turquoise-accented cowgirl hat she wore in the city when she felt homesick, grabbed a denim jacket, and hurried out the door.

Already out of the truck, he paused and his eyes widened when he saw her. "I didn't mind coming to the door."

"I didn't mind just coming on out to save you the trouble," she said.

He nodded, as if considering her motive, and walked around to open her door. "You look beautiful."

A shiver went down her spine, and she hoped he didn't notice. "Thanks." She climbed up into the truck and he shut the door. As he walked around to the other side to get in, she gave herself a stern talking-to. She was going back to New York soon. And Aaron had been right. Neither she nor Jeremy needed more heartache. So tonight it was just two friends out for pizza. And that's all it could be. An impish grin played across her lips. Even if one of the friends did tell the other one that she looked beautiful.

"Whoa, that's a mischievous grin. What are you thinking about?" Jeremy asked as he started the motor.

Crystal shrugged. "Just how funny life can be."

"I'm not sure I'm buying that answer, but I'll let it slide for now." He motioned toward her hat. "Finally decided you belong here, I see."

She touched the brim of her hat. "Just thought I'd give New York the night off and go as a cowgirl tonight."

"It suits you."

Crystal looked out of the window at the stars. For tonight, he was exactly right. It suited her perfectly.

When the pizza was almost all gone, Crystal grew serious. Jeremy was learning to watch her expressive face for a hint of where their conversations were going, but he was still caught off guard when she leaned forward and said, "Tell me about Lindsey."

He set his last slice of pizza back on his plate, his appetite gone at the mention of her name. "What do you want to know?"

Crystal's blue eyes were an odd mix of curiosity, sympathy, and something else he couldn't define. She sighed. "Everything."

"We were high school sweethearts." He hesitated, forcing himself to remember those days. "Her grandfather raised her, and besides him, she had no other family."

Crystal nodded, and he was struck again by how easy she was to talk to.

"Just out of high school, she got a job at the bank, and I went to the local community college. Her grandfather died and my parents just accepted her as family." His stomach lurched as he forced himself to remember how his parents had taken her into their home. "When I was about to graduate from the two-year program in agri, we set the wedding date."

He stared at the orange glow of the light on the wall beside their booth. How much should he tell her? He looked back at her. "Two weeks before the wedding, she left."

"Left?"

"Left town. Left me. Left me a note, actually, saying that she wanted to see the world, that she was too young to settle down."

"That had to be awful."

He nodded. "It was. But my dad pointed out that God has a way of working things out. And even though I never admitted it, I knew that deep down I felt a little relieved. Like maybe I wasn't ready either."

"So she let you off the hook?"

He nodded. It sounded simple. And except for Beka, he could wish it had stayed that simple.

"Then how did. . ." For the first time she looked a little uncomfortable. She dropped her gaze. "I'm sorry. This is really none of my business."

"I want you to know," he said. "Some of it's just not easy to talk about."

"I understand."

And he knew she did. Taking a deep breath, he picked up where he'd left off. "She came back about six months later." His mouth twisted. "She'd changed. Apparently, one of the bank customers had talked her into leaving town with him. But as soon as they got out on the road, he found a new conquest and left her. She found some new friends. That didn't last long either, though. They kept her strung out on drugs. But then one day she got clean enough to come home."

"So she wanted you back."

He nodded. "She said she'd always loved me and it was all a mistake. She wanted to get married right away. When she kept pressing me to hurry and set a new date, I figured out what was really going on." He pushed the pizza plate away from him. "She was pregnant."

Crystal put her hand to her mouth. "Oh no."

"I didn't have to marry her. But she convinced me that we could get back what we had and the baby would be ours, right from the beginning." He glanced over at a family of four at the table next to them. The man was cutting up pizza for a toddler in the high chair. "That part was true." He looked back at Crystal. "Beka was mine from the beginning."

Crystal nodded. "I can imagine."

"I was so relieved when she was born with no birth defects from her mother's drug use. But when Beka was still a baby, Lindsey took off again for two weeks. She came home and went into rehab. When she got out, she said it would never happen again. It didn't for two years. Then she left and never came back. The last I heard from her was when divorce papers arrived by courier a few months after she left." His heart tightened. "Until ten months ago. Right after Beka turned five."

"And Lindsey came back?"

"We'd moved here since the last time I saw her. But thanks to the wonders of the Internet, she found us. She showed up, clear-eyed and sorry, wanting nothing more than to be my wife and Beka's mother." He could hear the bitterness in his voice. He took a deep breath and spoke more quietly. "And to help me spend the money we got from selling the gas rights on my family's land."

"Oh, Jeremy."

"I made it plain that I had no romantic interest in her, but I offered to help her find a job and an apartment. And to figure out a way that she might fit into our little girl's life."

"But instead she took her?" Tears sparkled in Crystal's eyes.

Anger clenched the muscle in his jaw. "Beka was at a birthday party when I told Lindsey that we had no hope for a future together. Lindsey picked her up early. And just kept going."

"You must hate her."

He stared at the family next to them again. "I try not to. The first six months I spent just trying not to lose my mind. The past six months I've worked to keep from losing my relationship with God. Logically, I know hate has no place in that relationship. So some days I think I can forgive her." He watched the dad hold a sippy cup up to the toddler's mouth. "And other days, I'm sure I can't. But I have to keep trying." He glanced back at Crystal. "Because if I lose Him, what's left?"

Crystal bent down and picked her napkin up and set it on the table. "Morning's going to come early."

They left the pizza place without talking much more.

Halfway home, he glanced over at her. "Sorry for being such a downer."

She took her hat off and shook her hair out, then ran her fingers through it. "I'm the one who asked. But I'm not sorry. I think it's incredible how you've gone on."

He snorted. "What choice did I have? I'm not a noble man, Crystal. I'm just a guy trying to deal with what life's handed him. No different than you dealing with your own tragedy and going on. It's what you do."

She looked away from him and shrugged. "Some people deal better than others."

"Hey, you're doing fine." He drove up in front of the ranch house. "You're not sleeping on the porch anymore, right?"

Just as he'd hoped she would, she smiled. "No, I'm camping out on the couch now, so no more scary early morning discoveries for Slim."

"Then that's progress." He jumped out and ran around to her door and opened it.

"Emily Post really did teach you well," she teased as she climbed out.

As they walked up to the porch, their hands touched, and the next thing he knew they were walking hand in hand.

The third step squeaked as he stepped onto it, and Crystal giggled. "When we were teenagers, we'd come home from a date and Daddy would listen for that step to squeak. After that, he'd say we had one minute. Then the porch light would come on."

"One minute, huh?" he said, his voice husky as he held her hand and looked into her huge eyes. Her hair was spun gold in the moonlight. He pulled her gently closer and with his free thumb, he brushed a few strands of hair away from her face. "Does this count as a date?" he whispered just loud enough to be heard above the crickets' song.

A mischievous grin played across her face. "You tell me," she said softly.

He leaned toward her and barely brushed his lips across hers.

What was it about being with her that felt like he was coming home to his favorite place? "Yes, I'd say it more than qualifies," he murmured, his face still close to hers.

The sound of a truck motor broke through the cricket symphony, and headlights shone across the porch. They both turned toward the light. He squinted. "Is that Luke?"

"Yep," Crystal said wryly, releasing his hand. "Perfect timing, as usual."

The truck honked and went on by to the barn.

Jeremy turned back to Crystal, but she was unlocking the front door. "Thanks again for the pizza," she said, a little formally, he thought.

"I had a good time."

She looked back over her shoulder. "Me, too. See you in the morning."

And with that, she was gone inside. He heard the lock turn behind her.

He stood on the porch for a few seconds, wondering why he hadn't kissed her properly before they were interrupted. It was probably just as well. But he couldn't deny that he was disappointed.

CHAPTER 15

Ten long months of waiting for a middle-of-the-night phone call brought Jeremy awake on the first ring. "Jeremy Buchanan," he growled as he sat up and turned on the bedside lamp.

"You need to get here to Memphis. They've found a woman they think is Lindsey."

"Sam? Where? Is Beka with her?" Jeremy wiped his palm across his eyes, trying to clear the fog of sleep from them, as well as from his brain.

"Whoa, whoa. Nobody's seen Beka. But the woman they think is Lindsey is at Baptist Hospital. I'll meet you there, but hurry."

"Wait." He grabbed his jeans from the cedar chest at the end of the bed and yanked them on with one hand. "Was she in an accident?"

"Drug overdose."

"Is she. . ." He clutched the phone to his shoulder as he shrugged into a shirt.

Sam hesitated. "She's still alive, but barely."

"Has she said where Beka is?"

"You need to be praying, because right now she's unconscious."

"I will be."

And he did, the prayers tumbling on top of each other as he

131

wrestled his socks and boots on and grabbed his wallet and keys. Any romantic feeling he'd had for Lindsey had dissipated to dusty memories years ago. But even as angry as he was that she'd taken Beka, he'd never wished for her to die. He was ashamed that the next thought came so quickly, but it did. If she did die, how would they find his little girl?

In the garage, he jumped into his truck. As he backed out onto the road, his gut clenched. *What if it isn't her?* But an equally awful thought pushed into his jumbled mind. *What if it is?*

The dashboard clock read four a.m.

"Beka, where are you, honey?" he whispered to the empty truck.

As he passed through Jonesboro at five thirty, the sky was barely starting to lighten. His dark imaginings lifted slightly. To distract himself, he thought back on the previous day. The day that was supposed to have been his last day "staying right with" Crystal as Aaron had requested. But he just wasn't ready to go back to the loneliness he'd been enduring before she came into his life. Had she seen through his decision to keep working a few more days?

Not that he'd be there now to check the cows this morning. He picked up the phone and scrolled to her name. She should be getting up about now. He punched Send.

"Hello?" Her voice was heavy with sleep.

"Crystal, I'm sorry for waking you."

"Oh, that's okay. I should be up, but I hit Snooze. Everything okay?"

"Not really." He ran his hand across the leather of the steering wheel. "I'm on my way to Memphis. A woman they think might be Lindsey is in the hospital from an overdose."

Crystal gasped. "What about Beka?" All traces of sleepiness were gone from her voice.

His chest constricted, but he forced the words out. "There's no sign of her."

"Oh, Jeremy," she whispered, "you'll find her."

"Thank you. I'll let you know when I get home. But I won't be at work today for sure."

"That's fine. I'll get Slim to help me check the cows out and let them go. Take care of what you need to." She hesitated. "Please call me, whatever happens. And know I'm praying."

He knew he should hang up.

"Do you want to talk for a while?" Crystal said softly. "I hate that you're alone."

"Thanks." Grateful for her understanding, he was embarrassed that he had no words to fill the gap right now. Every time he opened his mouth, he struggled not to give voice to his worse fears.

As if she knew exactly what he was thinking, Crystal began to tell rambling stories about when she was growing up. Specifically about how they got each of her brothers and sisters, starting with Aaron and ending with the twins, Kaleigh and Chance.

His breath was coming a little easier.

"Does Beka like the stars?" Crystal asked suddenly.

Jeremy blinked at her sudden subject change. "Yes. She loves them. We used to spread a blanket on the ground and lie out and watch them when we first moved up here."

"Can she find the Big Dipper?"

He chuckled. "Sometimes. Right before. . ." The fears came rushing back, but he pushed them away. "She was getting to where she could find it sometimes."

"I had a book when I was her age. . ." This time Crystal's voice faltered. "I'm pretty sure it's here somewhere. Anyway, it teaches an easy way to find some of the constellations. I can't wait to read it to her."

"She'd love that. But she might give you a run for your money reading. She could already read some simple books when she turned five."

"Sounds like she's smart like her daddy." The warmth in Crystal's voice pushed away the coldness of being alone.

"I don't know about that. But I know she'll love you. She always colors her princesses with blond hair. And you know. . ." He paused, and to his amazement, felt a little bit of a smile tilt his lips. "I told you Sleeping Beauty's her favorite."

Crystal groaned. "Are you ever going to let that rest?" She giggled. "Pun intended."

"Probably not. You're too much fun to tease." He stared at the interstate sign in amazement. The exit for the hospital was straight ahead. "I'm here. I'll call you later."

"So you haven't heard from him since day before yesterday?" Elyse rubbed her dog's head.

"Right. He called me Thursday morning on his way to Memphis." Crystal sighed. "I'm about to go crazy not knowing. Thanks for walking down to keep me company." An engine roar in the distance brought her to her feet. "Somebody's coming around the barn."

Elyse stood, too. "It's Luke."

"Oh. It is." Crystal sank back to the swing.

"You know, Crys, if you're feeling like this now, how are you going to feel when you go back to New York and leave him a thousand miles behind?"

Crystal jerked her gaze to her soft-spoken sister, irrational anger welling inside her. "Feeling like what? I'm concerned about his little girl. Just like I would be if it were any friend." *Any friend who kissed me on this very porch*, she thought, her face growing hot.

"Ohh. . . Sorry for misunderstanding." Elyse stared out at the front yard.

Luke's truck screeched to a stop in the driveway. He got out and slammed the door. Crystal and Elyse sat without speaking, listening to the sound of his boots click-clacking loudly on the gravel.

Another sound caught Crystal's ear. She and Elyse, their own awkwardness forgotten, looked at each other in amazement. Their brother who had been so tense lately was whistling. A happy tune.

He stepped up on the porch and grinned. "Mornin'."

Crystal narrowed her eyes suspiciously. "What's going on?"

"Doc Westwood found out there's a big festival or something the same weekend she was having her grand opening, so she decided to move it out a month."

"Oh, Luke!" Elyse jumped up and hugged him. "That's wonderful!"

Crystal stood and hugged him, too. "It's good to see you looking more relaxed."

"I even thought of taking the day off, but I didn't have anything else to do, so I figured I might as well work."

"How sad," Crystal said automatically then thought of how that sentiment had pretty much been her own for the last seven years. "You deserve a Saturday off. Life's too short to work all the time."

"Let's do something together today." Elyse pointed toward the sunny sky. "It'll be so much better than fighting the rain."

Luke cast a sideways glance at Crystal. "Want to see if Jeremy wants to hang out with us? We could drive over to Hardy, see if there's any live music."

Crystal shook her head. "He's out of town."

"You sure? I saw his truck in his driveway when I went out to get a newspaper early this morning."

"Jeremy's truck?" Crystal tilted her head. "Is in his driveway?"

Luke nodded. "Something wrong with that?"

Her heart felt like lead in her chest. The news must have been bad for him not to call her. "I don't know." She picked up her cell phone and punched the button to dial Jeremy. After five rings, it went to voice mail. "I'm going to drive by there," she said to Elyse.

"You can tell Luke what's going on."

"Thanks," Luke drawled, still standing. "I was starting to feel like I was invisible."

Crystal didn't respond as she snatched her keys from inside the door and ran out to the farm truck. If she was staying around, she'd have to see about getting a car or an SUV like Elyse's. But in the city, she wouldn't need one.

Ten minutes later, she felt like a stalker, parked out in front of his house. She'd driven slowly by twice and finally pulled in. Luke was right. Jeremy's truck was here. But there was no sign of life.

She finally got out of the truck and walked up the driveway. On the porch, she hesitated. What would she say if he opened the door? She'd improvise. She raised her fist and hammered the door. On the fourth blow, she saw a small white button on the door facing. A doorbell. Why didn't she think of that? She pressed her finger on it, and inside the house, she heard it play a loud tune. No one could *not* hear that.

She waited and rang it again. "Jeremy," she yelled, feeling unreasonable panic.

When no one came, she stopped, suddenly feeling foolish. What if his parents had come back to town early and taken him out for breakfast? Or what if he was out at the barn, feeding the cat? Did he even have a cat?

The door creaked open.

He looked terrible. His eyes were bloodshot and swollen and his face was covered in short stubble. And he looked as if he'd been asleep.

She took a deep breath. "I'm sorry for waking you."

"That's okay," he said dully.

"Have you been home long?"

"Since about two this morning." He just stood there, not coming out, not inviting her to come in.

Why had she come? Surely he'd have called her when he woke up. Although he hadn't in the last two days. So maybe not.

"I was going to call you later."

"Oh." She shifted her weight backward, ready to bolt. "Then I'll just go on home and wait for you to call."

He winced. "No, I didn't mean that."

She stared at a little butterfly fluttering back and forth from a shrub next to the door. It couldn't seem to make up its mind.

"She died."

Her heart lurched. Beka? Her mouth opened, but no sound came out.

"Lindsey, I mean. She didn't make it."

"Oh no."

He ran his hand across his face. "I just kept hoping she'd bring Beka back safe and sound as Luke prayed last Sunday. Then disappear quietly into the night. Without me having to have her prosecuted. But also without me or Beka ever having to deal with her again."

"Nobody could blame you for hoping that," Crystal said.

"No? Why not? No life is disposable. But that's how I thought of her at this point. A means to an end. I hated her." His laugh was humorless. "Truth is. . .I'm still so mad at her I can hardly stand it."

"Jeremy, you prayed for her. You told me last night that you tried not to hate her." She took a step toward him. "You didn't want her to die."

The haunted look in his eyes tore her heart out. "I didn't. She looked so. . ." His voice drifted off. "It was terrible seeing her like that."

"I know it was."

After a few seconds, he took a deep breath. "Since she never regained consciousness, no one knows where Beka is."

CHAPTER 16

Crystal's legs wobbled. But he was still standing, so she wouldn't give in to her weakness. "Oh no. What can we do?"

"The police are trying. And I knocked on as many doors as I could in the area around the fleabag hotel where they found her. I did that all day yesterday until it got too late last night."

"Nobody knew anything?"

"If they did, they weren't talking. But it was hard to cover a lot of area." He ran his fingers through his hair that was already standing on end. "I'm about to take a shower and drive back over there to start again."

"Have you told your parents about Lindsey?"

He shook his head. "I can't. This is the first time they've even tried to get away from everything. I'll call them later."

"Hopefully, soon you can call and tell them that Beka's back home with you," Crystal said absently, an idea germinating in her mind. "You need a flyer. Do you have a picture of her? The most recent one?"

He nodded. "I have one I took door-to-door with me yesterday."

"Give me your phone."

He squinted at her, but he handed her his phone. She quickly mashed some buttons and handed it back. "I set your alarm. That will give you an hour and a half more sleep."

He looked like he was going to protest but she shook her head. "You can't help Beka if you're dead on your feet. Right?"

He nodded.

"So you'll sleep until the alarm goes off at nine then get up and take a shower?"

"Okay."

"Good. Now I just need that picture and a pen and paper."

He stepped into the house then back out with a small notepad, a pen, and a framed photo of the cutest little girl Crystal had ever seen. Blue eyes, blond hair, and adorable dimples. "She's beautiful." She clicked the pen and poised it over the paper. "Do you know the address where they found Lindsey?"

He gave her the name of the hotel. "Why?"

"I'm going to get you a map of the area and I want to know where the central point is."

"Oh." He looked confused but didn't argue.

"Now go to bed."

He nodded again and stumbled back into the house.

She practically ran back to the truck. If she was going to put her plan into action, she was going to have to hurry.

Jeremy slipped into his clean jeans and shirt and rubbed his hand across his clean-shaven jaw. He wouldn't have taken time to shave, but he figured the more respectable he looked, the more likely someone would be to help him. Although in that neighborhood it might work the opposite. Still, he felt better.

Partly because Crystal had insisted he go back to bed. As he put on his socks and boots, he wondered about how knowing she was doing something—even something as small as making a flyer—had made it easier for him to sleep.

The doorbell rang and he jumped up. Perfect. Another minute and he'd have been on edge waiting. Any earlier and she'd have been waiting for him.

He opened the door. "You have perfect ti–ming," he finished weakly as he took in the crowd on his porch and in his driveway. There were at least thirty people, mostly from church. They all held up papers, the clear bright picture of Beka smiling at him.

"I—" He cleared his throat. "I don't know what to say."

Daniel Montgomery held out his hand. Jeremy took it gratefully. The big man looked out at him through sorrowful eyes. "I'm so sorry, Jeremy."

"Me, too," Jack Westwood echoed.

Jeremy nodded to the local deputy. Jack had been a big support when Lindsey had first taken Beka and in the long months since, rallying the sheriff's department around the search. It was amazing how many people hadn't seemed to care since the kidnapper was the mother. But Jack had.

Jack's wife, Rachel, had tears in her eyes, but she nodded.

Luke clapped him on the shoulder. "We're with you, man." Behind him, sympathy shone in Elyse's brown eyes.

"Thank you." He still couldn't believe all these people were here to show their support. He was overwhelmed.

Crystal stepped forward. "We've already divided into teams of two. We'll carpool to the area and go on foot door-to-door around the place where Lindsey was found."

He stared out at the crowd. "Everyone's going to Memphis?"

"Yes, Memphis," Crystal said, readjusting her white cap over her blond ponytail. "Vans are filling up first, folks. Then we'll go to cars. At one o'clock, we'll meet at Corky's BBQ for lunch and report in." She turned to Jeremy. "If it's okay, since your truck is a crew cab, Luke and Elyse and I will ride with you. We're willing to stay as long as you want to."

He nodded, not trusting himself to speak.

Crystal started off the porch.

"Crys, wait."

She turned back and tilted her head to the side.

He cleared his throat again. "You'll never know how much this means to me. This morning. . .before you got here. . .it looked pretty hopeless." He waved out at the people climbing into vehicles. "And now this."

She brushed aside his thanks and rushed off to make sure everyone had directions, but he wasn't fooled. He was blessed that Crystal McCord had come into his life.

For however long she chose to stay.

Crystal glanced over at where the others were wearily climbing into their vehicles then back to Jeremy's tense face. "Do you want to stay a little longer and keep knocking on doors? Elyse and Luke said they don't mind at all."

"I guess we may as well go on home." Defeat punctuated his words.

"We left some flyers. Maybe somebody will recognize her and call."

He nodded tersely. "Maybe."

"Someone knows where she is." She kept her voice hopeful. "Maybe we'll get some calls tonight."

"Maybe." Jeremy's attempt at a smile faltered just before reaching his eyes, as though the effort proved too great.

Crystal would have given just about anything to take away his fear, his anguish. Anything to bring back that little girl for him. The depth of her emotions took her aback, frightened her a little.

The trip home was unbearably quiet. She searched her brain to find something. . .anything to say that might make a difference.

Jeremy's anger and despair were almost palpable.

Outside of Jonesboro, about an hour from Shady Grove, he spoke suddenly. "I can't believe so many people from church went all the way to Memphis."

She nodded. "Everyone was glad to help." And they had been. Thrilled to be able to do something hands-on to try to find Beka. Crystal had to admit she'd been impressed. It had been a long time since she'd felt the presence of a church family. She hadn't realized how much she'd missed it.

"I called this morning and made the arrangements for Lindsey." Jeremy's voice sounded tight.

Crystal could feel his anger and she didn't blame him. "That was good of you."

His face inscrutable, he turned his head slightly away from her. "Don't give me any praise. I didn't feel like I had a lot of choice. When Beka grows up and wants to know where her mother is buried, how would I explain to her that I have no idea?"

"So what did you decide?"

"We're having a graveside service Tuesday afternoon at the Shady Grove cemetery. That way Mom and Dad will have time to get back."

Luke leaned forward and touched him on the shoulder. "I can't imagine how rough this must be. Wish there was more we could do."

Jeremy glanced in the rearview mirror. "Today was enough, man. Thanks."

"If there's anything else you need, let us know," Elyse said, her voice sleepy. "If we need to feed the family. . ."

Jeremy blew out his breath and kept his gaze on the road. "No family. Just me and Mom and Dad. And I doubt we'll be hungry. But thanks."

"I'm sorry," Crystal said softly and rested her hand in the seat between them. Just in case. A moment passed and she felt a little silly, but then his warm hand enfolded hers. In the darkness of the truck interior, they maintained that connection the rest of the silent trip home. She didn't know if he got any comfort from the simple act of holding her hand.

But she definitely did.

Back at Jeremy's house, Luke and Elyse said quick good-byes, jumped in Luke's truck, and were gone.

"Want me to stay around for a while?" Crystal asked softly as they gathered their things out of the truck.

The look he gave her was one of apology, as if he had anything to be sorry for. "I'm probably better off by myself right now."

She nodded. "I understand. It's been a long day."

He walked her to the farm truck.

She set her purse inside and turned to face him. Worry and anger etched lines in his face so deeply she could see them in the moonlight. "Jeremy, don't give up."

His jaw muscle tight, he shook his head. "I can't."

She started to turn to climb into the truck, but he took her hands and pulled her to him. In his arms, she tried to memorize the rhythm of his heart. Maybe it was just the solemn mood of tonight, but she had a foreboding feeling that someday she'd want to remember.

When he released her, she shivered. He looked down at her, his eyes tender. "Thanks again."

She stood up on tiptoe and kissed him on the cheek. "Take care."

She jumped in the truck, revved the motor, and fled down the driveway. Who was she kidding? She glanced in her rearview mirror. She was the one who needed to take care. Her heart was in imminent danger of being lost to the cowboy standing back there in the moonlight, still watching her.

It was natural, she reminded herself firmly, as the farm truck bounced along in the ruts, for him to lean on her right now. But when he didn't need her anymore and it was time for her to go back to the city, what would keep her heart from shattering into a million pieces?

CHAPTER 17

Jeremy gazed out at the endless current of the river rushing over the boulders. In a hurry but never getting anywhere. That's how he'd felt since Beka's kidnapping. *Lord, why isn't anything happening?*

"You do know this is private property, don't you?"

He spun around to face Crystal.

Her mischievous smile froze on her lips. "I'm sorry. I probably shouldn't have interrupted you."

He forced his lips into an answering grin. "That's okay. I'm glad you did." And he was. "How'd you find me?"

"I was actually driving over to your house to talk to you when I saw Nacho standing patiently down here by the bridge. I figured you couldn't be far away."

She'd been coming to see him? For some reason, he'd thought she was avoiding him at church this morning. She'd slipped in even later than he had and sat on the opposite side of the aisle from him and her family. "What did you want to talk about?"

"I had a brilliant idea." She narrowed her eyes as if gauging his interest. "How do you feel about being on TV?"

"TV? Me?" He shook his head. "No, thanks."

"Wait. It's for a great cause. The best cause, actually. I talked to the station manager at Channel Six, and they'd love to do an

145

interview with you to help get the word out about Beka." Her blue eyes sparkled.

He frowned. "I approached them when Lindsey first took her. They reported the kidnapping on the news but weren't interested in helping me. I asked them to let me do a televised plea for Lindsey to bring her back." He'd begged actually. His gut tightened at the memory.

Crystal's face clouded. "Yeah, apparently the anchorwoman is a divorced mother and she was sympathetic to Lindsey. But now that she knows the real situation. . ."

"And Lindsey is dead." Bitterness he couldn't hide dripped from his words.

"I know it's hard. But Daddy always said, 'Don't look a gift horse in the mouth,' Jeremy. She wants to make it right now. And it could really make a difference."

"So how will we do it?"

"They'll run the interview four times—morning, noon, and at six and ten in the evening. Channel Six broadcasts all over northern Arkansas, southern Missouri, and part of western Tennessee and Mississippi. It's not a huge area, but she thinks it's big enough that we'll need to set up a local search center to field calls after the interview runs."

His heart pounded at the possibility of that many calls about Beka. He stared out at a leaf in the water whooshing away on the current. Things were happening. He just couldn't always see it. He sent up a silent thank-you and nodded to Crystal. "Okay."

"I called Mama and Daddy while I was trying to find you, and they said we should use their house as a search center. There's an extra phone line there already—from when we were teenagers. The phone company will just need to activate the second line and fix it so that calls will roll over to the next line when one is busy."

"That sounds great. Tell them I really appreciate it. When can we do the interview?"

"They want to tape Thursday and run it Friday."

"We can't do it sooner?" Patience was the one commodity he was running short of these days.

"She thinks Friday is the best day to catch more people watching. Besides, that'll be after the funeral. And it'll give us time to get the phone lines ready."

He nodded, and in unspoken agreement they turned to walk back to where the four-wheel drive "ute" was parked beside Nacho. He couldn't believe he hadn't heard Crystal coming. When their hands brushed, he slid his easily around hers. She glanced over at him but didn't say anything.

"I'll need to let the sheriff know what we're doing. He'll probably want to have his deputy, Jack Westwood, or somebody available to check out tips as they come in."

She squeezed his hand. "It's good to see you this way."

"What way?"

A grin lit her face. "Hopeful."

They stopped beside the utility vehicle, and he reluctantly released her. "You make me feel hopeful."

"Unless we're playing Razorback trivia."

"I'll beat you next game." He hoped there'd be a next game.

As he watched her drive away, he wondered what it would take to talk her out of going back to New York.

"Yes, I'm coming back." Crystal clasped the cell between her shoulder and her ear as she stretched to make one more swipe at the ceiling fan blades with the long-handled brush. "Mia, I've got to go. There's a lot going on here. Just trust me. Mama and Daddy will be home in less than four weeks, and I'll be on a plane right after that."

After Mia said good-bye, Crystal hunched her shoulders and

relaxed them as she walked into the kitchen, where Elyse was standing on a chair cleaning the light fixture.

"So, what do you say we start a cleaning business on the side? Who knew we could get so much done at night after working all day?"

Elyse pushed her long brunet curls away from her face. "I think I'll pass."

"Sad thing is this house was clean before we started, as far as I could tell."

Elyse nodded as she finished wiping the fixture. "That's what I said."

"I know. But you should have heard the panic in Mama's voice when she realized we were going to have a houseful of people here with her halfway around the world. I had no choice but to promise we'd clean." Crystal glanced at her cell phone while she was talking. "Thanks for helping me."

"I'm guessing the call you just got wasn't the one you've been carrying your phone around waiting for all night." Elyse stepped down from the chair, breathless.

Crystal chuckled. "No. That was Mia on the phone. And it's nice to know my agent hasn't forgotten me. But you're right." She grabbed a pitcher of tea from the refrigerator and pulled two glasses from the cabinet with her other hand. She plopped down at the corner booth. "I'm as bad as I was back in high school. Michael Miller would say he was going to call, and I'd spend the whole night by the phone." She poured a glass of tea and scooted it across the table as Elyse sat down then poured herself one. "Wonder what ever happened to him."

"He married Marianne Rogers. I think he sells insurance."

Crystal snorted. "I can see it now. You call in with a claim, and it takes him ten days to get back to you."

Elyse snickered and took a sip of her tea.

Crystal sighed. "Today was Lindsey's funeral, so I called Jeremy this morning to let him know I was thinking about him."

"Oh good." Elyse smiled at her. "That was sweet of you."

"He sounded glad. But he said he'd call me later. And it's like. . ." Crystal looked at the kitchen clock. Seven thirty. "Twelve hours later."

Elyse ran her finger around the rim of her glass. Probably thinking up a good excuse for Jeremy. "Didn't his parents just get back in town? Maybe they're catching up."

"Yeah. Or maybe he didn't feel like talking to me." Crystal pushed to her feet. "Who cares? He'll call if he wants to. I'm going to vacuum."

"Do you want to work in here and I'll vacuum? So you can hear your phone if it rings?" Elyse stood.

"No, thanks." She left Elyse scrubbing the countertop and hurried to the utility closet to get the vacuum cleaner. She'd prove she wasn't afraid to make a little noise, that she wasn't waiting around for a call.

Just before she turned the vacuum on, she glanced around to make sure Elyse wasn't looking then dug her phone out of her pocket and turned it on vibrate. Chicken.

When the downstairs rugs were all vacuumed, she put the machine away and fished her phone out again. Eight o'clock and no missed calls.

She could write a one-person play about this. A woman who waited for a phone call that never came. The idea caused her to freeze in her tracks. She used to have those mini-brainstorms all the time. Especially when she was doing house chores. Self-defense to keep from passing out from boredom, probably. But that was before. . . She forced herself to follow the thought through. Before Cami died. Before Crystal moved to New York and left all of her works in progress locked away in the room upstairs.

Her phone rang. She glanced at the caller ID. A smile tilted her lips as she slumped down on the couch and answered. "Hi."

"Hi." Jeremy's voice was like slow molasses. "How are you?"

"I'm fine. How'd it go?"

"Pretty good, actually."

She sat up. There was something different in his tone. "The funeral?" She'd fretted all day over not offering to go with him.

He gave a soft chuckle. "I know. Hard to believe."

She pulled her knees up to her chest. "What happened?"

"We met at the cemetery. Dad, Mom, and me. And Brother Tom. Just the four of us."

"I bet that felt odd." At Cami's funeral, even at the graveside, there had been people as far as she could see, standing and crying.

"Yeah. A little. But Brother Tom kept it short. Dad and Mom had told him some things about Lindsey. So he talked about her life. Before. How, even as a teenager, she always tried to help people who were down on their luck. And she couldn't stand to see anybody hurting."

"That was really nice of your parents to tell him good things."

Silence. She didn't know what to say, so she just stayed quiet, too.

Finally he spoke. "They were true, though. She used to be like that. And when we got back to the house, Mom had a couple of scrapbooks she'd put together. For Beka, she said."

"Scrapbooks of Lindsey?"

"Yeah. She'd spent a lot of time on them, so we sat down and looked through them."

"You did?" Crystal was having a hard time reconciling the anger and bitterness she'd always heard in his voice when he spoke of his ex-wife with this mellow-sounding man on the phone. "That was nice."

"Don't sound surprised," he said with a hint of teasing. "Sometimes I can be nice."

"You're always nice to me. It's just that. . ."

"I know, just not about Lindsey. But Mom was really hurting today." She heard him sigh. "I've been so wrapped up in my own pain since Beka's kidnapping that I haven't really stopped to think about how she and Dad have been feeling. Mom said those books were for Beka, but I could tell when I was looking at them that she really loved Lindsey once. Like the daughter she never had. Mom always thought Lindsey's grandfather's death changed her."

Crystal closed her eyes and rested her head against the couch. "Do you?"

"I do now." He sounded bemused by the fact. "Looking through those pages of her life, you can see she became a different person after he died."

"That's really sad."

"Especially because that's the last thing he would have ever wanted. He loved her so much."

"But you know"—Crystal didn't know why it was so important to her to point this out, but she had to—"she had a choice. She didn't have to leave you and turn to drugs. And especially, she didn't have to take Beka from you." She could hear the anger in her voice at the end.

Silence. She clutched the phone and held her breath.

"You're right," Jeremy finally said, slowly. "It was her choice. But once she made the decision to leave God and all she knew was right, even though she tried sometimes, I think she couldn't ever find her way back."

Crystal's eyes stung and she pushed to her feet. Her throat ached too much to talk. Was he speaking her own epitaph? Had she let Cami's death change her to the point of no return?

"Thanks for listening. I'm going to go make some notes for my interview."

"Hey." She finally found her voice. "I'm so glad you're able to forgive Lindsey."

"Yeah, well, it's a process. I'm not quite there yet."

"But you're on the road to peace. And that makes me happy."

"Thanks." He paused. "Are you okay?"

"I'm just working through some things. But I will be."

"Anything you want to talk about?"

"Not yet. But thanks."

"Okay, I'll let you go, then. Talk to you soon."

"Take care," she said softly and broke the connection.

She sat on the couch staring off into space, thinking about their conversation.

Elyse found her there a few minutes later. "Hey. Everything all right?"

Crystal jerked her head up to meet her sister's concerned gaze. "Huh? Oh, I'm wiped out."

Elyse collapsed on the couch beside her. "Me, too. The kitchen is clean. Perfect. You could eat off the floor."

"I'll stick to eating at the table if it's all the same with you."

Elyse groaned and tossed a sofa pillow at her. "Very funny."

"Hey, at least I still have my sense of humor." Crystal threw the pillow back.

"Such as it is," Elyse murmured, a dimple peeking in her cheek. She pushed to her feet. "I'm going home to bed."

"Sure, insult me and leave." Crystal stood and hugged Elyse.

"Better than insulting you and staying." Elyse gave her a saucy grin and a kiss on the cheek.

Later as Crystal made her bed on the couch, she thought about Jeremy's words that had hit her so hard. That once Lindsey had turned completely away from God, she couldn't find her way back.

Crystal shuddered. "Please don't let that be me," she whispered to the empty room, not sure her plea went any farther than the ceiling.

CHAPTER 18

So I'm asking. . ." Jeremy closed his eyes, took a deep breath, and opened them. "I'm begging you, if you have any information about my daughter, please call."

He stared at his own face on the TV screen. Maybe he should have shown more emotion. But he'd been so nervous about saying the right thing that he hadn't allowed himself to feel when he was recording the interview yesterday. As the camera broke away to show the anchorwoman, who was giving the phone number and reiterating the plea, he looked around the crowded McCord living room.

From across the room, sitting at the table with two phones on it, Crystal nodded and smiled. Beside her, Elyse stared at the phone in front of her as if it were going to open up and take a bite out of her hand. Jack and another deputy stood behind them, wearing headphones the phone company had provided, each monitoring a line.

Jeremy had wanted to take first turn at the phone, but the experts had advised against it. He was "too close" to the situation. Plus, a woman's voice apparently would put a caller at ease faster. So he'd wait and watch.

His mom and dad stood from where they were sitting on the

couch and came around to hug him. "You did a great job," his dad said, his voice husky with emotion.

On the TV screen, the anchorwoman was repeating the phone number.

The phone bleated out the special ring that came with the unique numbers the phone company had assigned for the search center.

His mother squeezed his arm.

Crystal answered the phone with the preplanned spiel. Then she waited and listened, pen poised above the notepad in front of her. The whole room seemed to be holding its collective breath.

"Yes, sir."

"No, sir, she's been gone for several months."

"This is a line set up for people who have information about Beka."

The other phone rang and Jeremy felt his mother's fingernails cutting into the flesh of his arm.

"Thank you anyway for calling," Crystal said and hung up, just as Elyse picked up the phone.

His gaze locked with Crystal's. She shook her head. "An older man who wanted to help search for her," she whispered. "He thought you said she's been missing since just last night."

Beside him, his mother released her grip on his arm and covered her mouth with a trembling hand. His dad put his arm around her. "We're going to step out on the porch and pray," he said to Jeremy. "Let us know if there's any news."

Jeremy pulled his gaze away from where Elyse was scribbling on a piece of paper with the deputy looking over her shoulder. "I will."

When Elyse hung up, she turned to him. "That caller said her neighbor has a little girl that looks just like the picture you showed. But the little girl was living next door when the neighbor moved in two years ago."

He wondered which was worse—these calls or the phone not

ringing at all? Two minutes later, he knew. When the high-pitched *b-r-r-ing* broke the interminable silence, his heart leaped with hope.

For the next hour, the calls came steady. Then they slowed to a trickle. None of them were real information about Beka.

At eleven, Blair, the anchorwoman from Channel Six, called his cell phone for an update.

He stepped out onto the porch to take the call. "No. No leads," he said softly, glancing toward his parents, who were sitting in the double rocker.

"Don't be discouraged." Her voice was thick with sympathy. "We'll play the interview again at noon. And at six. And at ten. So you should have another rush of calls after each airing."

"Thanks."

"I just got special permission to bring a crew out to tape the action at the search center for *Get Real, Shady Grove* in the morning if you haven't gotten a solid lead by midnight. That will give us a chance to run the phone number on the air one more time."

He knew she felt guilty about not helping him when Lindsey first took Beka, but he didn't care what her motives were. "That would be great. I'll let you know if we get a usable tip."

He looked up to see Rachel Westwood and Victoria Worthington coming up the steps. "Reinforcements have arrived." Rachel gave him a side hug. "We're next up to man the phone lines."

His mom and dad walked over, as behind Rachel, Allie Montgomery and Lark Murray held up trays of food. "And we're the lunch brigade," Allie added.

"Oh, this is so sweet of you," Jeremy's mom said.

Allie smiled. "We can't take credit. Everyone met at the church building and put the trays together. We just got to be the ones who brought them." She balanced her tray and hugged his mom. "Everyone's praying."

"I know they are. Thank you."

Jeremy looked at his mom as she chatted with the women. A year ago, she'd looked young for fifty. But the trauma of losing Beka had aged her, worry lines etched deep. He looked behind her at his dad and realized that he, too, had changed in the last several months. Yet they were willing to forgive Lindsey. He was humbled by their Christlike attitudes all over again.

He pushed the door open and showed Lark and Allie where to put the food. The phones were silent. Crystal and Elyse waved, and Rachel and Victoria hurried over to learn the ropes. Crystal's gaze met his and he felt like she was telegraphing him a silent "hang in there." He smiled and went back onto the porch.

"Mom, Dad, y'all come in and fix you a plate."

His mom put her hand to her stomach. "Honey, I don't think I could eat."

"You need your strength," he said, repeating the words she'd used many times to get him to eat in the months right after Beka's kidnapping.

She gave him a rueful smile. "You've heard that before, haven't you?" But she allowed his dad to lead her into the house.

Jeremy sank down in the porch swing and pushed it back and forth with one foot. He stared out at the cars and trucks parked in the driveway. As nerve-racking as this was, it felt good to actually be doing something. In the days right after Lindsey took Beka, it had been like this. But then life went on. For everyone else.

He dropped his head into his hands, remembering that awful time. And all the empty days since. Finally he began to pray.

Please, Lord, let it be different this time. My little girl is out there somewhere. And I know You're watching over her. But please, bring her back to me.

After he said, "Amen," he scrubbed his hands over his face and laid his head back against the swing.

The front door creaked open. He looked up to see Crystal, two plates in her hands. She tilted her head and handed him a plate. "Here. Your mom said to tell you that you need to keep your strength up, too."

He chuckled. "She's pretty smart." He patted the swing beside him.

Crystal sat down. "I really like your parents. Just talking to them at breakfast, I could feel their strength."

He nodded. "It's a good thing they're strong, with all they've had to go through."

"Or maybe they're strong because of all they've had to go through," she mused.

He glanced over at her. "Is that why you're so strong?"

She stared down at her plate. "I'm probably the weakest person I know."

He reached over and touched her chin and gently brought her face up to meet his gaze. "Don't believe that lie. I don't know what I would have done without you to lean on these past few weeks."

Her blue eyes softened. "I'm glad I was here."

"Me, too."

Just as they finished eating, the door banged open and his dad stuck his head out. "They're playing the interview again."

Crystal gave him a crooked grin and collected an unsteady breath as she reached out. "Ready for round two?"

Jeremy nodded, weaving his fingers through hers. He closed his eyes for a minute to center himself. After a quick repeat of his earlier prayer, that this time the calls might actually produce something relevant, he opened his eyes and smiled at Crystal "Let's go."

As the grandfather clock started to chime midnight, Crystal jabbed her pen toward her notebook and Elyse's. "How could we have so many calls and no real leads?"

"Rachel and Victoria got some good ones during their shift. There were a few I thought might be just what we were waiting for. But the sheriff said none of them panned out." Elyse sighed. "The closest I came was the woman who thought she saw Beka at a local preschool."

Crystal eyed her speculatively. "Someone checked that out, didn't they?"

"Yes, they took a day care group picture to the caller's house, and she picked out the child she meant." Elyse pushed her chair back and smothered a yawn. "Jack said the girl favored Beka, but she was Roger and Linda Howard's granddaughter."

"This has to be horrible for Jeremy, knowing the day is over." Crystal glanced toward the window where she could see the shadows of the men on the porch. They'd been out there for the last hour. She knew he just hated to see the day end with no success.

"At least Blair is coming in the morning with a camera." Elyse picked up her phone. "We're supposed to set this to go directly to voice mail at midnight, right?"

Crystal nodded and punched in the buttons on her phone, too, keeping an eye on the moving figures of the men.

Luke came in first, looking grim, with Jack Westwood behind him.

Jeremy came last. Stubble shadowed his jaw, and his eyes showed a distance that nearly broke her heart. His shoulders slumped, Crystal knew, from lack of sleep and discouragement.

She stood and walked over to him. "Hey," she said softly, while Luke and Jack were talking to Elyse about the phone lines. "You'd better get home and try to sleep. You have to go live at seven in the morning."

He raised his head to look at her. Exhaustion and worry covered his face like a mask.

She wanted to smooth out the wrinkles on his forehead with her hand, but she just stood helplessly. "I'm sorry, Jeremy."

He nodded. "You did your best. Thank you all for everything." The words were dry and brittle, but he reached out and touched her arm. Crystal took the gesture for what it was—all he had to offer at the moment.

Luke turned around and frowned. "Hey, Jer, why don't you let me give you a ride home? Then I'll pick you up in the morning and bring you back."

Jeremy's lips stretched into what might have been a grin on another day. "Thanks, man. I'll be fine." He left without looking back.

Crystal followed him outside. But by the time she reached the porch, he was getting into his truck. She stood and watched him drive away. It was hard to realize how important hope was. Until she saw it dying right before her very eyes.

She trudged back into the house and said good night to Luke and Jack.

After they left, she hugged Elyse. "Want me to walk you home?"

"Then I'd just have to walk you back."

Crystal smiled. "True."

Elyse patted her pocket. "I've got my phone."

"Call if you need me."

As soon as Elyse was gone, Crystal opened the front closet to get her bedclothes out. She reached up to get the pillow off the top shelf, wincing at a spasm in her back. What she wouldn't give for one night of sleep in a bed.

She froze and drew her hand back. Was she really so cowardly that she couldn't sleep upstairs? She didn't believe in ghosts. At least not any kind other than the one that lived inside her heart. But that particular ghost wasn't limited to a certain room.

A memory of today on the porch with Jeremy shot through

her foggy brain, sharp and clear. He'd said she was strong. She looked down at the patchwork quilt in her arms. Where was that strength now?

She shoved the blankets back in the closet and shut the door. She had a choice. Why should she let herself be held captive by her own fears and sorrow? Jeremy was a wise man. She headed for the stairs. Maybe she was stronger than she thought.

At the top of the stairs, she went straight to the closed door. Her hand trembled on the knob. Mentally she chided herself, until finally she opened the door. She stared at the dark room. Moonlight streamed in the window and she could make out the outline of two beds, still arranged with their heads together as they had been seven years ago. Nothing had changed.

But everything had changed.

Tears edged her tired eyes. She shut the door softly and slipped into the bathroom to get ready for bed. When she finished, she stumbled into Elyse and Kaleigh's old room, now Mama's sewing room with a double bed in the corner. Kaleigh still slept there when she came home for weekends and holidays. But she wouldn't mind Crystal borrowing the bed tonight. She set her phone alarm and snuggled under the covers with a sigh.

At least she'd opened the door.

CHAPTER 19

I'm Blair Winchester with Channel Six, live from Shady Grove, on this beautiful Saturday morning. As I told you before the break, this morning we're doing something a little different with a live newscast featuring a plea from a heartbroken father. Jeremy Buchanan's little girl, Beka, is missing. So here we are live from the McCord Ranch with Jeremy Buchanan. Jeremy." The heavily made-up anchorwoman stuck the microphone in his face.

He stared at her. She'd said the word *live* so many times that his tongue felt permanently glued to the roof of his mouth at the thought of all the people watching him right this second. He only had one chance to get this perfect. "Um. You've done a great job explaining the facts, Blair. And many of your viewers saw my interview yesterday. Thanks to everyone who called in. But I'd like to say one more time"—his gaze caught Crystal's, and she was looking at him like she knew he could do it—"if anyone out there has any idea where Beka is, please, please call." He held up a portrait that he'd had taken of him and Beka two Christmases ago for his mom and dad. "She's my little girl and I'm her daddy. And neither one of us will ever be completely whole until we find each other again."

He took a deep breath. He hadn't run this by anyone, not the anchorwoman, not the missing-children experts, not even Crystal.

He looked directly into the camera and smiled at his daughter. "Beka, honey, if you're out there and you can hear me, listen up, Little Bit." He winked as he said his pet name for her, forcing himself to imagine her looking straight at him. "I'll always love you. Never give up. When you get old enough to find me, I'll be waiting." He could feel a tear trickle down his cheek. He handed Blair the microphone and shrugged his shoulder up to wipe the droplet on his flannel shirt.

Blair took the microphone and cleared her throat. "Thank you, Jeremy." Her smile looked a little trembly as she faced the camera. "Folks, you've seen the local search center here set up at the McCord Ranch on the outskirts of Shady Grove, Arkansas. You've seen the operators inside ready to take your calls." The cameraman moved in toward her and she lowered her voice. "And you've seen a heartbroken father pleading for his daughter's return. Operators will be here until noon today. Please call the number on the screen or notify your local police department if you know anything at all about six-year-old Beka Buchanan."

When the camera stopped rolling, Crystal hugged Jeremy. He pulled her close and breathed in her strength. They hurried into the house to the phones.

As he braced himself for the roller coaster of hope and despair to start again, he was glad that he'd talked his parents into waiting at home for word. The stress was killing them.

Elyse and Rachel were taking calls and the phones were already jangling. After an hour, they slowed down to an occasional ring. Rachel looked at her notebook then over to where Jeremy was pacing by the couch. "Other than a couple of obvious crazies, I think most of this morning's callers were just touched by your plea and want you to know they're praying for you."

He ran his hand through his hair and sighed. "I appreciate their prayers."

Someone knocked on the door, and Crystal jumped up from the couch to answer it. A plump woman Jeremy recognized as his barber's wife stood on the doorstep with tears in her eyes. "Oh, honey," she said when she saw him. "I'm so sorry." She rushed past Crystal and handed Jeremy a plate with a sliced loaf of some kind of bread on it. "I made this for the flower club meetin'. But after I saw you on TV. . ." She shook her head and pulled a tissue from the pocket of her smock. "I wanted you to have it."

"Thank you so much." Jeremy held the plate and nodded toward the phone lines. "I'll share it with everyone."

She nodded and backed out the door and down the steps.

Crystal took the plate from him. "I'll put this in the kitchen."

Luke sauntered in the front door, looking over his shoulder. "Hey, what's going on out there?" He zoned in on the plate Crystal was holding. "That smells like banana nut bread." He reached out and scooped up a slice.

She slapped at his hand, but he was too fast.

In spite of his nerves, Jeremy smiled.

Luke jerked his thumb over his shoulder toward outside. "Do y'all know there's a traffic jam out there?"

Crystal set the plate down, and she and Jeremy raced to the door. "Oh, my," she breathed.

At least seven vehicles were trying to get down the bumpy little lane, with the lead one right in the middle of the road, apparently straddling the potholes, refusing to go over five miles an hour. The barber's wife was trying to go back the way she'd come, but the little car coming at her wasn't giving her anywhere to go. Finally she came to a stop at the edge of the driveway and waited.

Jeremy could hear the horns start to honk. "Who are they and what are they doing here?"

Jack joined them on the porch and shook his head. "That's my mother in the front car, and unless I miss my guess, Rachel's mom is with her." He clasped Jeremy on the shoulder. "I'm sorry, man, but it looks like your plea touched hearts you weren't aiming for."

Finally the little car reached the driveway and pulled off to the side. Mrs. Westwood and Mrs. Donovan climbed out, both carrying baking dishes.

Jeremy groaned. "Not that I'm not grateful," he said quickly to Jack.

Jeremy glared at Crystal as she smothered a giggle with her hand.

The older women were teary eyed as they bustled up to the porch. They practically fell on Jeremy, patting his back and squeezing his arm. "Bless your heart. If there's anything we can do. . ."

He nodded. "Thank you so much." He looked over their heads at two vans pulling up close to the porch. A woman jumped out of the first van and ran around to slide the big door open. "Over here," she directed. Children ranging anywhere from five to fifteen poured out of both vans, many of them clutching musical instruments, some of them carrying papers that looked suspiciously like sheet music.

The driver, a no-nonsense-looking woman, walked up to Jeremy and stuck out her hand. "Mr. Buchanan, I'm Claire Mitchum, and this is our homeschool group band and chorus. When we saw you on TV earlier, everyone started wondering what we could do to help."

He shook her hand. What in the world?

She beamed proudly at a snaggletoothed redhead carrying a clarinet. "Carson came up with the idea that we could sing and play for you."

Jeremy's puzzlement must have been showing on his face, because she gave him a sympathetic smile. "To calm your nerves while you wait." She leaned in close. "I know what you're thinking, but they're really quite good. And they so wanted to help in some way."

He nodded, bemused but touched.

"You sit on the porch." She included Crystal, Jack, and Mrs. Westwood and Mrs. Donovan in her motion. "You and your friends."

Crystal tugged on Jeremy's hand and led him to the double rocker. Jack guided his mother and mother-in-law to chairs and leaned down to slap Jeremy on the knee. "I'd better go check on the phone lines." He glanced out at the driveway where there were several other vehicles parking. "And see if Luke can handle crowd control."

The first note sounded and Jack rushed into the house.

Crystal slipped her hand into Jeremy's and squeezed. "This was really sweet of them," she whispered.

He nodded, wondering if she realized how desperate he was to know what kind of calls were coming in right now. But he had to admit to himself that he was better off out here being distracted instead of inside, driving himself crazy each time the phone rang.

He saw Luke slip out the door and hurry out to the driveway, not making eye contact with the group surrounding the porch. Jeremy grinned. In his midtwenties and a confirmed bachelor, Crystal's brother probably thought there were way too many women and children around for comfort.

Still smiling, Jeremy brought his attention back to the show. The kids and their song reminded him of the Von Trapp family from *The Sound of Music*. Except there were twice as many children. His heart squeezed. The little one on the end looked a little like Beka when she smiled.

When the song was over, everyone clapped, including Mrs. Westwood and Mrs. Donovan, along with a few other women who were now standing on the porch, most of them holding covered dishes of some kind.

The children bowed and curtsied, which almost caused a girl

in braids to drop her bass guitar, but she recovered in time to start another song. He tensed. What if there was a phone tip but they were waiting for the music to be over before they told him?

Crystal leaned toward him as if she were straightening his collar. "If there's anything, they'll come tell you immediately."

He relaxed. She was right.

When the third song ended and the applause was over, Claire Mitchum directed all the performers back into the vans.

Jeremy stood and pulled Crystal to her feet. Still holding hands, they walked over to where the children were loading their instruments.

"Y'all did a great job." Crystal's smile lit up her face. Jeremy could tell she was genuinely happy they'd come.

And truthfully, he was, too. "Thanks for taking my mind off things for a bit."

The little girl he'd noticed earlier tugged on his shirt.

He looked down at her and smiled. "Yes?"

"When your Beka comes home, can she come play with me?"

His breath caught in his throat. "I bet she'd love that."

A woman he assumed was her mother put her hand on the girl's head. "We'll check back with Mr. Buchanan about that when Beka gets home, okay, Hannah?"

Hannah nodded and skipped off to the van.

"Did you call the whole flower club?" he heard Mrs. Donovan say to Mrs. Westwood as he and Crystal walked back up on the porch.

"Just to let them know why we wouldn't be having cake for the meeting. How was I supposed to know that Eleanor would beat us over here with her banana nut bread?"

"Or that everyone else would follow our lead?" Mrs. Donovan muttered.

Crystal glanced at him. Apparently reading the panic on his face,

166

she sprang into action. "Thank you all so much for coming." She took command of the porch like it was a stage. "I know our hearts all ache for Jeremy today, and it was so sweet of y'all to come out and offer him your support." Still holding his hand, she gently maneuvered Jeremy toward the house door. "He's needed inside right now, but I'll get someone to help me take the dishes into the kitchen and. . ." He saw her eyes light on Luke as he came up the steps. Jeremy could hear Crystal's sigh of relief, but she covered it well. "Luke, if I get a notebook from inside, would you mind writing down everyone who is here and what they brought?"

Luke looked a little confused. "You want me to take names?" Jeremy heard him ask before he stepped inside and shut the door.

Elyse looked up from the phone when he walked in. She shook her head.

"Thank you for calling." She hung up. "Another well-wisher."

"We're running five to one, well-wishers," Rachel grumbled beside her. "And the tips aren't even logical. People are just desperate to help."

Jeremy glanced at Jack. "Not anything worth checking out so far?"

Jack shook his head. "Sorry, man."

Crystal walked in carrying two cakes and saved him from having to lie and say it was okay.

She bustled into the kitchen and came back out with a notebook and a pen. On the way out the door, she brushed Jeremy's shoulder with her hand. "It's still a couple of hours until noon. No giving up."

He nodded, but he could hardly stand to look at Elyse and Rachel or Jack and the other deputy. He knew they couldn't help it, but the pity in their eyes made him feel like he was going to suffocate. Especially when the phone didn't ring as Crystal made trip after trip into the kitchen with food.

Twenty minutes later, Crystal came in with a casserole. She

looked around at the gloomy bunch. "This is the last of the food. So far. It looks like one more car is coming up the lane." She disappeared into the kitchen for a second then hurried back out the front door.

Jeremy brushed his hand over his face and sank down on the couch. He dreaded going into the kitchen. Bringing food was kind, but in a way it reminded him of funerals and wakes. He shuddered.

The front door opened again, and he glanced up to see Crystal standing there, her face white.

He jumped to his feet. "What's wrong?"

"Nothing." She looked over at Jack as if trying to communicate something without Jeremy seeing her.

His heart pounding, Jeremy sprang to his feet and looked at the deputy and back to Crystal. "No secrets in this room. Tell me what's going on. Did something come over the deputy's radio?"

Crystal shook her head, her eyes wide. "There's a woman out here who says she's from Memphis and has information about Beka. But she'll only talk to you."

He darted for the door, but a hand clasped around each of his arms. "Whoa there, Jeremy. Let's slow down a minute." Jack's manner was easy, but his hands were like iron bands. "Think of all the crazies that have called in," he said, next to Jeremy's ear. "You can't just go out there and believe everything she says."

Jeremy stopped struggling and studied Crystal's face. "Does she look like a crazy?"

Crystal shook her head. "She's really young. Maybe early twenties. And she just looks scared. For some reason I think Luke trusts her."

Jack let go of Jeremy. "We'll go together, okay?"

Jeremy nodded.

Jack glanced back over his shoulder and motioned for the other deputy to follow.

Outside on the porch, Luke had laid his notebook on the table and was sitting beside a crying girl on the double rocker, talking softly to her. He looked up when they came out.

The girl looked up, too, her hazel eyes wide and frightened. "Please don't freak out. I didn't do anything wrong."

Even though his heart was pounding like a sledgehammer, Jeremy squatted down next to her as if she were a skittish calf. He even held his hand out toward her. "It's going to be okay. What's going on?"

She swiped her eyes with the unbuttoned cuff of a denim shirt. "You're so nice. Lindsey told me that you were terrible."

Hearing Lindsey's name rocked his balance, but he quickly reminded himself that they'd announced her name on TV. "How do you know Lindsey?"

The girl acted like he hadn't spoken and he realized that he'd learn more if he just let her talk. Harder to do than it sounded. "She said that you lost custody of Beka"—another knife, but again he knew his daughter's name was public knowledge, too—"but that you were so abusive they still had to hide from you." She drew in a shuddering breath. "So when Lindsey didn't come back, I didn't know what to do. . . She stayed gone a month once before." She pushed her hair back from her wet cheeks. "Working out of the country, she said. And sometimes she couldn't be in touch." She shrugged and, clasping her shirt cuffs, rubbed both eyes with her knuckles. "But then this morning, Beka saw you on TV and she was so excited."

Jeremy pushed to his feet. "You know Beka? Where's Beka? Where's my daughter?" He reached to grab the girl by the shoulders.

Jack stepped closer and put a warning hand on his arm.

The girl unfurled her fist and pointed.

CHAPTER 20

The deputies and Jeremy whipped their heads around to look at a small newer-model economy car parked in the driveway.

Jeremy heard the girl's voice behind them. "She fell asleep on the way over here. My roommate's with her."

He leaped the porch railing and bolted across the driveway, mindlessly praying as he ran, his boots barely touching the gravel.

"Jeremy, wait," he heard Jack call, then more words, but Jeremy wasn't listening.

The brunet in the front shrank back against the seat as Jeremy skidded to a halt just before he connected with the hood. Her eyes were wide in a pale face.

But his gaze quickly went past her to the blond head in the backseat. He stepped around to the side, and through the window he could see that the little girl was asleep on the opposite side of the backseat in a "big girl" booster seat, very similar to the dust-covered one he had in his garage. Her blond hair hid her face, but everything about her looked like his Beka.

He opened the door softly, his pulse pounding in his ears. His hand trembled as he reached over and gently brushed her hair back. Joy filled his heart so full he thought it might burst. A choking noise came from his throat as he tried to keep from yelling her name and thanking God at the top of his lungs. He slid in beside her and put his arm around her.

She stirred and her eyes popped open. He stared into those familiar pools of blue for a split second before she reacted. "Daddy? Daddy!" she squealed and wriggled against the seat belt.

He fumbled with the seat belt and finally she was in his arms. Out of the car, he clutched her to him and buried his face in her silky hair, breathing in the baby shampoo scent. With both hands, she pushed his face back and kissed him on the nose. He laughed and kissed her on the cheek. He ran his hands over her arms and little legs, not as pudgy as he remembered, but longer and stronger. He touched her feet.

"Do you like my pink toenails?" Her smile was shy.

"I love them, Little Bit."

"Amanda did them. And she let me wear my sandals today, even though it's not May yet, so you could see them."

For the first time, Jeremy remembered the girl who had been crying on the porch. He glanced toward the porch. There she was, now talking earnestly to Jack, with Luke still sitting beside her. The other deputy had apparently gotten the roommate out of the car and was questioning her over by the deputy's car. Jeremy's eyes went back to the porch.

Crystal stood on the bottom step, watching him and Beka. He waved to her, feeling as giddy as a kid at Christmas.

"Want to call Grandma and Grandpa?" he asked Beka.

"Yes." She ran her soft little hand over his razor stubble and turned his face toward her in a way she'd done a thousand times before. In a way he'd been afraid she'd never do again. "Are they at home?"

He nodded and put his finger to his lips. "Shh. . .let's surprise them."

Her eyes twinkled.

His dad answered the phone brusquely. "Did you hear anything?"

"Y'all need to come down here right now."

"Is it something bad?" The fear in his dad's voice made him regret not blurting out the news immediately.

"No, it's something fantastic." He heard the click in his ear before he could say another word.

He smiled at Beka. "I think they're on their way."

She wriggled in his arms, and he let her down but held onto her hand.

"Who's that?" Beka whispered as they walked toward the porch. "She's pretty."

"I call her Sleeping Beauty," Jeremy joked when he knew Crystal could hear him. "But you can call her Miss Crystal."

Crystal squatted down and stuck her hand out, tears wet on her cheeks. "Pleased to meet you, Beka."

"Pleased to meet you, too." Beka touched Crystal's hair. "Are you really Sleeping Beauty?"

Crystal cut her gaze at Jeremy, but he could tell she was too happy to even pretend to be mad at him. "Not really. But I did fall asleep on the porch once."

"This porch?" Beka looked at the porch. "Hey. Why is Amanda crying?" Before Jeremy could stop her, she broke free of his grasp and ran over to the girl, who wasn't actually crying anymore but had red swollen eyes. "Amanda, what's wrong?"

Jeremy followed her, unable to let her get out of touching distance.

Amanda smiled at Beka. "Are you happy to see your daddy?"

Beka bounced on the balls of her feet as she nodded. "Um-hm. I am." She touched Amanda's arm. "Can I go home with him?"

Amanda nodded. "Yes, honey. I think that's what you should do."

"Will you come, too?"

Amanda shook her head. "I don't think so." She looked over at Jeremy. "Maybe when things are all worked out, Michelle and I can come visit you sometime."

"When you don't have classes?" Beka said.

"Right."

Beka glanced around. "I want a drink."

"Please," Amanda said then glanced up at Jeremy, and a sheepish expression crossed her face. "Sorry. Habit."

"Please, may I have a drink?" Beka said, her sweet smile never faltering.

Jeremy ruffled her hair.

"How about lemonade?" Crystal asked.

Beka nodded and Crystal disappeared into the house.

Jeremy heard the roar of a truck motor and glanced toward the lane. His dad's truck careened into the driveway. Before he killed the motor, the passenger door flung open and his mom jumped out.

Jeremy looked down at Beka, half-expecting her to be shy, but he watched the realization of who it was dawn on her face. "Grandma!" She ran down the steps and into the arms of her grandmother.

Jeremy stood on the porch steps and smiled as his dad came running up behind them and swooped them both up into his arms. His heart overflowing with thankfulness, Jeremy rushed forward and added his own arms to the four-way embrace.

"You're squishing me," Beka's thin little voice protested.

He laughed and stepped back a little.

Just enough not to squish.

But still close enough to touch.

Crystal stepped off the porch, a cup in her hand.

His gaze met hers over Beka's head. Suddenly he knew what it would take to make this circle complete. The question was. . .did she know it, too?

When the front door opened, Crystal looked up from where she was helping Elyse and Rachel pack up the phones and fold the table.

Luke stood in the doorway with an odd look on his face. "I'm going to fix Amanda and Michelle a plate," he said.

She nodded. In a totally uncharacteristic move, her brooding brother had stayed right with Beka's babysitter ever since she'd shown up on the porch earlier. He reminded her of a German shepherd protecting a child.

He turned and motioned. The two girls stepped inside. They looked straight ahead and followed Luke to the kitchen.

Elyse, Rachel, and Crystal exchanged looks. "It doesn't look like they're charging her with anything," Rachel murmured.

Crystal glanced out the window where Beka was on the porch swing between her grandparents, enjoying her lemonade.

The door opened again. "Crystal? Could you come here for a minute?" Jeremy's face looked so young. From the second he'd seen Beka, the years had just seemed to fall away from his face and his stature.

"Sure."

Out on the porch, he guided her to the opposite side of Beka and his parents to where Jack Westwood stood waiting.

"So what's going on?" Jeremy said.

It occurred to Crystal that he'd waited for her to be there before he found out the details about Beka's return. The thought warmed her.

Jack glanced at his notebook then back at them. "As Beka said, her name is Amanda. Her roommate is Michelle. They're University of Memphis students. We believe they had no idea Beka was a missing child."

Jeremy frowned. "So you really don't think they had any part in the kidnapping?"

Jack shook his head. "They answered all the questions the same, over and over. No stumbling over facts, no getting mixed up. Even though we questioned them separately, their stories agreed completely. And I didn't get the feeling that their answers were rehearsed."

Jeremy glanced at Crystal as if asking her opinion. "I just can't imagine they didn't suspect something."

"Amanda said that lately she'd started to wonder if Lindsey was doing drugs." Jack put his hand on Jeremy's shoulder. "Amanda answered an ad for a babysitter last June. Two weeks after Beka was taken. Apparently your little girl was left in Amanda's care, at the house she and Michelle share, most of the time since then, with Lindsey just popping in and out occasionally."

Crystal looked across at Beka on the other end of the porch. She had moved to her grandma's lap and was happily drinking her lemonade. "Which is probably a good thing."

She felt Jeremy relax beside her. "Beka does seem happy and not. . ." He seemed to fumble for the words. "Not hurt." He ran his hand across his face. "I'm so thankful."

"The sheriff's out of town, but the other deputies and I don't see any reason to take Amanda in for further questioning. Do you?"

Jeremy hesitated then shook his head. "No. I guess as far as I'm concerned, she's free to go."

Crystal put her hand on his arm. "Have you thought about how Beka's going to react to Amanda leaving? After living with her for all those months?"

Pain flitted across his face, and she almost wished she hadn't brought it up.

"I'm going to have to figure out a way to make that easier, I guess."

Crystal nodded toward the house. "Oddly enough, Luke's sharing food with her in the kitchen. Something he normally wouldn't do with anyone, much less a single girl. Why don't we go in there and try to get to know her a little bit?"

"I don't know. . ." Jeremy glanced at his daughter.

"Your parents will stay right here with Beka. And when you take her home, they'll have to go to their own house. So it's nice for them to have some time with her."

"You're right." He followed her into the house.

No one was in the living room, but laughter from the kitchen drew them forward.

Rachel, Elyse, Luke, Amanda, and Michelle were sitting at the big table eating when they walked in. In an instant, the room grew quiet.

Amanda's smile faded. "I'm so sorry," she said to Jeremy. "I wish I'd known."

"I wish you had, too." His words were curt, but Crystal knew it was just because he needed someone to blame. Someone alive and here.

Luke stiffened.

Amanda dropped her gaze to her food and kept it there.

Across the table, Michelle let her fork hit her plate with a clatter and gave Jeremy a hard look. "You know, Amanda arranged her class schedule this year to match Beka's school hours. Not to mention the dates she turned down. And half the time Lindsey would 'forget' to pay her."

Amanda jerked her head up. "Michelle, I enjoyed having Beka around. It was no trouble."

Michelle's face softened. "I know you did. But I don't get why you're letting him treat you like a criminal. You did what you thought was right. And you'd die to protect that little girl and we both know it."

Elyse, ever the peacemaker, hopped up. "Let me fix y'all a plate."

Crystal put one hand on Jeremy's arm and motioned Elyse away with the other one. "You're exhausted from answering the phone. Sit down and eat. We can fix our own plates."

Jeremy's gaze took in Elyse and Rachel. "Speaking of answering

176

the phones, thank you both for doing that."

He looked at Michelle then at Amanda. "And thank you for keeping Beka safe." He and Crystal filled their plates without speaking then walked over to the table, where conversation still hadn't resumed.

Jeremy slipped in next to Amanda. "I'm sorry I made it seem like this was your fault."

She gave him a shy smile. "Thanks." She turned back to her plate then stopped and looked up at him again. "Is there any chance I could see Beka from time to time?"

He frowned and his eyes met Crystal's. She knew he wanted to say no. But how could he really?

"It'll be hard on Beka not seeing you, Amanda," Crystal said softly, in a not-so-subtle hint to Jeremy.

Jeremy's jaw stiffened but he nodded. "I think we should be able to set something up."

"Really?" Amanda's eyes lit up. "I'd love that." She gulped her lemonade, and Crystal sensed she was trying to hold back tears. "I'm going to miss her."

Jeremy fidgeted, visibly anxious to get back to Beka. "I'm going to go back out and see how Mom and Dad are doing." He pushed his chair back and excused himself.

"I'm finished, too." Amanda glanced at Michelle. "We'd better get on the road. You've got that big test Monday."

On the porch, Amanda crouched down in front of Beka. " 'Bye, sugar. I'll miss you." She blinked several times and smiled. "I'm going to come back and visit pretty soon, okay?"

At first Beka's expression reflected uncertainty, but then her face crumpled, tears flowing. "I don't want you to leave."

CHAPTER 21

Jeremy looked stricken. He squatted down next to Beka. "Hey, Little Bit, Amanda has to go home for now, but we'll drive over and see her next week"—he shot Amanda a questioning look and she nodded—"and pick up your stuff. . ."

Beka's tears dried some but still trickled down her face.

Amanda smiled and poked Beka gently in the tummy. "I'll get your things ready. So when you come, you can bring them back with you."

Beka sniffed and wiped her nose with the back of her hand. "But I want to go with you." It was more of a token protest than anything. The tears had stopped.

Crystal watched as Amanda forced a happy expression to her face. Her heart must be breaking. Sometimes love involved sacrifice with a smile. "If you go with me, you won't have your daddy. Remember how sad you were when you weren't here with him?"

Beka wrapped her arm around Jeremy's neck and nodded.

Amanda smiled. "I'll see you soon, okay."

"Okay," Beka said in a small, thin voice that touched Crystal's heart.

After Amanda and Michelle left, Elyse and Luke walked with Rachel and Jack out to their cars.

Crystal cut her gaze over to Jeremy, who was leaning against the wall beside her, watching his daughter, now sitting on the swing with his parents. "You need to take the food home with you."

He shook his head. "There's just the two of us. You keep it."

"There's just one of me." How pitiful sounding. But true.

He stared at her as if he wanted to say something. But instead he turned to his mom. "How about you and Dad take most of the food to your house?"

Mrs. Buchanan smiled. "Under one condition. That all three of you come eat lunch with us tomorrow after church."

"You know Beka and I will be there," Jeremy said.

Everyone looked at Crystal. Hey, who was she to bring a happy moment down? She smiled. "I'd love to. Thanks."

"Want to help me load up the food?" Jeremy asked her.

"Sure." She followed him into the quiet house. "I think there's a cardboard box that one lady brought her food in. Maybe we can pack it in that."

As they walked into the kitchen, he stopped and she almost plowed into him.

He turned around to face her and the kitchen suddenly seemed much smaller.

Her eyebrows drew together. "What's wrong?"

"I just wanted to thank you again for helping me find Beka." The expression in his eyes was unreadable. "You're an incredible person, Crys."

The familiar nickname sounded different on his lips, affectionate and intimate. She shivered. How had she become so attached to this man so quickly? And more importantly, how could she slow down the tide of emotion he always seemed to bring? She'd have probably been better off if she'd just gone along with his offer to take care of things and hurried back to New York when she had a chance. She stared up at him. "Thanks."

179

He gently pushed her hair back from her face. "I'm glad you decided not to let me take care of the ranch alone."

Her heart pounded in her throat. He had an uncanny way of knowing exactly what she was thinking. As a matter of fact, when she looked into his eyes, she had the feeling he could see all the way into her soul.

He cupped her cheek with his palm. "I've never known anyone like you."

She gave him a tremulous smile. "Is that a good thing?"

"You tell me," he murmured as he pulled her close and lowered his lips to hers.

The thought that she was leaving and that this was a complication she didn't need surfaced, but only for a split second, then she relaxed in his embrace. His kiss was the sweetest she'd ever known, and for a minute, everything else faded away.

He raised his head and brought his hand back up to her face. "So? Is it a good thing?"

She nodded, still frozen in place.

He dropped a kiss on her forehead and walked on into the kitchen. "So where's the box?"

She stood where he'd left her. Excuse me. Had the best kiss of the century not just happened on this very spot? Surely that deserved a few seconds of savoring. Her mind raced. Or had it just been a thank-you kiss?

The kitchen door burst open and Beka came running in. "Can I help, Daddy?"

"Sure you can, Little Bit." He set her up on the counter. "As soon as Miss Crystal gets us a box, we'll pack it all up."

Crystal unfroze and hurried over to retrieve the box from the utility closet. She handed it to him, hoping he wouldn't notice that her hands were shaking. Or that she wasn't a lot of help.

"Strawberry cake. Lemon cake. Yum. . ." He winked at Beka.

180

"We'll slip these home and not tell Grandma."

Beka giggled.

"Green bean casserole, broccoli and cheese. . .those can go to Grandma's."

Crystal handed him a bowl of banana pudding and he took it without looking at her. She studied him and he still didn't meet her gaze. She had a strong hunch that she wasn't the only one who was nervous. And what was there to be nervous about a thank-you kiss? She grinned. She didn't think she'd misjudged after all.

"All packed." He set Beka on the floor and handed her a loaf of bread. "Now don't get this smushed, okay?"

Beka giggled again and scampered out. Jeremy scooped up the box and tried to wrangle two grocery bags.

"Hello? Remember me?" Crystal couldn't resist.

He finally looked at her, and she could see the reflection of her own confusion in his eyes. She definitely wasn't the only one who'd been taken off guard by their kiss.

She reached for the grocery bags. "I can help."

He nodded. "Thanks."

"Anytime."

He walked out and she followed him.

Out on the porch, she blushed, suddenly sure that his parents knew what had happened in the kitchen. *Don't be ridiculous*, she scolded herself. *She* didn't even know what had happened in the kitchen.

They packed the food into his dad's truck, and Jeremy lifted Beka up on his shoulders. "Let's head home, kiddo." He turned toward his parents. "Want to come by for a while?"

His dad laughed and took his mom's hand. "Took you long enough to ask, boy."

His mom giggled like a giddy teenager. "We'll meet you there." She reached up and dropped a kiss on Jeremy's cheek. "I'm so happy."

She reached higher and squeezed Beka's pudgy hand. "See you in a few minutes, sweetie." She waved at Crystal. "See you tomorrow."

They climbed into their truck and left.

Jeremy turned to Crystal, still holding Beka on his shoulders. His smile was genuine but a little unsure. "Thanks again."

She hung on to the porch post and watched them leave, pushing hard against the loneliness creeping into her heart.

This had been the perfect day. All was as it should be. Jeremy seemed happy to act like that amazing kiss in the kitchen had never happened. Which meant that even though her Broadway path had taken a short detour, it was back on track. Her heart needed to stop longing for what it couldn't have.

"The end." Jeremy closed the book and leaned forward to kiss Beka's cheek. "I'm so glad to have you home."

She clung to him. "Don't go. Stay with me till I go to sleep, Daddy."

He kissed her hair. Like there was any way he was going anywhere. "Okay, Little Bit. Say your prayers. I'll be right here." He released her and sank into the rocker beside her bed.

Beka snuggled into the covers and closed her eyes. He'd thought she might protest that she didn't know how to pray, after all those months away, but her sweet voice rang out strong. Probably had Amanda to thank for that. "Dear God, thank You for everything You give us. Thank You for Daddy and Amanda and Michelle. And Mommy. Please watch over me while I sleep and keep me safe. In Jesus' name, amen."

His heart twisted that he had to figure out how to tell her that her mommy was dead. Even as he thought it, he realized that Lindsey was almost an afterthought in Beka's prayer. Her mother had been a stranger when she'd abducted her, and then she'd promptly dumped her with a babysitter. But it would still be hard to tell her. He knew that on the level that all children love their parents, Beka loved Lindsey.

As he watched Beka toss around and try to get comfortable in a strange bed, he faced the terrible truth. Lindsey hadn't really wanted Beka. She just hadn't wanted him to have her. As Beka stilled and her breathing evened out, he said his own prayer. He'd come so far toward forgiving Lindsey after the funeral. For his own good, and for Beka's, he couldn't afford to let the bitterness seep back in, no matter how tempting.

And, really, tonight, how could he be mad at anyone about anything? He rested his head against the rocker. Tomorrow they'd go to Sunday school and worship. And after that Crystal was coming to lunch with them at his parents.

His face grew hot as he remembered the few minutes after their kiss. Even though he'd initiated it, he hadn't expected their connection to impact him so deeply. Because of that, he'd reacted like an idiot. She deserved more. But he hadn't known how to disguise his confusion without just getting away from her.

He slipped his phone out of his pocket and stared at the time: 9 p.m. Texting wasn't his strong suit, but he could manage a few words to keep from waking Beka by calling. He scrolled to Crystal's number, pulled up a blank message, and typed, CAN'T WAIT TO SEE YOU TOMORROW.

He stared at the words and inhaled deeply. Was he ready to move forward like this message implied? Now that Beka was home, there was nothing standing in the way of following his heart. He hit SEND.

In a couple of minutes, his phone vibrated. He pushed the button to view the message. ME, TOO.

A smile tilted the corner of his lips, but he wasn't sure what to say. What if she was busy and didn't want to talk? SEE YOU AT CHURCH. NIGHT.

When her message came back, he felt like a kid in high school, fumbling to open it. *SWEET DREAMS.*

He chuckled in the quiet room. *YOU, TOO.*

From the top of the cedar chest at the end of the bed, he pulled a blanket across him. He stuck a stuffed elephant behind his head and looked at Beka one more time. Then he closed his eyes and sighed.

The perfect end to a perfect day.

Crystal sighed and floated upstairs, humming a love song from *Making a Splash*. She seemed to remember Aaron trying to make her promise that she wouldn't flirt with Jeremy. Did *Sweet dreams* constitute flirting? She grinned at the phone. If it did, then so did *You, too*. So Jeremy was as guilty as she was. And after what happened in the kitchen, she was pretty sure that conversation with Aaron was irrelevant.

She glanced at the closed door at the top of the stairs and hurried into the sewing room. Her satchel and suitcases took up so much space. She glanced at the big dresser on the wall. Feeling a little like a snoop, she walked over and opened the drawers. The first two held patterns and fabric, but the other four were blissfully empty. She knew her mother would be happy if she made herself at home. She sang loudly while she unpacked her suitcases into the drawers. When the job was done, she sat back with satisfaction. Now her hanging clothes were in the closet, and everything else was in the drawers.

She glanced over at the double bed. As long as Kaleigh didn't mind sharing if she came home for an overnight visit, Crystal had a place to stay until her parents came home. And if today was any indication, it could be an exciting three weeks.

She clutched her phone and stood, unable to stop herself from reading Jeremy's text messages one more time. She'd been sure that he regretted the kiss, but now she wasn't sure at all. Had he set out to drive her crazy? Or did it just come naturally?

She slapped the phone down on the dresser and walked out of the room. She needed a distraction.

In the hallway, the closed door pulled her attention just like it always did. "I don't need that big of a distraction." Her voice echoed in the quiet house.

Or did she? Last night, she'd opened the door. That had been a logical step. No sense in ripping off the hide with a Band-Aid that had been on for so long. Slow and easy, that was more her style. Maybe she should just turn the light on and look in.

She twisted the doorknob. Before she could reconsider, she flipped the light switch on.

The first things she saw were the posters. THE LION KING. MAMMA MIA. HAIRSPRAY. That last one had been a graduation present. And Cami had barely gotten to hang it on the wall before she was gone.

She forced herself to look at the picture above her own bed. An amazing aerial photograph of the ranch. Crystal had loved the small one so much that she'd asked for a framed enlargement for Christmas and had gotten it. She'd planned to take it to New York with her to stave off the homesickness. But her family had spoiled her, gathering her clothes for the funeral and the ones she wanted to take to New York with her. She'd never come back in this room.

Still standing in the doorway, she allowed herself to look around a little. For some reason, she'd expected dust on the furniture, but there was none. She immediately thought of her mother's quiet strength. Facing her daughters' room on a regular basis. One gone forever. The other gone for all intents and purposes.

What was it Jeremy had said about his parents? That in his own pain about Beka's disappearance, he hadn't considered theirs? Crystal knew she'd been equally guilty of that.

185

On the dust-free oak nightstand, Crystal spotted her well-worn Bible. Exactly where she'd left it seven years ago. She stared at it for several moments without blinking. If only getting right with God were as simple as just picking it up again.

Before she considered what she was doing, she darted in and grabbed the Bible then darted back to the doorway.

Breathless and feeling more than a little silly, she ran her hand over the grainy leather and traced her name, embossed in gold. Her parents had given her this when she'd gotten baptized. In her hand, it felt light. But her heart knew better.

She flipped through the pages. Her eyes immediately fell on a highlighted verse. " 'I can do all things through Christ who strengthens me,' " she whispered. One of the many verses she'd committed to memory back then. At the time, she couldn't imagine ever going a day without reading the Bible. Much less seven years. Of course at the time, she couldn't have imagined losing her twin, either.

Her cell phone chimed in the sewing room and, still clutching the Bible, she hurried to answer it, relieved to leave her uncomfortable thoughts. "Hello?"

"Crystal, it's Mia. Honey, I have fantastic news. That new Broadway play we heard was opening? *Sisters*? You've got a private audition for a supporting role."

CHAPTER 22

Crystal's legs went weak and she sank to the bed. "Really?"

"No, I'm kidding. Of course really. You audition first thing Monday morning. They faxed over the information, and I need you here early tomorrow to meet with the audition coach I've lined up."

"Tomorrow?" Her mind raced. She could eat lunch with Jeremy and his family right after church then rush to the airport. . .

"Call the airport and get booked on the first flight out in the morning. I want you well rested for this audition."

Crystal considered arguing, but she knew Mia was right. She sighed. This opportunity was too important for her to give a less-than-peak performance. "Okay. See you tomorrow."

She slipped the Bible into her overnight satchel and turned to the dresser. Apparently, she'd been a little premature in her unpacking.

"So you'll call me and tell me what time to pick you up Tuesday?" Luke handed her the overnight bag and glanced around the busy terminal.

"Yes. Or I can get a rental car if you're working."

"Elyse or I will pick you up. And don't worry about the ranch. I'll get Slim and the boys started in the morning and go into work a little late." He grinned. "I can do that since I'm the boss."

Crystal smiled, but she knew the truth was that he worked harder and longer hours than his crew. "Right." She hugged him and watched him walk away then got into the ticket line. She glanced at her phone: 7:30 a.m. She'd put off this call as long as she could.

She pulled up Jeremy's number and hit SEND.

She could hear the happiness in his voice when he answered.

"Hi," she said softly. "I'm sorry to call at the last minute, but something's come up. I won't be able to eat lunch at your mom's."

"What's wrong?" The concern in his tone tugged at her heart. "Anything I can help with?"

She shook her head even though he couldn't see her. Nothing he could help with. "No. I just have to fly back to New York for a couple of days to take care of something." She'd decided not to advertise the fact that she had an audition until she knew something for sure. It was just easier that way. "So I'm at the airport."

He didn't speak and she pulled the phone away from her face and looked at the screen to be sure the connection wasn't broken.

"You're at the airport right now?" He sounded bewildered.

"When I found out last night it was too late to call you. Would you tell your mom I'm sorry?"

"Sure." Was it her imagination or was his tone cooler? "I'll tell her."

"Thanks, Jeremy. I really am sorry."

"No problem. Have a safe flight."

She disconnected, and an uneasiness crept into her bones. Maybe she should have told him why she was going back to New York. Or maybe that would have made things worse.

"Where's Miss Crystal?"

Jeremy froze in the act of passing the green bean casserole to his

188

mother. He'd hoped Beka wouldn't even notice that she wasn't here, or at least wouldn't be curious enough to ask about her.

"Crystal had to go out of town today. For work." As soon as he said the words, he realized that he really had no idea if it was for work. The trip could be purely personal. Maybe Brad had talked her into giving him a second chance. He winced. Some thoughts were better left unthought.

"Oh. . ." Beka picked at her broccoli. "Like Mommy."

Jeremy's breath whooshed out of him. He wanted to protest that Crystal's trip, whatever the reason of it, was nothing like Lindsey's disappearances. But he picked up the basket of garlic cheese toast instead. "Here, honey, have some toast."

Beka wrinkled her nose. "I don't like that."

"Yes, you do. It's your favorite." Which was precisely why his mom had fixed it, even though they had a whole kitchen full of food, already prepared.

Beka shook her head. "Nuh-uh." She stuck her bottom lip out slightly. "It stinks."

Jeremy set the basket down and fought to get past the surge of anger at Lindsey. Even the simple things weren't simple anymore. He felt a hand on his shoulder and looked up into compassion-filled eyes.

"It's just going to take a while," his dad murmured.

Jeremy nodded. With his head, he knew that. But patience had never been his strong suit. So with his heart, he wanted everything to be back to normal. Now.

His mom and dad engaged Beka in conversation and he just concentrated on getting through the meal, listening to her chatter with one ear.

He should be thankful that she was as unchanged as she was. And he was. He knew enough about kids to know that even if she'd lived with him for the last ten months, she could have easily changed her preference for garlic cheese toast.

When they were finished, he pushed back from the table.

"Is Mommy coming today?" Beka asked as she climbed down from her chair.

His mom gasped then covered it with a cough.

"No. No, she's not, honey." Jeremy stood and put his hand on Beka's head, lightly ruffling her hair. "Let's go in the living room and talk for a minute."

Beka skipped ahead of him into the living room and clambered up onto the couch.

He sank down beside her, praying silently for the right words. "Do you remember Ralphie?"

The barn cat had been a fixture on the farm when they'd bought it. Last year, right before Lindsey had taken Beka, Ralphie had gone off to another farm exploring and apparently gotten into some rat poison. Beka bobbed her head up and down. "Um-hum. He died."

Jeremy nodded. "And we were sad."

Beka twisted around and looked up at him. "I cried."

"And that's normal. Because when animals or people die, we're sad."

Beka's eyes were wide as if she knew what he was going to say. "The lady on the TV said Mommy died."

Jeremy sucked in his breath, shaken that she'd heard that and not said anything. He put his arm around her. "That's right. She did."

Beka rubbed her eye with her fist and sniffed. "So I won't see her anymore?"

He shook his head. "I'm sorry, honey. But it's okay to be sad." He pulled her onto his lap and she didn't resist.

She buried her head in his shirt and cried.

He stroked her hair and looked up at his parents standing in the doorway. His mom wiped at her eyes and disappeared into the kitchen. His dad followed her.

"Why don't we pray about it?" Jeremy whispered.

"Amanda says. . ." Beka stopped to choke out a shuddering sob. "That God cares when we're sad."

"She's right." Not for the first time, Jeremy thanked God silently for Amanda. "Amanda's pretty smart."

He held Beka tight and prayed aloud for peace and comfort for her. When he finished, she climbed off his lap and pulled some books from the wicker basket at the end of his mom's couch. She held them out to him. "Read me a story?"

He nodded and took the books, a grin teasing the corner of his mouth as he saw the title of the top one. *Sleeping Beauty.* "I'd love to." She reclaimed her place on his lap and snuggled against him.

After the third book, Beka wandered into the kitchen to help her grandma make some cookies. He pulled out his phone. No missed calls. No text messages.

He opened Crystal's last message. SWEET DREAMS. Should he text her to be sure she made it safely to New York? It was odd knowing he wouldn't be seeing her for the next couple of days. Unsettlingly odd.

He flipped his phone shut. When he saw Crystal by the river that first day, he'd known she was a complication waiting to happen. And now he couldn't quit thinking about her. Somehow the fact that he'd been right gave him no satisfaction at all.

"So y'all are really getting married?" Crystal tucked the sheet under the couch cushion and stared at Tina, unsure the Texan wasn't pulling her leg.

"Unless I chicken out." Tina smoothed out the sheet on the other end and spread a blanket across it. She picked up a pillow and tossed it to Crystal. "When this temp job ends in a couple weeks, we're supposed to fly down to Texas and tie the knot." She smiled. "Too bad we're not taking the bike. We could buzz by Arkansas and see your ranch."

"I'd love that." Crystal laid the pillow on the couch and sank down beside it. "I'm so happy for you."

Tina sat down in the small armchair. "Me, too. God has really blessed us. So how did it go with the audition coach today?"

Crystal moaned. "It went fine, but I'm so tired I can't wiggle. When I think about Mia saying she wanted me to come today so I could be rested for the audition, I feel like laughing. Or I would if I had any energy."

"Poor you." Tina motioned toward the couch. "It's fun having you sleep over."

"Thanks, but I'm a little worried about coming back in three weeks. I don't know how long it'll take me to find a place."

Tina frowned. "I said it's *fun* having you. What part of that didn't you understand?"

Crystal sighed. "But will you still feel that way when you swap your roommates for Zee? I can't really see me bunking with newlyweds."

"Get real, girl. We'll have a couch just the same as I do now. You'll be welcome to stay with us for as long as you want. And if we're in Texas when you come back, you can stay at Zee's until we get back."

"A place to myself in New York." Crystal pretended to swoon. "Maybe you could just extend your honeymoon a little bit."

"Very funny. Other than being tired, are you excited about the audition tomorrow?"

Crystal picked at the blanket. "Sure."

"Uh-oh. What's wrong? Did you fall in love with a cowboy while you were in Arkansas?"

Even as Crystal shook her head, she felt her face burn. "Nothing's wrong."

Tina squealed and scooted closer. "Ohh. . .tell me about him."

"There's nothing to tell." Crystal could see from Tina's animated expression that her protests were useless. "I'm not in love with him."

She thought about their kiss yesterday in the kitchen. Was there any way that could have been just a thank-you? In as few words as possible, she told Tina about Jeremy, ending with his daughter's coming home.

Tina ran her hands through her pink highlights and collapsed back against the armchair. "Wow. You've been busy since you left the city."

"Hey, I'm not the one getting married."

"Not yet."

Crystal shivered and pulled the blanket up around her arms. "Not for a long time to come. Right now, I've got one thing on my mind." Her heart beat faster as she thought about the audition and all the implications of the outcome—good or bad. "Broadway."

Tina pushed to her feet. "I'm going to go to bed and let you get some rest." She bent down and hugged Crystal. "See you in the morning."

"Night, Tina. Thanks again for letting me stay."

When Tina was gone, Crystal stretched out on the couch and listened to the city noises. Honking horns, motors zooming by, the occasional trill of laughter, and from somewhere close, probably the club the next block up, she could hear the faint sounds of reggae. The city didn't sleep. It just moved from morning to night. Daytime folks gave way to nighttime folks and the cycle moved on.

Amazing how quickly she'd gotten used to the quietness of the ranch. She used to think she couldn't sleep without tires squealing, horns honking, and basses thumping. But she'd learned to.

She stared at the dark room. She'd learned to get used to talking to Jeremy Buchanan every day, too.

Some things she was just going to have to unlearn.

Crystal had been to Broadway auditions before, but they'd been open auditions—mile-long lines and a very short time to impress. This was a definite step up from those cattle calls—a private audition for a supporting role. Apparently the director was close friends with Herman Lowder, the writer and producer of *Making a Splash*. He'd caught a showing and been impressed with Crystal's performance. So when Mia contacted him about an audition, doors had opened.

The play focused on four sisters, and Crystal was auditioning for the part of the best friend of one of the sisters. Not the lead, but a lot of stage time. On Broadway.

It was a start. And if she was lucky enough to be offered the role, she'd definitely take it. But first she had to get that far.

She was supposed to be reading a scene with her friend, the sister. The burly bored-looking man holding the script didn't look like anyone's sister. Crystal groaned inwardly when she saw him.

When they were in high school, Cami had read in one of the acting magazines that she subscribed to that the worst thing you could do was to assume that your reading partner in an audition cared whether you got the part or not. The two of them had practiced together, one of them reading in a flat, distracted monotone while the other one auditioned.

For years, Crystal had counted on that early experience in situations like this. She tried her best to view the burly man as her friend and respond accordingly, but the director kept stopping her and asking her to try it again a different way. She almost got the feeling that she was a disposable experiment in figuring out what they wanted the role to be like. When she finished, the casting committee gave her a polite thank-you and no emotional response whatsoever.

She smiled and thanked them profusely for allowing her to audition, but her feet felt like lead as she trudged toward the exit. What a waste of time and money.

CHAPTER 23

As she pushed the glass door open, she called Mia.

"How'd it go?" Excitement bubbled in her agent's voice.

Crystal stepped out into the bright spring sunshine and hurried down the sidewalk to the subway station. "Awful."

"Oh no. What happened?"

"I think I was too bubbly. . .or too subdued. . .or too *something* for the part. They had me do it a hundred ways."

"So they were just using you to figure out what they were looking for."

Crystal ducked her head and watched her feet as she walked. "Yep."

"Crys, I'm sorry." She could hear the genuine sympathy in Mia's voice and it did make her feel some better. "That's no reflection on you as an actress. The play's not supposed to open until July. Apparently they're still in the preliminary stages of auditioning."

"I know. And there'll be other auditions. . ." Or would there? Even as tired as she was, she'd read a little in her Bible last night. Maybe God had decided that Broadway wasn't for her. "Probably."

"Probably?" Mia sounded panicked. "There's no probably. There *will* be other auditions. Other *Broadway* auditions. Just hurry home and I'll show you."

Hurry home? That's what she wanted to do right now. But she knew Mia meant hurry back to New York. "Okay."

"Listen, why don't you let me take you out to dinner?"

"Thanks, but I can't. I have an early flight back to Arkansas in the morning." The aroma of freshly cooked hotdogs wafted to her, drawing her over to the rolling cart. Crystal shifted her phone to the other hand and fished some dollar bills from her pocket. "Talk to you later."

As soon as she hung up, she ordered a hot dog from the vendor. Some moments called for comfort food. And this was definitely one of them.

Dog in hand, she made her way to a bench and took a big bite. When she and her brothers and sisters were in junior high, they used to have wiener roasts down by the river. In all the years she'd lived in New York, she'd never had a hot dog that compared to those. But that didn't stop her from trying one about four times a year.

She took another bite. *Wonder if Beka and Jeremy would like to have a wiener roast?* When the dogs were gone, they could bring out the marshmallows.

She glanced over at the vendor. Maybe she should tell him that's what he was missing—roasted marshmallows. He'd probably think she was crazy. And if this sudden longing to see Jeremy again was any indication, he might be right.

"Luke McCord here."

Jeremy smiled in the rearview mirror at Beka and spoke into his cell. "Hey, man, it's Jeremy. Beka and I are on our way to Memphis today to get her things from Amanda's. I wondered if you needed me to pick up anything for y'all while I'm in town."

"You have perfect timing."

"Great. I can haul whatever you need in the bed of the truck.

What do you need me to get?"

Luke laughed. "My little sister. But I won't tell her you were going to throw her in the back. Seriously, though, you could save me a trip and pick Crystal up at the airport. Her flight should land in about four hours. I was just about to leave to go get her."

"So she's in the air now?"

"Yep."

Jeremy considered the fact that Luke wouldn't be able to make sure it was okay with Crystal for him to pick her up. He hated to force himself on her. On the other hand, the thought of seeing her in a few hours made it worth taking a chance on her being unhappy with the chauffeur switch. "We'll be there when she lands, then. Do you have the flight info?"

Luke told him which baggage claims conveyor belt they were supposed to meet at. "Thanks a lot. She wanted to rent a car. I told her I didn't mind driving to Memphis. Still don't, but no sense in it if you're going." He laughed. "Especially with you having plenty of room to haul her in that empty pickup bed."

Jeremy laughed. "Why do I have the feeling I'll never live that down?"

After he hung up with Luke, he thought about the phrase "*never live that down*." Crystal had said something similar after he'd found her asleep on the porch. Never was a long time. He had a brief flash of him and Crystal, old and gray, her blue eyes still sparkling, as she teased him about hauling her in the bed of the truck or blushed about falling asleep on the porch.

"Why are you smiling?"

Jeremy glanced in the mirror at Beka, who was watching him intently. "I'm just happy, I guess." He winked at her. "Are you happy?"

"Um-hum. I can't wait to see Amanda."

"She's supposed to be there when we get there. But she won't have long to visit before she has to go to school."

Beka beamed. "I can tell her I'm going to school tomorrow."

"That's right."

"I hope my new class has a goldfish."

"If they don't, we might have to ask your teacher about getting one for the class." Jeremy had debated sending Beka to school with only three weeks left in the school year, but she needed normalcy in her life. And this way when she started first grade at the small Shady Grove Elementary School, she'd already know several kids from kindergarten.

"I bet Miss Cindy will be sad that I'm leaving."

"I bet she will, too."

Their first stop in Memphis was going to be the preschool/day care Beka had attended there. She should have been in kindergarten, but Lindsey had enrolled her in Miss Cindy's Day School near Amanda's house and told the teacher that she was going to homeschool after this year. She'd neatly sidestepped the lack of records by procrastination. He'd spoken to Miss Cindy, and she'd assured him that Beka would have no trouble adapting to kindergarten. When they left the preschool, they'd head on to Amanda's.

"Maybe she'll let me feed the goldfish today since it's my turn."

"We'll see."

To Beka's delight, Miss Cindy did let her feed the goldfish and read a good-bye story to the class.

And Amanda, thankfully, kept things upbeat when they got to her place. She opened the chipped-paint door with a big smile. Beka squealed and ran into her arms. While they were hugging, he glanced past them. What he could see of the tiny house was run-down but neat, the threadbare carpet clean.

Amanda stood and followed his gaze. "It's not much, but it's home." She motioned to a stack of plastic tubs next to the door. "I have Beka's things all packed." She hefted the tub nearest her and started out to his truck.

When they'd loaded everything, Amanda turned to Beka and held up a stuffed bear. "I thought you might want to keep Booboo Bear out to keep you company on your trip home."

Beka scooped the bear out of Amanda's hands. "Thanks, Amanda." Both she and Booboo kissed Amanda good-bye. Beka scampered cheerfully into her seat.

In the driveway, Amanda looked at Jeremy. "She seems happy."

He nodded. "She's really well adjusted, considering what she's been through, thanks to you." He pulled out several bills. "I'd like to pay you a little toward the income you missed this year. Your friend mentioned that Lindsey didn't always pay you."

Her eyes widened and she shook her head. "Thank you, but that's not necessary."

He grinned. "Actually it is necessary. I really appreciate your being here." He shoved the bills into her hand.

She shrugged and smiled. "Thanks. You know college students. Always broke. And of course I'm job hunting this week."

As he and Beka drove away, he made a mental note to speak to his parents about the three of them setting up a scholarship fund for Amanda.

Crystal leaned against the side of the escalator, clutching her carry-on bag. Somewhere over Kentucky, defeat had given way to exhaustion. She wanted to get back to the ranch and sleep for a year.

As she stepped off, she scanned the crowd in front of the conveyor belt for Luke. She froze. Even from the back she recognized the cowboy holding the hand of an adorable little girl.

Hoping they wouldn't turn and catch her backtracking, she made a beeline for the ladies' room, fumbling to get her cell out of her bag as she went.

"Luke McCord."

"What is Jeremy doing here? Where are you?" She glanced in the mirror at her travel-ravaged face, sleeplessness showing in every line.

"The phone sure is echoing. Are you in the bathroom?"

Crystal stomped her foot and growled. The woman at the sink next to her gave her a strange look.

"Yes, I'm in the bathroom. Did you ask Jeremy to come pick me up?" As she remembered the coolness in Jeremy's tone Sunday when she'd called to cancel lunch, she cringed.

"No. I was just about to leave when he called to say he was going to Memphis and did I need him to pick up anything."

"Oh." So he hadn't actually offered to come to the airport and get her. But at least he was going to be in town anyway.

"Yeah. . ." Luke laughed. "Ask him if you're going to have to ride in the back of the truck."

"The back? What are you talking about?"

"Just ask him. Or better yet, just climb up in there."

Crystal looked down at her gauzy black pants and stilettos. "I don't think so."

"You're no fun. See you tonight. Tell Jeremy thanks again for me."

Crystal held the phone out and looked at it. She'd offered to rent a car. But no. . .Luke had insisted on coming to get her. She put the phone back to her ear. "Bye, Luke."

"Bye, kid."

She disconnected and pulled out her makeup bag. Lip gloss and under-eye concealer might not make a big difference in how she looked, but they'd make her feel better. Years of theatre experience gave her speed, and in less than two minutes, she was walking across to greet Jeremy and Beka.

They were facing her this time, and unless she was seriously delusional, Jeremy's face lit up when he saw her. Of course, more likely, he was just tired of waiting. Still clutching Beka's hand, he pulled Crystal to him in a loose embrace and kissed her cheek.

Her heart, bruised and weary as it was, skittered at the closeness.

She bent down and hugged Beka, almost overbalancing as her carry-on bag shifted forward.

Jeremy reached and slipped it off her shoulder. "Let me get that."

She grinned up at him. "Thanks."

Beka bounced up and down on the balls of her feet. "I fed the goldfish."

"You did?"

"Um-hum. And we went to see Amanda."

"Oh, honey, that's great. Sounds like you've had a busy day already."

"You're going home with us."

Jeremy stepped forward. "If you don't mind."

Crystal smiled. She didn't mind at all. While she was in New York, she'd remembered the excitement of their kiss. She'd forgotten how comfortable he always made her feel. "As long as I don't have to ride in the back."

Jeremy put his palm to his forehead. "Luke has a big mouth." He winked at her just as the buzzer went off to signal that the conveyor belt was starting to move luggage out to be picked up. "I'll explain that later. Right now, we should probably find your suitcases."

She glanced up just in time to see her big duffle bag come into view. "I only have one and there it is."

He put his hand on the handle and looked back for confirmation. At her nod, he hefted it off the belt. "Ready?"

"Let's go." She felt a little hand slip into hers and looked down. Beka, seeing her daddy had his hands full, had apparently decided that Crystal would be an okay substitute for now.

Crystal smiled at her, but when she glanced back up at Jeremy, her breath caught in her throat at the tender look in his eyes.

"Thanks for coming to get me," she stammered.

Jeremy stepped back to let her and Beka get on the escalator first. "It was my pleasure."

Why did that sound so much better than "You're welcome"?

They didn't speak again until they were in the parking garage, walking across to the truck. Jeremy glanced over at her. "How did your trip go?"

"Fine." She wrinkled her nose. "Not really. It was kind of a bust."

"I'm sorry. Personal or business?" He grimaced. "Or personal and none of my business?"

She laughed. "It was business. But it turned out to be nothing worth talking about." Someday she might tell him. But for today, she didn't feel like sharing her humiliation with anyone. Let what happened in New York stay in New York.

CHAPTER 24

"Is Miss Crystal asleep?" Beka's voice rang out loud in the quiet truck cab.

"Yes, she is," Jeremy whispered and put his finger to his lips.

"No, she's not," Crystal mumbled. "I'm just resting my eyes." Her voice drifted off.

He chuckled. Obviously exhausted, Crystal was still a fighter. One of many things he'd grown to love about her. The laughter died on his lips. Love? He looked across the seat at her, her face glowing with childlike innocence as she slept.

She'd come into his life like a whirlwind and turned everything upside down. Now she was never far from his thoughts, and he'd do anything for her. But what made him think she was any different than Lindsey in the stability department? When he'd found her by the river, it was because she'd left New York upset and decided to come home on the spur of the minute. Then she'd canceled lunch Sunday without an explanation and flown off to New York. He couldn't help but wonder what that had been about.

He lifted his eyes to the mirror where he could see Beka looking at a picture book. He had a precious responsibility in the backseat. His heart was no longer his own to give without consideration of that. And when he gave it—if he gave it—it would be to someone he knew would help him provide Beka with the love and security she deserved.

He prayed silently until they reached the Shady Grove city limits. Ultimately he knew there was only One who could give Beka security. So Jeremy asked for wisdom.

"You look like you've got something serious on your mind." Crystal's sleepy voice startled him just as they entered town.

He glanced in the mirror. Now Beka was the one zonked out. "Just thinking."

"I did a lot of that on the plane trip home."

"Really?" He kept his gaze on the road and strove for casual. "About what happened in New York?"

There was no mirth in her drowsy chuckle. "What happened in New York? You mean watching my dream die on the vine?" She laid her head against the seat and closed her eyes again.

"What was it? Some kind of audition?" He knew he shouldn't keep pushing. But if he was going to protect his heart—and ultimately Beka—from history repeating itself, he felt like he had to.

She blinked her eyes several times then nodded slowly. "Possibly my last audition. And suffice it to say, it didn't go well."

"You're giving up acting?"

She shrugged. "I'm thinking seriously about it."

The raw pain in her voice kept him from feeling any pleasure. "I'm sorry, Crys. That must be tough."

She sat up straight and rubbed her hand across her face. "It's my decision."

"I'll be praying you make the right one."

She mumbled something he didn't catch.

"What?"

She shook her head. "Nothing. Thanks for your prayers. I need them."

He could sense her defeat and it hurt. "Sometimes dreams just need to be redefined."

She looked over at him. "What about you? What's your dream?"

He shrugged. "When I was growing up in south Arkansas, Dad worked in a factory. Everybody assumed I'd work there, too, when I got out of school. But Dad and I wanted to own a cattle ranch. He socked away every cent he could save. And when I got out of high school, I went to college to get an agri/business degree. Dad and I went over the things I learned together."

"Then they discovered natural gas on your land. . ."

He nodded. "And we were able to go ahead with our plan a little sooner than we'd thought."

"That's really cool."

They rode in silence for a half mile or so, then Crystal shifted around in her seat to face him. "Let me ask you a question."

He glanced over at her. "Okay."

"What if your dad had changed his mind and decided to retire to Florida? Or died?" Her voice grew soft. "Would you still have bought a ranch?"

He stared out at the road, searching for an honest answer. "You know, it's impossible to say what we'd do in a situation until we're in it, but I think so. We're just two people who happen to have the same dream. Sharing it is a bonus but not a necessity." He looked at her. Was she thinking of her and her sister and their joint dream to go to Broadway? Was that why she wanted to quit? Because she felt guilty for doing what her sister wasn't here to do?

"I guess if Dad changed his mind, that's when my dream would have to be redefined. Instead of the two of us owning ranches side by side, I'd have to concentrate on my own love of the outdoors and of cattle in particular." He grinned. "I'd learn to be the Lone Rancher."

She groaned. "That was bad." But her lips tilted back up into a smile as they turned off the highway onto the gravel road.

When he pulled up in front of the ranch house, he jumped out and lifted her bags out of the back.

She walked up on the porch and unlocked the door. "You can just set the bags inside the door. I'll get them later."

He started to argue but he hated to leave Beka asleep in the truck. One of the repercussions of the kidnapping—even though Lindsey was dead and he knew the McCord ranch was a safe place—he panicked when Beka wasn't in his sight. Hopefully that would pass with a little time. He set the bags down and stepped back onto the porch.

Crystal's smile was bleak as she turned to face him. "Thanks again. For everything." She stood on tiptoe and kissed his cheek.

He wanted to pull her into his arms and kiss away her sadness. But he had just prayed for wisdom. And he knew that wouldn't be wise right now.

For either of them.

The music woke her from a dream where the last curtain had fallen but the orchestra wouldn't quit playing. She rolled over and felt around on the floor by the sofa until her hand closed around the phone. "Hello."

"Crystal?" The tender concern in Jeremy's voice sent shivers down her spine. "Are you okay? Did you get a nap?"

"Yes. I guess I was so tired I fell asleep on the sofa." She sat up and rubbed her eyes with her free hand. "I'm wide awake now though. What's up?"

"Beka and I were wondering if you were hungry." She could hear the smile in his voice. "She fixed tuna salad sandwiches and thought you might like us to bring you one."

"That sounds wonderful. Tell her I'd love one." Crystal stuck her feet into her sandals. "Bring yours, too, if you haven't eaten, and we'll eat together."

"Sounds perfect. We'll be right over."

She hurried to the bathroom, washed her face, and put her hair up in a ponytail. At least she didn't look as tired as she had earlier.

Ten minutes later, the doorbell rang and she rushed to answer it.

Jeremy had his hands on Beka's shoulders. Beka, wearing a white apron with CHEF emblazoned on the front of it, grinned broadly and held up a plate of sandwiches. "I made these myself."

Crystal stepped back and Beka sashayed by her, heading to the kitchen as fast as her chubby little legs would carry her. "Don't come in yet," she called over her shoulder.

Jeremy gave Crystal a rueful grin and shrugged. "She has a plan."

Crystal raised her eyebrow. "That's what I like. A girl with a plan."

"She insisted on my calling her 'miss' after she put on the apron."

Crystal almost laughed at the confusion on his face. "She's playing my two favorite games. Pretend and dress up."

He leaned around as if he could see through the crack of the kitchen door. "Do you think we should check on her?"

"Nope. I think she's just fine."

A minute later, the kitchen door swung open and Beka motioned them in, her eyes sparkling with excitement. She held up a small notepad and pencil Crystal recognized as the ones they kept by the phone. "Have a seat. Here's a menu." She handed them a sheet torn from the notepad. It said "MENU," then a few lines down it said "TUNA SALUD." The S was backward. Under that it said "TEE."

Jeremy pulled Crystal's chair out at the tiny corner table where they'd shared her mama's beef stew a few weeks ago. She sat and he walked around and sat across from her.

"Miss," Crystal waved her hand in the air.

Beka jogged over to the table. "Yes?"

"I have a question about this wonderful menu."

A little grin teased at the corners of Beka's mouth, but she lifted her nose into the air. "What is it?"

"Is the tuna good?"

Beka considered her for a second. "Oh yes, ma'am. It was made by a world-famous chef."

"Oh, that's wonderful." Crystal put her hand to her face and looked at Jeremy. "We should truly be honored."

He grinned. "I'd say we are." He looked at Beka. "Aren't you going to sit down, honey?"

Beka gave him a stern look. "Waitresses don't eat with the customers." Quick switch to big smile. "Now"—she waved the notepad and pen—"what do you want to eat?"

Crystal studied the menu. "Okay, miss. I'll have a tuna sandwich."

Beka giggled but wrote on her pad. "Sir?"

"Hmm, I'll have the same." A mischievous grin flitted across Jeremy's face as he entered into the spirit of the game. "And may I have some potato chips with that, miss?"

"That's not on the men—"

He pointed to the chips on the counter.

She put her hand to her forehead in an "oh, duh, silly me" motion so reminiscent of Jeremy that Crystal couldn't keep from chuckling.

"Yes, you may have chips." Beka scribbled on the paper. "What would you like to drink?"

"Tea." They both answered at the same time.

"Good."

Beka tore off four paper towels and spread one carefully in front of Jeremy and one like so in front of Crystal and gave each of them one to hold. Then she brought the plate of sandwiches over to the small table and set it down. She put one sandwich on each paper towel in front of her "customers." "There."

Crystal was enthralled watching Beka, memories flooding in of doing this very thing in this very kitchen. Except her parents had two waitresses.

Beka carefully poured their tea into the plastic disposable cups kept on the counter for easy access.

Crystal bit back a gasp as the liquid sloshed dangerously close to spilling once, but every drop stayed contained.

Jeremy wiped his brow with the back of his hand in mock relief when he was sure Beka couldn't see him.

Beka set their plastic cups in front of them and stood back. "Oh, chips."

She hurried to the counter, retrieved the bag of chips, and brought it over.

"Thank you so much, miss. This is a lovely place you have here." Crystal took a sip of her tea, holding her pinky finger extended. "I'll have to tell all my friends."

"Thank you, ma'am." Beka swept away, her head held high.

"You really get into this, don't you?" Jeremy murmured.

Crystal shushed him. "You can't play pretend halfheartedly."

"Miss?" Jeremy called.

Beka turned back toward him.

"Are you sure you wouldn't like to sit at our table and eat with us?"

Beka put her nose in the air. "Sir, I told you, waitresses don't eat with their customers."

Jeremy covered his grin with his napkin. "Oh. I see." He pointed to a stool at the counter. "I guess that's where waitresses eat, right?"

Beka looked where he was pointing, put her finger to her chin, and tapped it. "Yes," she said decisively. "That's the waitress spot."

After Beka was settled in at the "waitress spot" with her food, Jeremy glanced at Crystal. "Is it okay if I offer thanks for the food?"

Crystal nodded.

He said a short prayer for the food, and at the end he asked God to "Bless the hands that prepared it."

When he said, "Amen," Crystal looked up at him with a grin. "Think she noticed?" she asked in a low voice.

"And bless me," Beka said happily.

Jeremy grinned. "She doesn't miss a trick."

"Miss, this tuna is delicious," Crystal said.

Beka stopped eating and looked over at her. "Thank you, ma'am."

When they'd all finished, Crystal looked out the window. It was another hour at least until dark. She glanced over at Jeremy. "Do y'all have time to go for a walk?"

Jeremy looked pleased. "Sure."

Crystal smiled at Beka. "Beka, let's walk out to the barn. I want to show you something."

Beka slipped her apron off and walked over to Crystal. "What is it?"

"You'll see when we get out there."

All the way out to the pole barn, Beka peppered Crystal with questions. "Is it big?" was followed quickly by "Is it tiny?"

Crystal shook her head and stepped to the side of the door to switch the outside breaker on. They kept the electricity turned off when they weren't using this barn. Which was most of the time now.

She pulled on the rectangular wooden button, and the big door creaked open.

"Is it an animal?" Beka's voice was quiet. She slipped her hand into Jeremy's.

Crystal laughed. "No. No animals in this barn. Although my daddy used to say we sounded like laughing hyenas sometimes."

As they walked into the dusty barn, just like Crystal had the day of the private meeting, she imagined the McCord Players up on the stage acting their hearts out. They'd had so much fun here.

"What is this place?" Beka whispered.

"It's a theater my daddy built for my sister and me when we were not much older than you." Crystal pointed toward the stage. "We'd get up there and pretend to be anything you can think of." She hurried over to a closet in the corner, next to the bathroom. When she opened the door, she spied the big trunk of costumes in the corner, but the smell of moth balls propelled her backward. She turned to Jeremy and Crystal. "We'll let this air out a little while I show you the stage." She left the door ajar and led the way up to the stage.

"You'll get dusty," she warned.

Jeremy ruffled Beka's hair. "We'll wash, won't we, Little Bit?"

Beka nodded and bounded up the steps and onto the stage. She pranced from one end to the other, giggling all the way. "Miss Crystal, watch this." She jumped up in the air and spun around. "I'm a ballerina."

Crystal and Jeremy clapped.

"You come play." Beka motioned to them.

Jeremy grinned at Crystal. "You should feel right at home up there, but I don't remember the last time I was on stage." He stepped back and let her go up the short stairs ahead of him. "Probably graduation."

She looked over her shoulder at him. "That doesn't count. When's the last time you were on a stage and pretended?"

"Fifth grade. We put on *Cinderella*. Or our version of it, at least."

"And you were Prince Charming?"

He laughed. "I was one of the footmen."

Beka, who had been listening intently to their banter, clapped her hands together. "You be a prince, Daddy."

He looked down at her. "If you'll be my princess."

She shook her head. "I'm going to be the evil fairy, Malevolence."

"Ah. . ." Crystal said. "So we're doing *Sleeping Beauty*?"

"Yes." Beka bobbed her head once. "And you"—she pointed at Crystal—"can be Princess Aurora."

"I think you have a director in the making," Crystal said under her breath to Jeremy.

Beka pulled Jeremy to one side of the stage. "You stand here. It's not your turn yet."

Crystal watched with amazement as the little girl breezed through Aurora's birth and the evil fairy's curse. She jumped around acting out the parts and directing Crystal until she pricked her finger on an imaginary spinning wheel.

Crystal fell onto the stage with a plunk. Through her eyelashes she saw Beka look at her in surprise then look at her daddy.

"Now she'll have to sleep for a hundred years." Jeremy's voice sounded amused.

"Nuh-uh. You have to kiss her."

CHAPTER 25

Crystal cringed inside. How had she not seen this coming? She considered her options. Jump up and greatly disappoint a six-year-old director. Lie really still and hope that Jeremy had a diplomatic solution. She decided on the latter. She held her breath as she waited to see what he'd say.

But all she heard were heavy steps on the stage. Her heart pounded against her ribs. From under her eyelashes, she saw cowboy boots coming toward her. She felt him bend down over her.

"You don't have to—" she whispered, breaking off as his lips brushed hers gently.

"Awake, fair princess." His voice was very princelike.

Startled, she jerked her eyes open and stared into his amused gaze. Who was the professional here anyway? She fluttered her eyelashes. "Thank you, my prince."

He stood and offered her his hand. When she took it, he pulled her to her feet.

"The *end*," Beka yelled and clapped loudly.

"You're a quick study," Crystal said quietly through her smile.

Jeremy nodded. "It was an easy role."

"Prince?"

"Kissing you."

"Oh."

Before she could say any more, Beka almost knocked her down with a hug. "That was fun, wasn't it, Miss Crystal?"

Jeremy quickly turned away, but not before Crystal heard him snicker.

Crystal was in the sewing room, unpacking her things from her trip, when her cell phone rang. Her heart jumped and she scolded herself. Jeremy had only been gone two hours. It wasn't likely he was dying to talk to her. Sure enough, a glance at the caller ID showed it was Aaron.

She flipped it open with a grin. "Hey, big brother, how's it going in the Windy City?"

"Great. We're getting settled in. How's Home on the Range treating you?"

"Still good, actually." Her voice softened. "I love it."

"I'm glad. That eases my guilt considerably."

"Guilt?"

"About railroading you into doing it."

She laughed. "I knew you were giving me pointed looks that day in the barn. Was everyone in on it?" She balanced the phone on her shoulder while she slid her blouses from her duffel bag into a drawer.

"No. Just me. And only because I thought it would be the best thing for you right now, too."

She bumped the drawer shut with her hip and reached in the bag again. Her hand closed around her Bible. She walked over and placed it on the nightstand. "You were probably right. Why don't I just let you make all my important life decisions from now on?"

He chuckled. "That would last about two seconds. Then you'd get tired of it."

"Good point."

"I was actually calling to get your help in a decision. About Dad and Mom's welcome home party. Bree had an idea."

"Let's hear it."

"Considering their thirtieth anniversary was last week, what would you think if we made this a combination anniversary/welcome home barbecue and invited their friends and neighbors?"

"That sounds fun." And she was glad she was going to be here for it. She'd missed so much.

"Good. You know how iffy the weather can be the first week in May, though. What if it rains or turns off cool?"

She glanced out in the hallway of the simple two-story frame house. "I don't think the house could hold everyone."

Aaron sighed. "I hate to move it into town, but I don't guess the horses or Luke would take kindly to being run out of the barn so we could have it in there."

"No, but you know what? We could have it in the pole barn. We could put tables and chairs up on the stage even and have Mama and Daddy and their closest friends and family up there, then set everyone else up with tables and chairs on the floor."

"Cool," Aaron agreed. "I didn't pay much attention when we had our meeting out there, but it seems like it was pretty dirty."

Crystal looked down at her jeans, still streaked with dust. "Yes, I was out there tonight, and trust me, it's filthy. We'd have to have a workday."

"You were out at the pole barn tonight?" Aaron's voice was puzzled. "Why?"

Crystal hesitated. In their frequent e-mails, she'd purposely not mentioned her growing relationship with Jeremy. But she'd always been honest with her brother. "Jeremy and Beka came over and we went out to show Beka the stage. She's into pretend right now."

"Imagine a six-year-old girl into pretend. Hard to believe," he said teasingly.

She laughed. "Well, she's really into it. She was even our waitress all during supper."

"Ah, I see." His voice suggested he saw entirely too much. "So you and Jeremy are spending quite a bit of time together."

Why had she thought for a second that a secret could be kept in her family? Not that it was a secret, but she should have known Luke or Elyse would tell Aaron. "Quite a bit."

"I guess that first week didn't turn out to be such a hardship after all, huh?"

"Not so much."

He laughed. "Okay, I can tell when you don't want to talk about something. So how about Saturday for a workday?"

"Do you mean for those of us who are here? Or are you and Bree going to be able to come in?" She pulled her jewelry box from the bag and set it on the dresser.

"I think we could drive down Friday and spend the night. I think Bree would really like that."

Uh-oh. Crystal had sensed the last couple of times she'd talked to her sister-in-law that being a houseparent wasn't all sweetness and light, but she hated to pry. "Can y'all leave the boys?"

"We have a couple who will fill in for us any weekend. All we need to do is ask. So I'll take care of that tomorrow."

"Oh, Aaron, that would be awesome! I'll let Luke and Elyse know and call Kaleigh and Chance and see if they can get away." She caught a glimpse of her reflection in the dresser mirror, her smile huge, her eyes sparkling. How ironic that it hadn't been that long ago that she almost dreaded spending much time with her brothers and sisters. Now she couldn't wait.

"Great. I'll call Matthew. But make sure they know that if they have to choose, we'd rather them be at the party in two weeks than at the cleanup day."

"Boy, you sure are bossy. What do you think you are, the oldest or something?"

He laughed. "You said I could make all your decisions from now on."

"I take it back." She paused. "But seriously, I do need to ask a favor."

"Anything for you."

She walked over and ran her hand over the leather cover of her Bible. "Could you pray for me?"

"I've never missed a day of doing that since you left home, Crys. But it's good to hear you ask." He cleared his throat. "How are things going between you and God?"

She smiled at his directness, even as a lump came in her throat. "Well, I found my Bible. And I've been reading it again." She ran her hand over her eyes. "I know what I should do. I'm just having a hard time believing that He really wants me back after the life I've lived for the past seven years."

"I can relate to that. By the time Mama and Daddy adopted me, I'd lived a rougher life than most grown men ever do."

She sank down on the bed, grateful that he was trying to make her feel better but unwilling to let him make it seem like she was no worse than he had been. "Yeah, but Aaron, you were a kid who was in a terrible situation you didn't create. That's different."

"Just listen. Here's what I remember. One night, after I'd been in the family about a year, I wanted to get baptized but I was afraid to. I didn't want to let God down, and I was afraid I wouldn't be able to stop using the language I was used to. After all, I'd tried for a year and still slipped up occasionally."

She lay back on the bed and closed her eyes. She could remember her tender-hearted big brother and that night he was struggling as clearly as if it was yesterday.

"A wise little girl told me something that night that I've never forgotten."

"Me?" That part she didn't remember.

"Yes, you. You told me that Christians aren't perfect, but they are forgiven." She could hear emotion in his voice. "Hearing that changed my life."

She stared at the ceiling as tears leaked down the sides of her face onto the quilt. "Thanks, Aaron."

"Hang in there, sis. Better days are coming."

She swiped her eyes with the back of her hand. "I'll talk to you soon. Love you."

"You, too. And I'm praying for you."

When the connection was broken, she tossed the phone beside her on the bed and pushed to her feet. She needed air. And space. She needed to see the stars and think. She hurried down the stairs, grabbed a jacket from the hook by the door, and ran outside into the darkness.

She stepped off the porch and started walking down the lane. She looked up at the stars. They crowded together in the sky, like a huge audience gathered together to watch her. To cheer her on? Or to wait for her to mess up again?

Crystal had no idea where she was going until she glanced across the split-rail fence and saw the huge oak tree stump, illuminated by the moonlight. How many nights had she sat on that stump watching the stars? And praying?

She climbed over the fence and walked slowly over to the stump to sit down. She pulled her knees to her chest and thought of what Jeremy said about Lindsey after her funeral. That once she'd left God and everything she believed was right, she couldn't seem to find her way back. Those words had haunted Crystal ever since she'd first heard them.

Here I am, Lord.

A mess.

You know, I'm no different than Lindsey. Her sins were easier to see. But mine are just as black.

"I was just so mad." Her voice sounded loud in the empty night. "I didn't want to live without Cami. I thought You must hate me to do that to me." Hot tears fell on cold cheeks. She waved her hand at the sky and swiped at the tears. "Oh, I knew You didn't do it. You didn't make those kids drink and drive. But for as long as I can remember, I was taught that You are in control of everything. That made it hard to understand."

Aaron had talked to her about this every time he got a chance, but by the time she was past the initial anger enough to grasp the concept of a world where sin caused bad things to happen to good people and God made beauty from ashes, the chasm between her and God was so wide. . .

"That there was no crossing it," she whispered to the stars.

The tightness in her chest threatened to choke off her breath. "I wanted to come back." She lifted her face to the sky and let the tears cascade down her cheeks unchecked. "But then I'd ask myself, 'Why would You want me?'"

She sat without moving, looking up. So many dancing lights that they were uncountable. Suddenly she remembered a Bible verse her daddy had helped her learn when he was teaching her about the stars. "He counts the number of the stars; he calls them all by name."

Uncountable for her. But not only could God count them, He even knew their names.

She drew in a shuddering breath. Maybe there was hope for her after all.

Jeremy handed Beka her pink book bag and followed her into the classroom.

Kids darted here and there, making the most of their last few minutes of freedom before the bell rang. A freckle-faced boy chased a little girl with long black hair. "Give me that back!"

"Jessica, give Caleb his notebook." The teacher spoke firmly from where she stood at her desk, her back to them. Jeremy was reminded of the old adage about teachers and mothers having eyes in the back of their heads.

The little girl tossed the notebook at the boy and he fumbled it then picked it up off the floor. He stomped off to his desk in a huff.

Jeremy put his hand on the back of Beka's head and guided her gently toward the teacher.

Miss Davis turned around, her brown, shoulder-length hair swinging like a shiny curtain. "Beka, it's so good to see you again." She motioned to a desk near the front. "I've got your desk all ready." Beka carried her backpack to the desk.

Miss Davis smiled at Jeremy. "Mr. Buchanan, I didn't get a chance to tell you Monday when you stopped by but I'm so glad things worked out." She looked over at Beka, who was showing her book bag to the little black-haired girl. "We're thrilled to have Beka here." She lowered her voice. "I saw you on TV and my heart just went out to you." Her pretty, slightly round face reddened. "Your plea was so moving."

Embarrassed, Jeremy nodded. "I appreciate so many people caring."

"If there's anything I can do for you and Beka, if you need any help with anything. . ."

"Thank you. Right now we're fine." His answer seemed stilted, but he didn't know what to say.

"I'll keep a special eye on her." The woman really did seem sweet. And Jeremy was sure she was sincere.

After Lindsey left, it seemed like every single woman in the county made a point of offering to help the poor man left alone with a two-year-old. He understood they hadn't known he'd taken care of Beka largely alone even when Lindsey was still there. But he'd assumed that now they'd realize that he'd raised Beka for three years on his own before Lindsey took her.

The bell rang and the kids all hurried to their seats. He stepped over to Beka's desk. "I guess I'd better go."

She looked up at him and grinned. "Bye, Daddy."

No hug? No kiss? No "Please don't go"?

She turned to the little black-haired girl who was sitting beside her, and Jeremy knew he was forgotten.

Logically he knew Beka would be safe inside the kindergarten room, but he wanted to pull up a chair—even one of those tiny chairs—and sit in the corner and make sure.

He glanced up to see Miss Davis watching him with a sympathetic smile. She gave him a little wave and looked at the door. He guessed that was a not-very-subtle hint that he wouldn't be allowed to sit in the room after all. So he might as well leave.

In the school parking lot, he considered just waiting in his truck. It was only eight hours. His laughter echoed in the quiet cab. It'd be his luck Blair from the TV station would show up with her "live" camera crew and the noon news feature story would be "Paranoid Dad Refuses to Leave School Yard." He put the truck in reverse, backed out of his parking place, and slowly left the school grounds.

When he pulled up in front of his empty house, he had a sudden urge to check on the McCord cattle.

CHAPTER 26

Who was he kidding? He was going to see if he could find Crystal.

There. He had admitted it.

He bypassed the house for the barn and saddled Nacho.

As he trotted down the road, he thought of that day he'd first seen Crystal by the river. Only tiny sprigs of green had been scattered around then. Just enough to offer hope of a better time coming. And now all the greenery was in full bloom.

After he crossed the river, he scanned both sides of the road for any sign of humans. Finally, when he was about to give up and call her, he saw a small figure in the distance standing beside a horse.

He gave Nacho a signal and together they easily cleared the cattle guard and took off at a gallop down the field road. He slowed before he got to her, for fear she'd think there was something wrong—something other than his being lonely and wanting to see her.

She shielded her eyes and smiled up at him. "Hey, stranger. I wasn't expecting to see you today."

Holding the reins loosely, he shrugged. "Turns out they don't let dads stay at kindergarten."

She took off her work gloves and walked over to him. "Aww, you would have looked so cute in one of those little chairs."

He chuckled. "You don't know how close I came to trying that." He shifted the reins to one hand and slid easily to the ground. "But as nice as her teacher was, I was afraid she'd turn mean real fast if I tried."

Crystal touched his arm. "It must have been tough to leave her."

He nodded and kicked a twig, embarrassed to meet her eyes. "It's crazy how panicked I felt."

She shook her head. "Not at all crazy. You might be surprised to find that even parents who haven't been through what you have still panic on the first day of kindergarten."

He cut his gaze to hers. "I hadn't really thought about that. But I guess you're right."

She nodded. "Mama said when she left me and Cami the first day of school she just went home and cried her eyes out. Cleaned the house from top to bottom, sobbing the whole time."

He grinned. "Maybe I should go clean house."

She pulled the fencing pliers from her back pocket and held them out to him. "Or you could help me fix the fence."

He took them from her. "I'd do anything to get out of cleaning house. Now since Beka's all caught up in pretending, maybe she can pretend to be a housekeeper."

As he and Crystal worked without speaking, Jeremy marveled at how easy even their silences were now. He remembered all the lectures he'd given himself about not getting too attached to her, but those lectures were empty words compared to the fullness of his heart when he was with her.

He watched her hook the wire on the post, her hands enclosed in small leather gloves that were still too big. What would it be like to have forever with her? To be able to work and play and sleep beside her the rest of his life? His heart had no trouble imagining that. But when he stumbled across the opposite question—What would it be like not to have the rest of his life with her?—he couldn't wrap his mind around the possibility.

Crystal glanced at him. "So she liked the theater in the barn last night?"

"Hmm? Oh. Beka." He took a fence tie from her and nodded. "It was all she could talk about. Even this morning, she was almost as excited about that as she was about starting a new school."

"Wow. That's cool." She sat back on her feet. "And I have some good news. Next time we go out there to play, it should be a lot cleaner."

"Oh?"

"Yep. We're having a family workday Saturday to clean it up. We decided to turn Mama and Daddy's welcome home party into an anniversary barbecue bash for the whole county and have it in the pole barn. You're invited, by the way."

"To the barbecue or to the workday?"

A mischievous smile tilted her lips and her eyes twinkled. "Well, now that you mention it, it *will* take a lot of elbow grease to get that old barn cleaned up."

He groaned. "I thought that you were getting me *out* of housecleaning."

"Yes, but I didn't say anything about barn cleaning."

"I'll be there." As he said it, he knew he'd gladly scrub the dirtiest of barns if it meant spending the day with her. Realization slammed into him like a charging bull. He turned back to work before she could see the truth in his eyes.

He had completely fallen in love with Crystal McCord. And there was nothing he could do about it.

Crystal glanced around the campfire. Everyone looked tired but contented. And the barn was as clean as it had been back in the days of the McCord Players.

Chance and Kaleigh hadn't been able to come, but Matthew had made it in. He and Luke had built this wonderful campfire. At Crystal's request.

Jeremy shifted closer to her on the rock they shared with Beka, his breath warm against her ear. "Great idea ending the day with a fire."

Crystal grinned up at him. "You're the one who thought of the marshmallows."

He nodded toward Beka, who was letting Elyse's dogs lick the sticky marshmallow from her hands. "I think Beka has fallen in love."

What if Beka's not the only one? She quickly banished the thought from her mind.

Across the fire, Bree leaned back against Aaron as he whispered in her ear. They both looked so happy and relaxed. Bree had confided to her today that she loved the boys at the group home but was afraid she'd never be allowed into their inner city world because of her middle-class upbringing. She'd sounded so distraught when she said Aaron made fitting in look easy.

Crystal had reminded Bree that even though Aaron had been raised on those streets, love was the universal language. And once the boys realized that Bree was there because of love, they'd accept her. Crystal looked away from Aaron and Bree. Everywhere she turned her attention, it came back to love.

Beside them, Elyse pushed to her feet. "Is it okay if Beka walks with me to take the dogs home?" She grinned down at the sticky little girl. "And we'll wash her hands while we're there."

Crystal could see the hesitation in Jeremy's face, but he nodded. "Sure."

"Very brave," she said in a low voice as Elyse and Beka walked away. "I'm proud of you."

He shrugged. "Being able to let her go some is something I'm praying a lot about." He glanced over at Crystal, the reflection of the flames dancing in his eyes making them unreadable. "Among other things."

"What other things?" She wasn't sure she wanted to know, but she couldn't stop herself from asking.

Her phone rang before he answered. She considered just letting it ring. But the ringtone told her it was Mia and she'd already missed one call from her today.

"Hello?" She stood and stepped back from the fire.

"Crystal!"

"Yes, Mia. How are you?"

"I'm fine. But I have another private audition for you. And I think you'll get it. They specifically asked for you."

Crystal felt her throat constrict. She glanced toward the group around the fire and lowered her voice. "Broadway?"

"No, but close. It's barely off-Broadway and this time it's a lead role."

Crystal stared at the fire, particularly at Jeremy's back. Some things shouldn't be given up. She cleared her throat. "Mia, I've decided to take a break from New York for a while."

"A break?" Mia's voice went an octave higher. "You've had a break."

"I'm sorry. Just don't put me up for any more roles until you hear from me."

"Are you switching agents and this is your way of telling me?"

"No. You're the only agent I want. But right now, I'm just in a. . ." She looked back at the group. All her brothers and Bree were looking at her. Only Jeremy was pretending he couldn't hear her. She took another three or four steps away and turned her back. "I just need a break, Mia."

Mia gave a dramatic sigh. "Fine. Let me know when you're ready to start again."

"I will. And if you need to replace me with a working client, I understand."

"Don't be silly, Crys. We're friends. I'll be here when you come to your senses."

Crystal smiled. "Thanks. I'll talk to you later." She walked back to the campfire and sank down by Jeremy.

"You're turning down auditions, kid?" Luke looked puzzled.

She shrugged. "For now."

She glanced at Jeremy, but he appeared to be fascinated by the fire.

"So Jeremy. . ." Aaron gave Luke a hard look for asking personal questions in front of nonfamily, and Crystal couldn't help but smile. They'd been a tight-knit group in junior high and high school. Some things never changed. "Did I hear you say you're going to Oklahoma next week?"

Jeremy nodded.

Crystal glanced over at him. Oklahoma? This was the first she'd heard of it. "What for?"

"There's a herd of Black Angus for sale there that I'm interested in."

"Cool. So what will you do about Beka and school? Or is it a day trip?" It occurred to Crystal that if she ever wanted to switch careers, she could try law. She sounded like a cross-examiner.

"I'll be gone a couple days. Beka's going to stay at Mom and Dad's."

Wow. So he really was trying to get used to letting her out of his sight some.

Luke threw another log on the fire, and Aaron and Bree got into a long "smoke follows beauty" debate about the resulting smoke.

"You going to be okay leaving her?" Crystal asked softly under the cover of their loud banter.

He turned to look at her. "That remains to be seen. But like

227

I said, I'm praying about that."

"Among other things," she reminded him. Giving him every opportunity to share what the "other things" were.

But he just nodded.

Jeremy pulled into the unfamiliar barn lot and got out of the truck. The late afternoon sun, more show than heat now, did little to take the chill out of the unseasonably cool day. Jeremy lifted the backseat up and got his jacket out.

On the other side was a jacket his dad had left the last time they'd been out. Jeremy had always figured his dad would be with him when he got ready to buy livestock. They'd gone together a few years ago to get his dad and mom's cattle, with Beka and his mom in the backseat of the crew cab truck.

But this time, when his mom had offered to keep Beka so she wouldn't miss school, Jeremy had felt uneasy at the thought of his dad not being home, too. No matter how many times he reminded himself that Lindsey was dead and the threat to Beka was gone, he couldn't shake the unease. So even though he'd felt bad, he hadn't invited his dad.

Finally, right before he'd left home yesterday morning, his dad followed him out to the truck. "You know I'd go with you, son." His dad had rubbed his graying stubble. "But I think we'd both rest better if I stayed here and kept an eye on things."

Jeremy had smiled, glad that his paranoia wasn't his alone. "A burden shared is a burden halved," his grandpa always said, and that seemed fitting here.

So he'd headed to Oklahoma alone, in search of the perfect herd of cattle. He'd looked at several, but this last one he was scheduled to see had looked the best online.

The cattleman came out to meet him, right on time. The man's gruff voice matched his weather-beaten face. He stuck out his calloused hand. "H. B. Smith."

Jeremy shook his hand and introduced himself. "Glad to meet you."

Mr. Smith led the way to a small utility vehicle, much like the one the McCords had, and motioned for him to climb in. As they bounced across the bumpy hills, the older man talked about his cows. After he'd extolled their virtues, he looked across at Jeremy. "You probably wonder why I'm wantin' to sell. My daddy always taught me to ask that question no matter what you were buyin'."

"Yes, sir, I was curious why you'd sell the whole herd. Are you getting out of the cattle business?"

Mr. Smith pulled the utility vehicle up to the crest of a hill. The sun cast shadows across a small ranch house below. For a few seconds, the man didn't answer. Then he looked over at Jeremy. "Hard to believe, but I guess you could say I'm getting out of the business. For now, anyway. My wife, Evelyn, was diagnosed a few months ago with cancer. And her treatments are just wearing her out."

"Oh, I'm sorry," Jeremy murmured.

Mr. Smith gave him a crooked grin. "She's a fighter. And I have no doubt she's going to be fine. But you know that old saying, 'Seize the day'? That's what I'm doing. Life's too short for me to be out here messing with cattle while she's going through that alone." He looked around at the beautiful rolling hills surrounding them. "I've got enough money to make it if I never own another cow. But if I had to do without Evelyn, all the money in the world wouldn't matter."

Jeremy nodded, but the man's words hit him deep. Would he have the courage to "seize the day" with Crystal?

Two hours later, he left the ranch a poorer but happier man. The sun was setting at his back and he debated stopping in town for a quick supper or heading onward. Common sense finally won, applauded by a loud growl from his stomach. He looked for a drive-through, but the closest thing to it was an old dilapidated building that had big trucks parked all around it. Inside, he found a table and was barely seated when the waitress came to bring a glass of ice water and take his order. After she left, he pulled out his cell phone and called his parents' house.

When his dad answered, Jeremy said, "You're speaking to an official, honest-to-goodness cattleman now."

"That's great, son. I'm so happy for you."

Jeremy heard his dad call to his mom, "It's Jeremy. He's a real rancher now."

Then his dad's voice came back over the line. "What did you get?"

For the next few minutes, they talked specifics about the herd then his dad laughed. "There's a little monkey here climbing on me, wanting to talk to her daddy."

Jeremy grinned. "Put her on, please."

"Daddy?"

"Hey, Little Bit, how you doing tonight? You got your pj's on?"

"Daddy, Grandpa says you're a real rancher now. Are you? What were you before?"

"I am, kiddo. Before today I was just a man with a dream." Jeremy smiled. "Did you have fun today?"

He listened to her talk about her day. The third time a yawn interrupted her words, he knew what time it was. "Good night, sleepyhead. Gran will tuck you in and I'll be there tomorrow when you wake up." He'd be in sometime after midnight, but as much as he wanted to, he knew he shouldn't get Beka out of bed to take her home. He would eat breakfast with her before school, though.

"Good night, Daddy. Love you." After he hit the END button, he sent a heartfelt thanks to God for bringing Beka back to him.

His food still hadn't arrived, so he scrolled down to Crystal's number and stopped, his thumb poised over the SEND button. *"Seize the day,"* he remembered Mr. Smith saying. *Seize the day.* He looked around the greasy truck stop, with its vinyl-top tables punctuated by truckers, each one eating alone. This was the day.

CHAPTER 27

Jeremy hit the button to put the call through.

"Hey, cowboy, how's the trip going?" Crystal sounded happy to hear from him.

He picked up a straw and opened it, then slid it into the water glass. "Livin' the dream, babe. I'm officially a cattle owner."

"Oh, Jeremy, that's awesome. How many head did you buy?"

"Around five hundred. Some of them will be delivered tomorrow." He fiddled with the straw wrapper. "I spent a lot, but I think I got a good deal."

"I'm sure you did. I'm so happy for you." Crystal paused. "There's just something about living and raising a family on a ranch that can't be beat."

"Yep. That's what I always thought." Was she thinking about the future in terms of him? Or was he delusional? He glanced down at the straw wrapper. He'd shredded it.

"So when will you be home?"

Funny, how everything she said seemed personal, but then when he analyzed the words, they could be purely conversational. "Sometime after midnight. Since I stopped for supper, it will probably be closer to one or two."

"I bet you'll be on cloud nine when they deliver your livestock.

232

Want me to bring the guys over and help you get them settled in?"

"That would be good, Crys. Dad and I will be there. And Dad's two hired hands. But we can use all the help we can get." He took a sip of his water.

"Your food will be out in a minute, hon," the waitress called as she sashayed by him with an armload of plates.

He nodded.

"What time should the cattle be there?"

"The first batch will probably be in around noon." He hesitated. "If you want to come early, I'll have some coffee ready."

He wasn't sure if she realized that invitation was a personal one, but if she showed up early with Slim and the boys in tow, he'd just make more coffee.

"I'd love to." Her voice was soft. "It's been weird, you being gone."

Relief at hearing her say those words made his stomach do a flip. "We've seen each other a lot since that first day at the river. It's odd not seeing you, too." He took a big gulp of his water. "I miss you."

The waitress shoved his plate under his elbow. "Here you go, hon." Her loud voice drowned out any response Crystal might have made.

"Hold on a minute," he said into the phone. He forced a smile. "Thank you."

"Need anything else?" She waved her hand at the cheeseburger plate, overflowing with french fries.

"No, thank you."

As soon as she was gone, he put the phone back up to his ear. "I'm so sorry."

"Oh, that's okay. I'd better let you eat. I'll see you tomorrow. Drive carefully."

"Okay. 'Night."

" 'Night."

He stared at the phone in his hand. Had she said she missed him, too? Or not? Why hadn't he asked her to repeat it? He started to slip the phone into his pocket then yanked it back up. When was he going to learn? Seize the day. He hit REDIAL.

"Jeremy?" she said, her voice sounding puzzled. "Is everything okay?"

"Yes." He could feel his ears burning. "Everything's fine. I'm sorry for bothering you, but a minute ago when I told you I missed you, the waitress showed up with my food and I didn't hear what you said." He stared at his cheeseburger plate, his appetite gone. Why had he called her back? Seizing the day didn't mean losing his mind.

"I said I missed you, too." He could hear the amusement in her voice. She probably thought he was crazy. "I'm glad you called back to ask."

He grinned. "Oh. Well, good, then. Good night."

A muffled giggle came through the line. "Good night, Jeremy."

He hung up, suddenly starving again.

"I can't believe we're playing hooky." Crystal linked her arm with Elyse's as they walked down the sidewalk in old Hardy town.

"*We're* not playing hooky. *You* are. I just happened to have a cancellation."

Crystal grinned. "Either way, I'm glad you came with me."

"You just didn't want to drive the farm truck."

"Well, I admit I wasn't looking forward to bouncing and putt-putting all the way here. But mostly I'm glad for your company."

"I'll accept that." Elyse motioned toward the line of quaint little gift shops just ready to open. "Do you know exactly what we're looking for?"

Crystal shook her head. "The perfect gift for a new rancher. That doesn't cost a lot."

"So"—Elyse gave her a sideways glance—"nothing but the best will do. As long as it's cheap."

Crystal snickered at her blunt assessment. "Well, it's the thought that counts. And I *am* unemployed."

A woman, obviously a shopkeeper, stepped out on the sidewalk and turned her sign from CLOSED to OPEN.

"Let's go in here." Crystal dragged her sister into the store. "Look for anything that says *cows* or *cattle* or *rancher*."

"Look at this," Elyse said, pointing toward one of many small rectangular wooden signs.

Crystal read it aloud. "COW COUNTRY. . .WATCH YOUR STEP." She laughed. "Cute, but not exactly what I had in mind." Her gaze went to the bottom row of signs and she gasped. "This is it. It's perfect."

Elyse walked over. "That was easy. Let's see it."

Crystal held it up.

"HOME IS WHERE THE HERD IS," Elyse read slowly. "Oh, that is perfect."

Crystal carried the sign to the cash register and paid for it.

Back out on the sidewalk, she looked at Elyse. "It's really good, but it's not exactly what I was hoping for."

"What?" Elyse put her hands on her hips in mock indignation. "Are you this picky when you're buying me a gift?"

Crystal blushed but was spared answering when she spotted a junk store a few yards down the sidewalk. "This place looks neat."

Elyse chuckled but followed her in.

Crystal gasped. Stepping inside was like being transported back into the past. An old Radio Flyer wagon in the storefront window was filled with a Kewpie doll, a jack-in-the-box, a tattered copy of *Five Little Peppers and How They Grew*, and a variety of other old toys. A giant red ribbon was tied around the whole ensemble.

Crystal walked around in wonder. She'd been in antique stores before, but they'd been stuffed with high-priced furniture. On these shelves, Cabbage Patch dolls mingled with I LIKE IKE campaign buttons. Old copies of the *Farmer's Almanac* rested on a rickety turntable from several generations ago. Crystal picked up a set of jacks and a red rubber ball. For a buck or two, a person could buy a piece of her past and preserve it.

Of course in her case, most of her childhood was preserved in a bedroom at the top of her parents' staircase. Just waiting. She laid the jacks and ball back down.

Her gaze lit on an old doctor's bag and she smiled. An exact replica of the one she'd taken out in the pasture the day Anastasia had given birth. She picked it up and ran her hand down the uncracked brown leather. It was in excellent condition. She opened it. No unpleasant odor or rips in the lining. The price tag caught her eye and she nodded. The perfect gift.

Elyse, apparently mesmerized by the collection of old books, looked up as Crystal walked by. "Did you find it?"

"Um-hm." Crystal held it up.

"Oh. A doctor's bag. Interesting."

Crystal laughed at the droll tone in her voice. "I'll explain it later."

Elyse followed her up to the cash register. "I'll be looking forward to it."

After Crystal paid for the bag, she glanced at her cell phone. It was nine thirty and she wanted to be at Jeremy's at eleven for coffee. She explained the significance of the satchel to Elyse on the way to the dollar store.

"Ew. You're getting him a satchel full of stuff to use when his cows have a difficult birth?"

"Well, he can, but it's more of a joke. Or a remembrance, I guess. Of that day that Anastasia gave birth to Prince."

Elyse shook her head. "You make cows seem like so much fun.

Almost makes me wish they didn't scare the living daylights out of me."

"If you'll just go with me out to see Prince—"

" 'Almost' being the key word there," Elyse said firmly. "Thanks but no thanks."

After a quick stop at the dollar store, Elyse eased the car out onto the highway and headed for Shady Grove.

Crystal bounced in her seat. She never sped, but her cautious sister had a habit of driving three to five miles under the speed limit. Usually not a problem. But today. . .

"Any chance you'll move back to stay?" Elyse's gaze stayed on the road.

Crystal had been waiting for one of her brothers or sisters to ask her that question. But she wasn't expecting it right now. "There's a chance. I think I'll stay a while after Mama and Daddy get back."

"Oh good! You just need a break?"

Since Elyse had been gone with Beka to take the dogs home during the infamously overheard conversation with Mia by the campfire, Crystal stared at her suspiciously. Had one of the guys or Bree told her?

Elyse glanced away from the road long enough to give Crystal a puzzled look that surely couldn't be feigned.

"Yeah. A break."

"Mama and Daddy would be thrilled to have you around. We all would. And you're welcome to bunk with me after they get back, if you want to."

Crystal shrugged. "I'm pretty comfortable in the sewing room." She glanced at the speedometer and resisted the urge to ask Elyse to pick up the pace just to the limit. On the other hand, she'd considered talking to her sister about the future and here was the perfect opportunity. She respected Elyse's quiet wisdom and completely trusted her. "I've been thinking about something. But this is just between you and me, okay?"

"Sure."

"Remember when Allie Montgomery mentioned that drama day camp?"

Elyse nodded, still watching the road.

"Then we got those books at Coffee Central."

Elyse nodded again.

"So now we've cleaned up the pole barn. . ."

Elyse slapped one hand on the steering wheel and flashed Crystal a quick smile. "How perfect!"

Crystal chuckled at her sister's contagious enthusiasm. "But I'm not ready to commit yet. I'll decide by the time Mama and Daddy get home Friday night and talk to them about using the barn if I want to do it."

"So what play would you do?" Elyse whispered.

Crystal laughed. "You don't have to whisper. We're the only ones in here." She thought about the question. "I don't know. What do you think?"

"Remember that one we did where Spring didn't want to let Summer come? That would be a really good one. Simple enough for all ages, but you put humor in to appeal to the older kids."

Crystal nodded. She remembered it now that Elyse brought it up. Funny how she hadn't thought of her plays in years. She used to write one every six months or so.

Elyse gave her an appraising gaze. "I guess those plays are still in your bedroom?"

"I guess so." Crystal sighed and slumped against her seat belt.

"Do you want me to go look for them?" Elyse's voice was filled with sympathy.

"No, I'll do it. But thanks." She'd conquered a lot of the mystery of the room just by opening the door and then getting her Bible from the nightstand. She could surely go in and get the plays. Suddenly, she remembered how she'd told Elyse that she'd never be ready to go in the room. Maybe she needed to quit using that word so much.

Jeremy glanced at the kitchen clock as he put the coffee on to brew. One minute till eleven. He didn't know which he was more excited about—Crystal coming over early for coffee or the fact that his cattle were arriving in about an hour. He slid the filter holder in with a rueful grin and poured the water in. As much as he hated to admit it, Crystal probably trumped the cows as far as excitement factor.

When he heard her old farm truck pull into the driveway, his heartbeat accelerated. He was pretty sure the cattle delivery truck wouldn't cause that reaction. He took his best coffee mugs out of the cabinet and set them on the table then got the cream out of the refrigerator and put it by the sugar bowl. There. He was ready.

The doorbell rang and he walked slowly into the foyer to answer it. "Crystal, good to see you."

And it was. Dressed in faded jeans, a blue shirt that matched her eyes, and a beat-up cowboy hat that he'd guess was one of her brothers' castoffs, she was still prettier than any model he'd ever seen.

She slipped off her hat as she stepped inside. "The coffee smells delicious."

"Come on in." He motioned her to follow him. In the kitchen, he reached for the coffeepot. "Have a seat."

"Wait." She held up a familiar brown leather satchel. "I brought you something."

He stopped with his hand still extended toward the coffeepot and raised an eyebrow. "You thought my cattle might be sick?"

She smiled and blushed. For the first time he noticed a smattering of freckles across her nose. "No, silly. This is for you. I figured the Buchanans needed their own official calf-birthing kit to pass down through the generations."

He stared at it. "For me? This isn't the same one you had that day?"

She shook her head. "Nope. This is your very own."

He took it and opened it. She stepped close to him and watched him lift the items out. There were all the same things she'd pulled from the bag the day they'd helped the cow give birth.

He grinned. "This is amazing, Crystal." Something in the bottom caught his eye and he reached in and fished it out. "What's this?" It was rectangular and flat, wrapped in the Sunday comics.

She shrugged, her chin almost touching his shoulder. "Looks like the good rancher fairy left you a welcome-to-the-cattle-business present. You'll have to open it and see."

He ripped the paper away carefully, holding it out in front of him.

She gave him a look of feigned disbelief. "What? You don't trust me?"

He glanced down at her sparkling eyes. "Most of the time I do."

He held the sign up and read it. HOME IS WHERE THE HERD IS. He grinned at her. A couple of years ago, he'd have agreed. But today he knew his home was wherever Beka. . .and Crystal were. "Thank you," he said softly. "That's my kind of sign."

"It reminded me of you. I love how you've waited for this dream to come true."

He turned toward her and looked down into her unwavering gaze. "I love—"

"Knock, knock." His dad burst through the back kitchen door. "Got any coffee around this—" He stopped like someone had knocked the breath out of him. "Oh. Sorry."

Crystal casually took one step away, and Jeremy smiled. "Hi, Dad. We were just about to get a cup." He set the satchel on the counter and got another mug from the cabinet. "You're just in time."

"I saw y'all's farm truck out front and thought Luke had gotten

240

off work and come by to help unload cattle." His dad's smile was sheepish as he directed his words to Crystal. "I don't usually just barge in. I'm pretty excited about seeing Jeremy's cattle." He sat down at the table.

"I don't blame you," she said. "That's why I came early, too. For the cows"—she looked toward Jeremy, who was holding the coffeepot—"and the coffee."

Jeremy poured all three of them mugs of coffee.

They'd barely finished the first cup when an engine roared outside.

Crystal slipped her mug into the sink and turned to face him and his dad with a big grin. "Party's over. Sounds like the cows just came home."

Crystal leaned against the corral fence and looked out over the green hills, dotted with cattle.

"Hard to believe they're finally here." The pride in Jeremy's voice as he came up behind her made her smile.

She turned to look at him. "I've never seen prettier cows anywhere."

He coughed.

"What?"

"I know you didn't just call my cattle pretty."

She gasped in mock indignation. "Well, they *are* pretty."

He shoved his hat back on his head. "Whatever."

She laughed and pointed to two calves chasing each other. "Are they pretty?"

"You never give up, do you?" His grin belied his words.

"Rarely."

"In the spring, when we have a whole new batch of calves, *then* you can say they're pretty. And I'll agree."

She shivered in spite of the sun. He was talking like she was going to be here in the spring.

And in that moment, she realized she was counting on it.

CHAPTER 28

Crystal dropped the last empty box in the hall with a hollow *thump* and ruffled the dust from her hair. "This is all Jeremy's fault," she muttered to the closed door in front of her. She'd planned to just rush into the room, get her plays, and get out. But no. When she'd seen how excited Jeremy was about his future as he'd proudly unloaded his cattle, she'd realized how badly she needed to put the past to rest so she could face her own future. So she'd come home, taken a quick shower, and headed to the attic to get boxes. And now here she stood. Ready to put the past to rest. Supposedly.

She knew she could open the door. She'd done that twice already. *Third time's a charm*, she thought, as she twisted the knob and pushed the door open. From the doorway, her gaze took in the matching dressers, beds, desks, and, at the end of the room, a small bookshelf between the windows. She should have come back in here that first night after Cami died. By not facing the familiar, she'd let it become foreign and terrifying.

She grabbed a box in each hand and trudged over to her dresser. Might as well start with the easiest task first. As she reached to open the first drawer, she noticed an unfamiliar book on the oak dresser top. She picked it up and ran her hand over the shiny cover in wonder. The school yearbook from her senior year. Had Mama mentioned that it came in the mail after she went to New York? Maybe. Probably.

For the last seven years, Crystal had been especially adept at blocking out what she didn't want to face. But today was about facing something bigger. And if she opened that cover, she might never get back to the room. She set it over by the door to take with her when she was done.

Suddenly impatient to get the whole thing over with, she yanked open the first drawer. Neatly folded T-shirts, one or more of almost every color imaginable, were packed inside. As she pulled them out, she swallowed hard at the memories attached to a couple of pieces of fabric sewn together with a design on the front. She stacked them on her bed, remembering an online article about making a quilt out of old T-shirts.

Twenty minutes later, she was kicking herself for not working up the courage to do this when she'd first gotten to the ranch. Fashion had changed a lot in seven years, but these work jeans and shirts would have worked fine during her weeks of looking after things. She put several outfits over to the side to wear in the future when she needed to knock around with the cows and then scooted the two boxes to the middle of the floor. Even without the T-shirts and work clothes she'd saved out, they were full. And all her dresser drawers were empty.

She stood and carried a smaller box to her desk and opened the drawer. Her plays filled the space, some printed from the computer, some handwritten. She plunked down in the desk chair and flipped through them. As she skimmed the one about Spring and Summer, she smiled. She'd assumed that reading her compositions with adult eyes would make her realize they weren't as good as she remembered. But this wasn't bad at all. It would be great to teach and perform for a drama day camp. She scooped the plays into the small box, set it by the door with the yearbook, and snagged an empty box. All that was left in her desk were a few odds and ends—paperclips, ink pens, a neat stack of clean notebook paper.

She walked over to Cami's desk and opened the drawer. And shook her head. She should have known. A few wrinkled pages of blank notebook paper. A pen. And a pencil with the lead broken off. For Cami, school had been a nice place to meet friends. What studying she'd done had been done sitting on the bed. Or even the floor.

Crystal shut the drawer and faced the bookshelf. A corkboard half filled with snapshots was propped on top of it. A group shot of all the McCord kids caught her eye and she leaned in to get a better look. One of the last times they put on a "production" out at the barn. Cami was holding up two fingers behind Luke's head, totally unaware that Kaleigh was doing the same thing to her. Typical. She started to take it down then pulled her hand back. The pictures were part of their lives. And there was still a lot of corkboard to fill.

She squatted down in front of the small bookshelf she and Cami had split. Crystal's side had her favorites—classics old and new, like *Little Women, A Wrinkle in Time, Pride and Prejudice.* As she slid her fingers down the spines of the books, she stopped. Uh-oh. *The Adventures of Tom Sawyer* and *The Adventures of Huckleberry Finn.* Those were Kaleigh's. Borrowed and never returned. She slipped them out and dropped them on her bed. Better late than never.

Cami's top shelf was packed with acting magazines. Crystal glanced over her shoulder at the beds. There was no telling how many hours they'd spent sitting cross-legged on those beds while Cami read acting tips aloud and made Crystal repeat them back to her. People thought of Cami as the flighty twin, but she was serious about acting. And determined that Crystal be, too.

Oh, Cami, I miss your determination and your energy. A bittersweet smile played across Crystal's lips as she pulled the magazines off the shelf and put them in the empty box. *Who am I kidding? I miss you. Period.*

She dragged the box of magazines over to join the other boxes in the middle of the room and cast a wary glance at the closet. She'd taken all her own hanging clothes to New York. So what was left would be Cami's. That cute little blue sundress that she loved so much. The silver sequined formal she'd worn when she'd been crowned homecoming queen.

A lump formed in Crystal's throat, but she bit her lip hard and slid the door open.

She blinked and leaned in to examine the tiny space. It was empty.

Why would that be? Her mama had specifically told Elyse that she was leaving their room for Crystal to face.

Her heart pounded as she ran over to Cami's dresser and yanked open the top drawer. Empty. She opened the next one. Same thing. Each drawer she opened was as empty as her savings account. She fell down on her knees and opened the bottom drawers one at a time. Nothing. Until the last drawer. A folded piece of notebook paper was all that was inside. She picked it up and opened it, immediately recognizing the handwriting that filled the whole page as being her mother's. It was dated at the top. Four years ago.

Dear Crystal, she read and sank back to sit cross-legged on the floor.

> *If you found this letter, it means you finally faced your fears about your bedroom. I'm so proud of you. Cami would be, too. Honey, everyone deals with grief in their own way. Losing Cami has been hard on all of us. Especially you, her twin. The other half of her, she used to say.*

A teardrop fell onto the paper and Crystal swiped at her eyes. She hadn't even realized she was crying. She blinked to clear her vision and looked back at the paper.

You're probably wondering where Cami's clothes are. (If you haven't already run downstairs to ask me.) I hope the answer to that question doesn't upset you.

I always intended for you to go through her things. It seemed right somehow. I was hoping you'd ask me or one of the other girls to help you but I knew you needed to be there. Until today when Mrs. Shelton from church called and said a family down on Turkey Trot Road had their house burn to the ground last night. The dad is unemployed, they let their insurance lapse, and they lost everything. One daughter, a senior in high school, and she's the same size as you and Cami were three years ago.

Honey, I'm sorry, but my conscience wouldn't let me leave these clothes packed away upstairs when someone needs them. Cami would want her to have them. And I know you would, too, if you were thinking clearly. No one has a more giving heart than you do.

Crys, in a way losing you was worse than losing Cami. Because even though we'll always miss her, we know where Cami is and that she's better than okay. I hope the fact that you're reading this letter means you've come home to us to stay. At least in your heart. That would be an answer to my prayers.

Love, Mama

Crystal let the paper drop to her lap as the sobs shook her shoulders. She was glad her mother had put Cami's clothes to good use, but tears flowed freely down her face as she wept for Cami and the future on earth she'd never have. And for their family and the awful pain they'd dealt with—essentially losing two daughters at once. And for herself. And the confused thing she'd called life since she left here.

She got the message her mother was trying to send her, loud and clear.

Death with God was just the beginning of a journey. But life without God was no life at all.

Jeremy set his fork on his plate and pushed back from the table a little. "That was delicious, Mom. As usual."

Crystal nodded. "Mrs. Buchanan, everything was so good."

Luke and Elyse echoed her words. And Jeremy's dad nodded. "Just wait until you try her tunnel-of-fudge cake."

Jeremy's mom blushed, but she was beaming. "Thank you. If y'all like it, I thought that's what I'd bring to the party next Saturday."

Jeremy saw a slight frown flit across Crystal's face. "Are you sure the ladies from church don't mind providing the desserts and side dishes?" She smiled. "I know they'll be better if y'all make them, but we were prepared to pay someone to cater."

His mom put her napkin on the table. "Don't be silly. We're thrilled to be a part of this celebration. It'll be more fun this way."

"What about the barbecue?" his dad asked.

Luke cleared his throat. "Bart Davis from church volunteered to do all the smoking and barbecuing if we provide the meat."

"Well, then"—Jeremy's mom clapped her hands once as if that settled it—"he's the best in the country. So it sounds like the food is taken care of."

Elyse nodded. "We sure do appreciate it."

Jeremy's dad glanced into the living room, where Beka was playing with her doll. "Isn't Beka's teacher Bart Davis's daughter?"

Jeremy's mom nodded. "That's right, she is."

"Patti?" Crystal said. "I didn't know she was a teacher. We went to school together."

His mom smiled. "She's really taken with Beka."

"I think she's taken with the fact that Beka has a young, handsome, single daddy," his dad said.

Jeremy choked on the tea he'd just sipped. Had his dad lost his mind? "Oh, I don't—"

Crystal touched his hand. "Well, why wouldn't she be?"

Jeremy closed his hand around hers. "Thanks." He was startled that she'd spoken up, but it made him feel good down to his toes.

"I could think of several reasons why," Luke drawled. He grinned at Jeremy. "But then I'm not your parents or your girlfriend."

Crystal's face turned a pretty pink at the laughter that followed, but she didn't pull her hand away.

When the dishes were done, they all tromped outside to the patio to enjoy the early May sunshine. Jeremy slipped his arm around Crystal's waist. "So are you really my girlfriend?" he murmured against her vanilla-scented hair.

She looked up at him, her blue eyes wide. "You tell me."

He chuckled, as much at how his heart was slamming around in his chest as at anything else. "If it's up to me, then I know the answer."

She smiled. "Then I guess you know."

The sun suddenly got brighter, the grass greener, the sky bluer. How had one reluctant cowgirl breezed into town and turned his world on its end?

Elyse's brown eyes widened and she lowered her voice so that the whole restaurant wouldn't hear her. "You're really moving back into your room?"

Crystal smiled. "Well, not permanently. But yes, for the rest of the time I stay here. Kaleigh will be home tomorrow night after her finals and she'll need her room."

"Um-hum. And you're okay with changing rooms?"

"I really am, Elyse. The other night—cleaning things out—was tough. But I've let this go for too long. There's no reason not to sleep in my bed and let Kaleigh have hers."

"Do you want me to cancel my dog club meeting tonight and help you?" Elyse looked at the time on her phone.

"No. Especially since it starts in ten minutes. And what would your 4-H members think?"

"One of the moms could handle it."

Crystal shook her head. "No. I'm glad you asked me to meet you for an early supper before your meeting. It was great getting out for a while, especially since Jeremy had something to go to at Beka's school." As she said it, she felt a twinge similar to the one she'd had when he'd first mentioned he had plans tonight. After his big declaration Sunday, he hadn't referred to their relationship anymore. Which was fine. And he hadn't invited her to go to Beka's program with him. Which was fine, too.

Sympathy played across Elyse's face. "You're not worried about Patti Davis, are you? It's obvious Jeremy's head over heels about you."

Crystal sighed. "No. I'm not worried about anyone else. But between you and me, I would love to go to Beka's program." She smiled. "I mean. . .I am sort of into drama."

Elyse took one last sip of her drink and set it on the table. "Maybe he's afraid to rush you."

"Maybe." It could be. The thought made her heart a little lighter. "Thanks." She stood and gave Elyse a hug. "I'm going to run home, move my things from one room to the other, and turn in early."

Halfway home, bouncing along in the old farm truck, she heard her cell phone ring from somewhere in her purse. She seriously needed to get some custom ringtones. In New York, it hadn't mattered because she'd kept it on mute so much of the time, thanks to rehearsals and performances. She kept her eyes on the road as she slid her hand into her bag. But now she'd like to know who was calling instead of having to do it the old-fashioned way and answer it. She pulled it out and flipped it open. "Hello?"

"Hi." Jeremy's voice poured over her like warm sunshine. "Are you almost ready?"

"What?"

"Um. . .you were going to ride with us, weren't you?" He sounded hesitant. "Or were you driving?"

CHAPTER 29

A split second of panic exploded through her. Jeremy obviously assumed she was attending the program. She released a huffy breath. Well, good grief. How was she to have known? They definitely had to work on their—no, his—communications skills if this relationship was going to last. And she hoped it did, for say, a hundred years or so. She grinned at her thoughts and glanced down at her clothes. Acceptable for a school program. "Sure, I'll ride with y'all. Are you gonna come by and pick me up?"

"In about ten minutes, if that's okay."

"Perfect." She smiled at the phone. "Perfect," she repeated.

"Good. See you then."

Ten minutes later, she was a little breathless, but ready and waiting.

As soon as he pulled up, she ran out. Her mama would have croaked if she'd been here, but she wasn't. And Crystal was a little past the high school dating scene anyway. Plus, he'd have come in if she'd waited. She laughed as she hurried out to the truck. She was making excuses to the mama in her mind. Sad.

When she climbed in, a big grin spread across his face. "You look nice."

She glanced down at the jeans and her red shirt. "Thanks." She turned around to look at Beka. "You are a super-duper bumblebee."

"I'm going to put my antennae on when I get there." Beka held up pipe cleaners with fuzzy balls on the ends glued onto a headband.

"That's a good idea. Just to be sure they don't get smushed." Crystal bounced slightly in her seat. She was so excited about seeing a kids' play.

"So. . ." Jeremy said quietly. "Had you forgotten about the play?"

She raised her eyebrows. "No. Why?"

"Well, it sounded like you were driving when I called you a while ago. And right before we left the house, I saw the farm truck go by."

She studied his face, so kind, so sweet, so. . .clueless. "I didn't *forget* about the play. I just didn't know I was invited."

"You didn't—" He lifted one hand from the steering wheel and slapped his forehead. "I'm an idiot." He snorted and shook his head. "I'm sorry. I thought. . . I just assumed you'd go with us."

And in a New York guy that kind of assumption might have made her feel taken for granted, but with Jeremy, it just made her feel included and necessary. "Well, you did say Beka had a program tonight. But I thought you were just letting me know where y'all were going to be."

He gave her a rueful grin. "So is it okay? I mean, did you want to go?"

She glanced back at Beka, who was humming a song to herself. Then she brought her gaze back to rest on him. "More than anything."

His brows drew together. "You do know this is an elementary program? It won't be what you're used to."

She clapped her hands together and bounced a little. "I'm counting on that."

He blew out a laugh as he eased the truck into the school parking lot. "Are you excited?"

"Hey. We're all excited. It's opening night." She turned around and grinned at the bumblebee in the back. "Right, Beka?"

"Right!" Beka pumped her fist in the air and they all three laughed.

When they got inside the school building, a dark-haired woman rushed to meet them. "There's my other bumblebee." She looked up at Jeremy with a sweet smile that only faltered a little when she saw Crystal. "Crystal McCord. It's good to see you."

"Hi, Patti. You, too." Crystal had never been close to the bubbly brunet, but she'd always liked her.

"I heard you were back in town." Patti brought her attention back to Jeremy. "Temporarily."

Crystal stepped up beside Jeremy. "Yes, well—"

Patti took Beka's hand and waved over her shoulder at Jeremy and Crystal. "C'mon, sweetie. We need to get those antennae on and get you ready."

Jeremy winked at Crystal as they walked into the auditorium.

"I have butterflies," she whispered as they settled into the third-row center aisle seats.

He motioned toward the pulled curtain. "You planning on getting up there tonight?"

"No. But I always feel a little butterfly-ish for the people on stage. It goes with the territory." Not to mention that when it was over, she'd probably see several people she hadn't seen in years. Since the accident.

"Ahh. . .I see." His smile was tender, and she had a feeling he really did see.

Her phone rang and she jumped. "Glad that happened now," she whispered. She flipped it open. "Hello," she murmured.

"Crystal!" Mia screamed. "You won't believe it."

Jeremy and all the people sitting around them were looking at her.

"Mia, there's a performance about to start," she whispered.

Mia immediately took the cue and lowered her voice, but excitement still vibrated in her tone. "Performance?" she hissed. "Are you in the city?"

"No, I'm in Arkansas. It's a—"

"Never mind." She raised her voice again. "You have to be here by noon tomorrow. You got a callback. But they want you to audition for the youngest sister part."

Crystal blinked, trying to process what Mia was saying. "A lead role?"

"Yes. But you have to be here by noon. That's why I booked you a red-eye flight out of Memphis before I called you. Do you have a pen?"

Crystal reached for her purse. But Jeremy slipped his pen from his pocket and held it out to her. She looked up into his eyes, and the disappointment there took her breath away. He'd obviously heard every word, or at least enough to get the gist of the conversation.

She quickly scratched down the flight info on the back of a feed store receipt and hung up, trying to ignore the stares of the people around her. She realized belatedly that she should have gone out as soon as her phone rang.

She looked up at Jeremy again. "I'm sorry." It sounded so inadequate. "This is for a Broadway lead." She handed him his pen.

He took it and nodded, his jaw set as if chiseled from stone.

"Jeremy, I have to go for my agent. It would really let her down if I didn't. And she's worked so hard." She reached over and touched his arm. "But I'm *not* going to get the role. A lead role on Broadway." She laughed. "The chances of that happening after all

255

these years. . ." She shook her head. "You'd have a better chance of getting Luke to go on a blind date."

A smile tilted one corner of his mouth just for a second. He pulled his keys out of his pocket and stuffed them into her hand. "Take my truck back to the ranch. Dad and Mom will be here in a few minutes. We'll get a ride with them and come by and get it later."

"Are you sure?"

"Positive."

She leaned over and kissed him on the cheek. Let the gawkers talk. "I'll be back before Mama and Daddy's party Saturday."

He held on to her hand, and as she straightened, he gave it a gentle tug. "Be sure you are. Call me if you need me."

"I will."

He released her hand and she headed toward the door. In the aisle, she almost bumped into Jeremy's parents. "Hi." She answered their puzzled expressions with a weak smile. Jeremy would have to explain to them where she was going.

As she reached the door, the curtain parted jerkily, as if the strings were in the hands of a sixth-grader. Crystal stopped, seized by the certainty that she had to see one particular bumblebee before she left.

She stood with her back against the wall next to the door as the music started and a row of flowers walked out, singing as they came. A few minutes later four precious little bumblebees came skipping out singing a *bzz. . .bzz. . .*song.

When it was over, Crystal applauded wildly with the rest of the audience. She glanced across the auditorium to see Jeremy, gazing at her intently, an enigmatic expression on his face.

Her hands froze in mid-clap, her mouth dry. She had to get out of here while she still could. She yanked the door open and fled to the parking lot, afraid to look back.

Jeremy unfolded another chair then glanced over at Luke and cleared his throat. "So is someone picking your folks up at the airport?"

Luke shook his head. "They left their car there. Aaron and Bree are flying in and riding with them."

"Oh. And is Crystal coming with them?"

Luke's eyes were filled with sympathy as he slid a chair under the table. "She was supposed to, but apparently she's going to have to come in on the red-eye and rent a car. I guess things are takin' longer than she thought."

Jeremy picked up a table and moved it to the front of the room. He hadn't really expected to hear from Crystal. He knew she'd be busy and would call if she needed him. But he had thought she'd be home tonight.

Ever since she left the program the other night, he'd had a gnawing fear in his gut that refused to be calmed. It was there when he got up in the morning and when he went to bed at night. What if she didn't come back?

Elyse started unfolding chairs around the table he'd just set up. She gave him a sideways glance. "She doesn't know anything yet. About the part, I mean."

He nodded.

"We've only heard from her once, and that was tonight to say she'd be late. I think she's been really busy."

He appreciated the information, but his pride stung that her family obviously felt so sorry for him. "Just getting a callback for Broadway is a big deal."

Elyse nodded. "It is. We're really proud of her."

He tried to hold back a sigh. "I guess it's what she's wanted her whole life."

Elyse's brown eyes looked troubled by the question. "Cami

couldn't talk about anything else."

Only Cami had died. And Crystal had gone to New York alone. His heart ached for the loneliness she must have faced, eighteen and grieving in the big city, away from everyone she knew. He rubbed his hand across his face. "Crystal must have wanted it very badly, too, to go ahead after losing Cami."

Elyse regarded him again with an odd expression. "Cami was very determined that they do it."

He thought about that, later, after he'd picked up Beka at his parents' and gotten her into bed. Was Elyse trying to tell him that Crystal was in New York because of Cami's dream?

As Crystal eased the rental car onto the dark gravel road, she glanced at the dashboard clock. Almost midnight. And it would still take everything she had not to pull into Jeremy's driveway as she drove by. Not one waking hour had gone by in the city that she hadn't considered calling him. But as the original callback turned into one more audition and one more, she found herself less and less certain of what she'd say. And the truth was, she still didn't know.

Her phone vibrated. She slowed, and with one hand on the steering wheel, flipped it open. The screen said, NEW VOICE MESSAGE. She pushed the button to listen to her messages. According to the time/date stamp, this call had come while she was in the air.

"It's Mia. I hope you're sitting down." Mia paused dramatically and Crystal gripped the steering wheel tightly. "Because. . .welcome to Broadway, baby! You got the part. Rehearsals start Monday morning. Enjoy your parents' party but be sure you get back ASAP. We'll go over the details together Sunday. Love you, darling."

Crystal hit the brakes and came to a complete stop on the deserted gravel road. Her hands shook as she fumbled for the number to replay the message.

As Mia's voice came through the line again, Crystal stared down the dark road at the nearest guard light. Jeremy's ranch. And, even though she'd have never admitted it to anyone, the place that she'd already started thinking of as her future home. But now. . .

She'd gotten the part. A lead role. On Broadway. She tried saying it aloud. "I got a lead role on Broadway." Her voice sounded scratchy, like she hadn't used it in years. She eased off the brake and moved slowly down the road. She was afraid to even look at Jeremy's house as she drove by. If she didn't stop thinking about him, she'd throw caution to the wind and wake Mia up to refuse the offer.

And who in her right mind would turn down a dream come true?

The music woke her. Country music blaring in the distance. She opened her eyes and blinked at brightly colored Broadway posters on the wall. She smiled and gave a lazy stretch as she slowly came alive. Suddenly she sat straight up and stared at the clock. Eleven a.m.

Last night came flooding back. The phone message from Mia. "Broadway, Cami," Crystal whispered to the empty bed across from her.

The house had been quiet and still when she'd gotten in. Kaleigh had been asleep in the sewing room, Chance in the boys' room, Aaron and Bree already bunked at Elyse's, and her parents in their own room. It hadn't been that hard to climb into her old bed.

Instead of dwelling on the past, she'd lain awake in her childhood room most of the night, thinking about what the future would hold. And, more importantly, what it wouldn't. And now she'd overslept and was going to be late. No doubt her family had thought they were doing her a favor letting her sleep in, but she'd wanted to talk to Jeremy before the party started at noon.

As she gathered her clothes from her overnight bag, the deep *boom, boom, boom* of a bass guitar vibrated her room. Someone, probably Luke or Chance, or both, had apparently found the huge outdoor speakers they'd used for parties in high school and set them up outside the barn.

Even though it was almost noon now, she took extra care getting ready. Tina had always told her, "If you're going to make a late entrance, you'd better look like someone worth waiting for." Crystal was only interested in impressing one guest really. She was already thinking of ways that long-distance relationships *could* work.

She settled on a turquoise top and a knee-length denim skirt with strappy sandals. She smiled at herself in the mirror. Together, she and Jeremy would figure this out. At the last second, she grabbed her hat and slammed it on her head. Who knew when she'd get a chance to play cowgirl again?

Jeremy stood toward the back and looked up every time someone walked in the open barn doors.

"Daddy! Look." Beka came running across the barn holding her teacher's hand. "It's Miss Davis."

Miss Davis looked more than a little embarrassed, but she flashed Jeremy a sweet smile. "Hi. Fancy meetin' you here."

He nodded. "How are you today?"

"Fine. Daddy's just getting ready to pull the ribs out of the smoker, and I came in to get a platter." She held up a big plastic plate. "But Beka insisted I come see you."

Jeremy looked down at Beka and ruffled her hair. "Honey, Miss Davis probably didn't want to be dragged across the room when she was busy."

The brunet giggled. "I didn't mind. And you can call me Patti."

260

The polite smile froze on his lips as he looked past her. The girl he'd been waiting to see had just walked in the door, a vision in turquoise and denim. And cute as a button in that hat. One glimpse of her, and all of his concern about her not calling blew away like dandelion seeds.

CHAPTER 30

He wanted to run and sweep her up in his arms and swing her around. But he forced himself to keep his feet planted as he watched her eyes scan the room. Before her gaze landed on him, she saw her parents and ran to hug them. While they were hugging, he looked back at Beka's teacher.

"Well, um. . .Patti, I've heard your dad's barbecue is the best in the country. It sure was nice of him to do this." He nodded toward her. "And it was nice of you to help him."

She reached out and playfully swatted his arm. "That's sweet of you to say so."

He glanced to the side and saw Crystal staring at him from just a few yards away. Their eyes locked.

Patti followed his gaze. "Is it okay if Beka goes with me to take this platter to Daddy?"

Jeremy jerked his attention back to her. "Yes, sure, okay."

She and Beka left hand in hand, and he turned back to where Crystal was walking toward him. Way too slowly to suit him.

He held out his arms and she walked into his hug. He breathed in her vanilla scent. "I missed you."

"I missed you, too," she murmured.

He released her but held on to her hand.

"So how did your trip go?"

She leaned against him. "Fine. We'll talk about it later, okay?"

He felt a twinge of uneasiness in his gut, but he pushed it aside. She was home now and by his side. Whatever the future held, they'd deal with it together.

Crystal smiled and laughed and played the part. She and Jeremy flitted from table to table, greeting guests. She hugged Aaron and Bree, and Kaleigh and Chance, and never let her smile falter.

Not even when Luke said, "How'd the audition go, kid?"

She shrugged. "I didn't fall on my face."

She felt Jeremy watching her so she smiled wider. She'd come down to the barn prepared to tell him the news first thing then try to convince him that they could work things out. That he could come to New York once a month and when she could get away, she'd fly home. But then she'd seen him and Beka with Patti Davis, and just like that, she knew. What she had to offer wasn't enough. He and Beka had been through so much turmoil with Lindsey, both before and after the kidnapping. It was time for them to be settled. And weekend trips to New York didn't figure into that picture. She remembered how Amanda had forced a smile when she had to leave Beka with Jeremy that day. Sometimes love demanded a sacrifice.

Finally, Jeremy tugged on her hand. "Let's go for a walk," he whispered, his breath on her ear, making her shiver.

She nodded, but her legs trembled as she walked.

Outside, they headed toward the river without speaking. Finally he stopped and pulled her against him. Her hat fell off, but she didn't move to pick it up. Instead, she savored her moment in the shelter of his arms. If only this moment would never end.

"You got the part, didn't you?" His voice was husky.

She nodded, her face still buried in his chest.

He gently held her away from him and looked at her face. "Congratulations. I'm very proud of you."

She could tell he meant it. "Thank you."

"So you're going to accept the offer?"

"I can't imagine turning it down."

He let go of her and nodded, but not before she saw the pain in his eyes. "I can understand that. It's a big honor." What he didn't say was so loud, she could barely hear what he did say.

Now was the time she'd planned to pitch the idea of a long distance relationship, but she couldn't do it. He deserved more. Much more. "It really is. But I'll miss you."

"I'll miss you, too." He picked her hat up and handed it to her. "I wish you could see how much you've changed since you've come home."

She frowned at him. "What do you mean?"

He motioned toward the river in the distance. "The girl I found crying by the river that day was beautiful. In a porcelain doll way."

"And that's bad?"

He smiled and looked upward as if poking fun at himself, then looked back at her. "You seemed so fragile. Like one touch would break you."

"And now I'm different?"

"You're even more beautiful. But you look alive. And strong. You laugh more." He reached out and pushed her hair from her face. "Your skin has a glow to it that definitely wasn't there before."

She blushed.

His smile was bittersweet. "I don't want to see you go back to how you were."

She remembered how unhappy she'd been by the time she actually left New York. And she had to admit, only a small part of that had to do with Brad's betrayal. But this was a chance at Broadway. How long had she worked for that? "I'll try my best not to change. But I have to take the part. I'm sorry."

He nodded. "You have to listen to your heart, Crys."

She stared at him, trying to find a reply. Finally she sighed. "Well, I probably should go pack. I need to fly back tonight. Rehearsals start Monday."

"Okay."

"I'll be back out to the party in a little while." Swallowing against the lump in her throat, she turned away.

He touched her shoulder.

She spun back around.

He scooped her into his arms and hugged her tight.

Her heart was beating so loudly in her ears that she couldn't be sure, but she thought she heard him whisper, "I love you," against the top of her head. He let go of her and touched her face, his eyes tender. "Take care." He dropped his hand and walked quickly away.

She stared at his back. How long would it be before he moved on? Pain shot through her. Would she know? Or would she just come home some Christmas to find he was married?

Tears streamed down her cheeks. She stood and watched him until he made it all the way to the barn.

But he never looked back.

"Thanks." Jeremy forced a smile as Patti set a plate of ribs and a glass of iced tea in front of him. She'd seen him when he came back to the barn and had stayed by his side ever since, content not to talk. He didn't know whether she'd guessed what had happened or if his face just looked as gray as he felt inside. But he was glad for the buffer she provided. Crystal's family and his own parents had sent him a few inquisitive looks, but no one had approached him.

An hour later, Crystal walked back in. She had changed from

the skirt into jeans and apparently retired the hat. She was still beautiful, but her smile was gone. She glanced toward him and Patti.

He quickly averted his gaze toward his plate. When he looked up, she was talking to her family. He stood. "I need to go."

Patti stood, too. "Okay. Do you want me to bring Beka home later?" She nodded to where his parents were surrounded by friends. Beka was playing dolls on the table beside them with another little girl her age.

If he tried to take her now, his parents would want to know why. And he didn't want or need a scene. He nodded. "Or just ask Mom and Dad to bring her home."

She smiled at him, sympathy shining in her eyes. "I'll handle it."

"Thanks. Just make sure she doesn't get out of your sight."

"I'm a teacher," she gently reminded him. She touched his shoulder. "I'll take good care of her."

"I know you will." He forced his lips to tilt up. He glanced across the room and saw Crystal staring at them.

And for the second time in two hours, he turned and walked away from the woman he loved.

"Knock-knock."

Crystal glanced up from where she was zipping the last suitcase. "Hey. Come in."

Her mama walked in and looked around the room. "Have I told you lately how proud I am of you?"

The tears that Crystal had been keeping at bay for the last couple of hours crept toward the surface, but she blinked them back. "Not lately."

"Well, I'm very proud of you."

Crystal snorted. "I don't know why."

Her mama motioned around the room. "For facing your ghosts, for one thing. And wow, how many mothers can say their daughter won a lead role on Broadway?"

"I hope that's a rhetorical question." Crystal flashed her a smile.

"It is."

"So you're okay with my going back to New York?"

Her mother sat on Cami's bed and stared at Crystal as if weighing her answer. "I'm okay with your being happy. And like I said, I'm really proud of you. This role is something you've worked hard for and you deserve it."

"But?"

Her mama chuckled. "But, I hate to lose you again."

Crystal sat beside her without waiting for an invitation. "You're not going to lose me again, Mama. I'll be back more often." She nodded toward her overnight bag. "And you'll be glad to know I've been reading the Bible some every day."

Her mother smiled. "I am glad about that." She reached over and patted Crystal's knee. "I'm kind of impatient. I'm ready for you to realize how much God loves you."

Crystal made a grimace. She knew God loved her. Or at least that He had. But she also knew how she'd turned away from Him. "Mama, here's how I look at it. I'm going to keep reading my Bible and try to live right from now on. And in the end, maybe God will feel sorry for me and let me slip into Heaven with the rest of y'all. I figure that's the most I can hope for." That was an oversimplification, but it was pretty close to how she felt.

Her mama hit the bed with her hand. "That's where you're wrong, Crystal Marie. And until you get that through your thick head. . ." She stopped and sighed. "I promised myself I was going to let you and Him work this out on your own. And I am." She pushed to her feet. "I love you, sweetie." She started toward the door then turned back to face Crystal. "Do you know that?"

"Yes. I love you, too, Mama."

"Well, then. . ." She rolled her eyes. "Never mind. I'll send your daddy and your brothers up to carry your luggage down."

Crystal sighed. It was time to go. So why didn't she feel ready?

As they walked out of rehearsals, Crystal listened with one ear to Melissa's nonstop chatter. A member of the ensemble and also Crystal's understudy, Melissa had latched onto her during the first rehearsal. Now after five days of working together twelve hours a day, Crystal considered her a friend. With her enthusiasm and starry-eyed excitement about Broadway, she reminded Crystal of Cami. Which actually helped Crystal to stay focused on why she was here. It had been a long week.

Outside the theater, Melissa nudged her. "Do you know that guy? He's smiling at you."

Crystal followed Melissa's gaze to the man leaning against the building next to them and bit back a gasp. "Brad." No doubt Mia had told him where he could find her.

Brad pushed off the wall and sauntered toward her. "Hi, honey."

Melissa giggled. "I'd better go."

"No, you don't—" It was too late. Melissa was several yards down the sidewalk.

Crystal turned back to Brad. Before she could speak, he thrust a fresh bouquet in her hands.

"Daisies. Your favorite." He gave her that slow grin that used to melt her heart. Funny how fake it looked now. Tina had been right all along. "I remembered."

"Thanks." She looked down at the flowers. Way too little, way too late. "You know—"

He held up his hand and stepped closer. He reached out and touched her lips with his finger. "Don't talk."

She jumped back. "No!"

He looked stunned. "You're not still holding a grudge, are you? We had something really special."

Her stomach rolled. "No, we didn't. We had nothing special at all." She knew. Because she'd had something really special. And given it up. What she'd "had" with Brad didn't even begin to compare. "I'm sorry you wasted your money." She pushed the bouquet back to him.

He didn't take it and the flowers fell to the ground. He gave her a mournful expression. "Look. I'm sorry that happened with Sabra."

She stared down at the daisies scattered on the sidewalk then brought her gaze back up to meet his. "Brad, I accept your apology. But you and I have no future. So please don't waste your time, either." She spun on her heel and walked quickly down the sidewalk.

After a minute, she glanced back. He was gone. Hopefully for good.

"Push me, Daddy." Beka's sweet voice was tinged with irritation.

He jerked his mind back to the present and reached out to push the swing. "Sorry, honey. I was thinking."

"That's okay," Beka called over her shoulder as she went up in the air. "I like to think."

I don't, Jeremy thought sourly. He'd thought his life would be perfect if Beka were just home. And it was in so many ways. But Crystal had been gone one week today and he couldn't stop thinking about her.

His phone rang, and he retrieved it from his shirt pocket. "Hello?"

"Jeremy, it's Patti."

"Oh, hi." She'd had Beka over to her house a few times to play after school and had gotten his number in case of an emergency. But this was the first time she'd called.

"I was just thinking. . .I know it's Saturday night and you might have plans, but I thought you and Beka might want to eat supper with me. I'm making spaghetti."

Beka's favorite. "That's really nice, but I think we'd better just stay home tonight. Thank you, though."

"Oh, okay. I'll talk to you later then." She hung up quickly.

He felt bad. But he knew Patti was asking for more than supper. And it wasn't fair to make her think that was a possibility. Because the truth was he had nothing left to give.

CHAPTER 31

When Crystal walked into the kitchen Sunday morning, Tina had a piece of toast halfway to her mouth. She froze with it there. "Good morning."

Crystal smiled. "Good morning."

"I'm afraid to hope, but does the fact that you're wearing a skirt and carrying a Bible mean you're going to church with us?"

"If the offer is still open."

Tina grinned. "Of course it is. Zee's gone to get the keys."

Crystal smiled. In spite of the fact that her grandfather in Texas spoiled his only granddaughter, Tina was frugal. But she and Zee had splurged on an old car they only drove on Sundays. "I don't want to get to church looking like a tumbleweed," she'd said more than once.

"I'm so excited." Suddenly, concern clouded Tina's eyes. "Listen, our congregation is a little different. It's probably not what you're used to."

"Aw, c'mon. I've lived in the city for seven years. Surely you don't think I can be shocked." Considering Tina's and Zee's penchant for unusual hair coloring and piercings, she could only imagine. But she wasn't going so she could gawk. She was going because she was tired of being alone. And she had a strong feeling Tina and Zee would be moving to Texas soon. Being in Shady Grove had made her remember what it was like to have a church family. It would be nice to find that here.

Tina smiled up at her husband as he walked into the kitchen. "Crys is going with us."

"Cool." Zee gave Crystal a fist bump.

"She thinks no matter what our congregation is like she won't be shocked."

Zee drew his brows together. "You didn't tell her?"

Tina shook her head.

Crystal laughed. . .a little nervously, she admitted to herself. But she wasn't going to give Tina the satisfaction of begging to know what it was that was so shocking about their congregation. They'd discussed the Bible enough over the years that she knew it wasn't anything too outlandish. So she'd have to just wait and see.

In the car, Zee headed north. And just kept going. After half an hour, Crystal looked at Tina to see if she was worried, but she and Zee were holding hands and acting as relaxed as if they were out for a Sunday drive. Crystal smiled at her thoughts. Obviously, they were out for a Sunday drive.

The big buildings gave way to more trees and smaller houses. Until finally, Zee took a right at a small street and a right into a gravel parking lot. A tiny white frame building sat in the middle of the lot. Tina looked over at Crystal and smiled. "I'm sorry for making you sweat it. But you have to admit, this is definitely different than what you're used to."

"It reminds me of when we'd go visit my granny and papa and go to church with them," Crystal said wonderingly as she climbed out of the backseat.

Tina nodded. "That's why we started here a couple of years ago. I was homesick, and this is exactly like the tiny little congregation my grandmother took me to."

"Just wait until you get inside," Zee said. "It's like stepping back in time."

At the top of the steps, Tina stood back and let Zee open the door. He motioned Crystal to follow Tina in.

Several men and women stood in the foyer talking. Their faces lit up when they saw Tina and Zee. "You did come back," a bald man said and nodded toward his gray-haired wife. "I told Lila I wouldn't be surprised if you honeymooners got to Texas and decided to stay."

Tina shook her head. "And leave y'all? No way." She pulled Crystal forward and introduced her.

Every one of the forty or fifty members, including the preacher, shook her hand and told her how good it was to have her. Or at least it felt like it. She was shocked, even though she'd said she wouldn't be, but she'd never felt more welcome.

By the time the preacher got up to speak, Crystal knew why Tina and Zee loved it so much here. The fervor of the worshippers, young and old, couldn't be denied. The songs were old—most she hadn't heard since she'd visited her grandparents' church as a child—but the zeal was new and fresh. She breathed in an easy breath and opened her Bible. She was glad she'd come.

Twenty minutes later, Crystal stared at the scripture, the print slightly blurry, as the preacher recounted Jesus' parable about the son who had taken his inheritance and gone to the far country. She rubbed her eyes with her knuckles. She'd heard this story so many times when she was young. And she hadn't really forgotten it. She just hadn't thought of it in a long time.

The preacher stepped out from behind the pulpit, his voice low and filled with passion. "Can you see the Father watching? Waiting for His beloved child to return? Oh, don't kid yourself. He knows all the things that happened in the far country. But He just yearns for His child to come home. To let Him make everything right. And when He finally sees His long-lost child, what does He do?" The preacher paused and Crystal clutched the edge of the padded pew. "He runs to meet him," he said, almost in a whisper.

His eyes scanned the congregation's faces. "Today, if you need to come home, He's watching for you."

Crystal's ears were ringing as he made his final plea to anyone who needed to come. When everyone stood and began to sing, the words of the old song pierced the shell around her heart like a surgeon's knife. " 'I've wandered far away from God.' " She drew in a breath. " 'Now, I'm coming home.' " Her legs trembled and she thought she might have to sit down. " 'The paths of sin too long I've trod.' " As the congregation sang, " 'Lord, I'm coming home,' " she stepped into the aisle.

Tears coursed down her cheeks, but in that moment, she knew, beyond a shadow of a doubt, that God was running to meet her.

"Daddy, can I go home with Grandma and Grandpa?" Beka smiled up at him in the church parking lot. "Please."

"Honey, we were there all afternoon." And he'd enjoyed spending time with his parents. But he'd planned for him and Beka to go home after the evening service. He'd hoped to get her into bed early so he could have a little time where he didn't have to pretend that everything was okay.

"But Grandpa said he'd show me Snowball's kittens again if I go home with them."

His mom rested her hand on his shoulder. "We'd love to have you both, but we figured you might could use some down time."

He put his hand on Beka's head. "Okay, you can stay for a couple of hours. But no complaining when I come get you. You've got school tomorrow."

"That's right," a voice behind him said. "And I hear your teacher is really mean."

Patti walked up beside them.

Beka giggled. "You are not mean!"

"Oh. Well, that's good to hear. But you still have to get your rest."

"Okay." Beka curled her arm around Jeremy's neck and squeezed when he bent down to give her a hug and a kiss. "I love you, Daddy."

"Love you, too, Little Bit."

He watched her skip off between her grandparents. It still wasn't easy to let her go. But he was learning.

"It's hard being the one left behind, isn't it?" He looked up to see Patti smiling.

"It sure is."

"Want to go get a Coke or something?"

He considered it. She seemed like a really nice person. But she wasn't the one for him. "Um, Patti. . ."

Her face reddened. "It's okay if you don't."

He watched his parents' truck pull out of the parking lot. "I just can't." He closed his eyes for a second, praying for the right words. "You're sweet and caring. And very pretty." He smiled at her. "But I'm in love with someone else."

Her answering smile didn't waver. "Crystal McCord."

He nodded.

Her brows drew together. "I thought she moved back to New York."

"She did. But unfortunately, my heart can't let go."

She reached over and touched his hand. "I understand." Her eyes were filled with compassion. "Two years ago, I lost my fiancé in Afghanistan."

Jeremy squeezed her hand and released it. "Patti, I'm so sorry."

She nodded. "Everyone is." Her smile was sweet. "Still, that doesn't bring him back." She bit her lip. "Now don't take this the

wrong way. But the only reason I've. . .I guess you could say. . .
'pursued' you is because my sisters are driving me crazy badgering
me to get back out there before I'm too old."

Jeremy shook his head. "Don't listen to them. You can't be older
than twenty-five."

"You win the prize. I *am* twenty-five."

"Patti, you need to listen to your heart." He remembered telling
Crystal that same thing. And her heart had led her away from him.
But he knew it was sound advice. "You'll know when it's time to get
back out there. And when it is time, you'll have no trouble finding
the right person."

Patti kissed him on the cheek. "Thanks. Don't forget to take
your own advice."

As he got into his truck, he thought about what she'd said. He
knew one thing. His heart wasn't letting go anytime soon.

CHAPTER 32

Crystal didn't know how she'd let Melissa talk her into this. She'd only wanted to go home and rest. But Melissa had insisted that she was having a few of the cast members over to unwind. And that it would be very low-key. Just a few people talking about the play and hanging out. So here she was at Melissa's "after rehearsal" party.

The music was so loud she could feel the bass drumbeat. She leaned up against the wall and tried to shrink into it as people crowded around her, some moving to the beat, some just talking. Everyone but her seemed to be having fun. But then she'd mostly come to give the newlyweds some time alone at home.

"Hey." The guy standing over her had to yell for her to hear him.

She glanced up into soulful brown eyes.

He stepped closer. "You don't look like you're having much fun. Want to get out of here?" The smell of alcohol on his breath made her pull back.

She shook her head. *Not with you anyway.* "No, thanks."

He sipped from the drink in his hand then held up his glass. "Want one?"

She showed Mr. Clueless her Dr Pepper can. "No, I'm good." Melissa had assured her there wouldn't be alcohol served, but Crystal knew from experience that didn't stop people from bringing their own.

He pointed toward a small open spot in the crowd. "Want to dance?"

"No, thanks." Was she going to have to hit him over the head before he took the hint and buzzed off? He was a good-looking guy. She recognized him as being in the ensemble. He probably picked up a girl at every party he went to.

"Let's go for a walk."

"I'm a little tired." She wasn't any older than anyone else, and they'd rehearsed all day, too, but tonight she felt ancient.

"Oh, come on. Loosen up." He grinned, showing perfect white teeth. He reached for her arm to pull her away from the wall.

She shrugged his arm away. "Back off, okay?"

"Well, okay. You don't have to be so snarky. I don't beg a girl to be with me. I don't have to." He turned and walked away. At least she hadn't actually had to hit him over the head, but it had been touch and go there for a second.

She glanced at the clock on the wall. Had she been here only an hour? It felt like days. Okay. Fifteen more minutes and she was out of here. That would have to be enough "alone" time for Tina and Zee. They hadn't asked for it anyway.

She went into the kitchen where it was a little quieter. Melissa and her roommate were fixing trays of appetizers. She helped out for a few minutes while she drummed up an excuse for making her exit. Melissa looked disappointed when Crystal told her she was leaving, but she didn't argue.

As she walked back through the party, she saw that the perfect-teeth guy had moved on to the girl who played one of the other sisters. He had his arms wrapped around her and she was pressed against him as they barely moved in time to a blues tune.

When Crystal finally got back to Tina and Zee's, they were in the kitchen eating ice cream.

"What are we celebrating?" she asked as she walked in.

Tina laughed. "You know us too well. We just made the final decision. We're moving to Texas." She held up the carton of Rocky Road. "Want some ice cream?"

"No, thanks. But that's awesome news."

Zee put his hand on Tina's shoulder. "We're hoping to start a family before too long. And it only makes sense to move closer to Tina's grandpa."

Tina nodded. "But we're going to miss you, hon."

Crystal hugged each of them. "I'm going to miss y'all, too. But I think this is the right decision."

"We'll stay in touch," Tina assured her.

"I know we will. Some friends are for a season, but others are for life."

Zee groaned. "Did you get that off an e-mail forward?"

Crystal laughed. "Probably. So sue me. Sometimes those things have gems of wisdom hidden between those rows and rows of e-mail addresses."

She hugged them again and left them alone with their ice cream.

In the guest room, she got her Bible out and read it for a while. When she went to put it back into her overnight bag, her hand closed around something she didn't recognize. Her high school yearbook. She remembered now that she'd put it and her plays in the bottom of her duffel bag to look at later. She reached in and pulled out both the plays and the yearbook and carried them to her bed.

She stuffed the two pillows against the headboard and scooted herself up in the bed until she was sitting with the plays resting on the slanted table that her knees provided. After a few minutes of reading, she got a pen and started to edit. Two hours later, she relaxed her legs and stretched. She had to stop and go to bed.

Not because she was sleepy but because a twelve-hour rehearsal demanded a good night's sleep.

She set the plays on her nightstand, and her gaze fell on the yearbook. Curiosity welled up inside her. There was no use trying to ignore it now and go to sleep. She slid it toward her across the slick comforter and ran her hand over the embossed lettering on the front cover. Her heart pounded. Was she ready to take this walk down memory lane? She sent up a silent prayer and flipped the heavy cover open.

Just a few pages in, she stopped. Their senior pictures—hers and Cami's—were side by side. She stared at the blond hair, blue eyes, and their grins, Cami's a shade more confident. Even at the end of their Shady Grove High School careers, only a handful of their close friends could tell them apart.

She flipped another page and there were Cami and the rest of the court at the local beauty salon getting their nails and hair done for homecoming. And she and Cami and Phoebe in Farm Welding class, their helmets up, smiling for the camera. "What a waste," Cami had complained that whole semester. "Like we're going to ever weld on Broadway."

Phoebe had pointed out that at a crucial moment on stage, one of the poles that held the lights could break. And wouldn't it be handy if the star could bring in a portable welder and take care of that? Cami had wrinkled her nose, but she quit griping.

Crystal smiled at the memory. Phoebe had such a dry sense of humor. Crystal needed to find the card she'd given her at the bookstore and give her a call. She'd missed her.

Crystal flipped the page and froze. In the Shady Grove yearbook, tradition demanded that each senior had a page paid for by his or her family, featuring pictures of the graduate from birth to the moment of this great accomplishment. And including handwritten words of inspiration to the graduates. Crystal couldn't believe it had been seven years and she'd never seen her or Cami's senior pages. Until now.

Crystal studied the page the family had put together for Cami. Without fail, the brothers and sisters had mentioned Broadway. But at the bottom, Daddy had written, "Remember Whose you are." Cami had loved *The Lion King*, and Daddy always added his own twist to Mufasa's advice to Simba.

Crystal closed her eyes. How ironic that her dad had felt the need to encourage Cami to keep the faith. He'd probably never dreamed that Crystal would be the one who would turn her back on God when times got tough. She'd called him and Mama after she got home from church yesterday. They'd sounded so happy, and she was pretty sure she heard tears in her daddy's voice.

She turned her attention back to the yearbook. She looked at Cami's page one more time, and her eyes stung as she read what she'd written to her sister. "Whether on the barn stage or the Broadway stage, you'll always be a star to me. I love you."

She turned the page, and there was her name and date of birth with photos of her whole childhood parading across the page. Each of her brothers and sisters, as well as Mama and Daddy, had written her a note. They ranged from "Here's lookin' at you, kid"—Luke—to "You've got a big heart, so never let anyone tell you that you're too little"—Aaron—to "You can do anything you set your mind to"—Daddy—to "God loves you, honey, and He has big plans for you"—Mama. Down at the bottom, she recognized Cami's familiar scrawl. "Wherever life leads us, thank you for inspiring me to be better, to dream bigger, and to always follow my heart. I love you."

She'd signed it, "Broadway Bound, Cami." That's how her sister had signed everything for the last two years of high school.

The last two years of her life. Unshed tears ripped Crystal's throat raw.

Crystal had no doubt Cami would have accomplished her

dream if things had been different.

Crystal stared again at the quote. "Wherever life leads us. . ." She ran her hand over Cami's picture. She remembered the pain she'd felt when she'd stood in the field and watched Jeremy walk away. Who could have guessed where life would lead them? Or that Crystal would have so much trouble following her own heart?

It had been a long day. The cows had broken through the fence on the north side, and Jeremy and his dad had spent most of the afternoon getting them back in and repairing the break. He'd been grateful when his mom had volunteered to pick Beka up from school and take her home with her. But now that he was home and showered, the house was unbearably empty.

He grabbed his keys off the hook by the door and walked out onto the porch. He'd turned down his mom's offer for supper, but that was before he knew it was going to be one of those nights where he couldn't stop thinking about Crystal.

He stepped off the porch to get a better look at the sunset. The clouds billowed across the sky, a purple curtain lined in orange and yellow. Down at the bottom of the cloud bank, one star twinkled. His dad used to tease him that if he could see it before dark, it was probably a satellite. But if Crystal were here, she'd wish on it with him.

He sank down on the top porch step. Could Crystal see the sunset in the city? Or was she too busy to look? Did she still smile when something touched her heart? And laugh at anything silly? Or had she gone back to the tense, nervous girl she'd been at Aaron's wedding and later by the river? He prayed for her all the time. That she'd be happy and healthy. And even though it tore his heart out to think about it, he prayed for her to find love. A true love that would be good for her.

Sitting there on the step, he felt old and tired. He looked up at the crunch of gravel and stared as a small black car slowed and turned into his driveway. He stood, talking sternly to his heart. Begging it to realize that this was probably a lost traveler needing directions. Or an encyclopedia salesman. But his heart refused to listen and thudded against his ribcage as the driver's door opened.

He saw her blond hair first, blowing in the breeze, and then there she was staring at him. She gasped and took a step toward him.

A thousand questions swirled through his mind, but they fell to the ground as he ran to meet her. Only one thing mattered right now. She was here.

He swept her up in his arms and spun her around, holding her tight. For a few minutes, they hugged without speaking. Then finally he released her. "Is everything okay?"

Her smile was bright and clear. "Everything is wonderful now."

"How did you get time off so quickly?"

Her smile grew even brighter. "Funny you should ask. Because I'm not taking time off. I'm here to stay."

Jeremy opened his mouth, but no words came out.

Crystal let out a tentative laugh. "Cat got your tongue?"

"What about Broadway?"

"It's still there. But it's going to have to get along without me."

"I'm lost. Can you please help me wrap my head around this?" Jeremy knew he sounded like an idiot. His heart raced a million beats per minute at the hope that maybe, just maybe, this woman he'd willingly given his heart to might actually have given up the stage and come home to him.

Her eyes shone with unshed tears, and she reached out to take his hand. "It's really simple. I went in this morning and told the director that as much as I appreciated the opportunity, my heart was somewhere else. He agreed to release me from our agreement."

Two weeks' worth of tightness in his chest relaxed. "Really?

Where is your heart?" His own smile felt a little misty.

She gave him a slap on the shoulder. "You'd better be taking good care of it, you big lug."

"I'll trade you."

She looked puzzled for a second then he saw the realization dawn. "Or we could just leave them right where they are—yours with me and mine with you. Forever."

He cupped her cheek and stared into those beautiful blue eyes. "Do you have any idea how much I love you?"

She nodded, her eyes twinkling. "About half as much as I love you."

A laugh burst out of him. "Reverse that and you'll have it right." He dropped a playful kiss on her forehead, but when she stretched up on tiptoe to meet his lips, the laughter gave way to a kiss that left little room for doubt.

By the time they agreed they probably loved each other exactly the same, the night sky was scattered with stars. And he still held her in his arms.

Christine Lynxwiler

Award-winning author and past president of American Christian Romance Writers, Christine, her husband, Kevin, and their two daughters live in the foothills of the beautiful Ozark Mountains in their home state of Arkansas. Christine's greatest earthly joy is her family, and aside from God's work, spending time with them is her top priority.

THE RELUCTANT COWGIRL—DISCUSSION QUESTIONS

- Crystal allowed herself to be separated from her family emotionally even though she loved them. Why do you think she did this?
- Why can't Crystal sleep in the house? How does her progression of resting places parallel her healing process?
- Jeremy remembers how Lindsey would leave, then come home when things went wrong. What makes him decide Crystal really is different?
- Crystal believes in God but feels like He wouldn't want her back after she deserted him. Several different things that happen in the story make her see otherwise. What are some of those things?
- Why was Crystal's grief over Cami still so fresh after seven years?
- The McCord family is unique because most of the children were adopted at an older age, yet they're obviously close to each other. What do you think is the reason for that?
- When Beka was first kidnapped by her non-custodial mother, Blair (the anchorwoman) had little sympathy for Jeremy. Do you think Blair (and others) would have felt the same way if the tables had been turned and the non-custodial father had stolen the child? Or if a stranger had? Why or why not?
- If Cami hadn't died, do you think Crystal would have still gone to Broadway? What do you think might have happened in the twins' lives?
- Have you ever seen someone living another person's dream? What are the reasons people do this?
- The Reluctant Cowgirl is a story of homecoming. Why does that theme resonate so strongly with most of us? Do we have to actually go back to the place that we were born and raised in order to "come home"? Why or why not?